ALSO BY MEGAN ABBOTT

Queenpin

The Song Is You

Die a Little

Bury Me Deep

Megan Abbott

Simon & Schuster Paperbacks
New York London Toronto Sydney

SIMON & SCHUSTER PAPERBACKS
A Division of Simon & Schuster, Inc.
1230 Avenue of the Americas
New York, NY 10020

First Simon & Schuster trade paperback edition July 2009

SIMON & SCHUSTER PAPERBACKS and colophon are registered
trademarks of Simon & Schuster, Inc.

For information about special discounts for bulk purchases,
please contact Simon & Schuster Special Sales at
1-866-506-1949 or business@simonandschuster.com.

The Simon & Schuster Speakers Bureau can bring authors
to your live event. For more information or to book an event,
contact the Simon & Schuster Speakers Bureau at
1-866-248-3049 or visit our website at www.simonspeakers.com.

Designed by Davina Mock-Maniscalco

Manufactured in the United States of America

3 5 7 9 10 8 6 4 2

Library of Congress Cataloging-in-Publication Data
Abbott, Megan E.
Bury me deep / Megan Abbott.
p. cm.
1. Physicians' spouses—Fiction. 2. Female friendship—Fiction.
3. Phoenix (Ariz.)—Fiction. I. Title.
PS3601.B37B87 2009
813'.6—dc22   2008030676

ISBN-13: 978-1-4165-9909-8
ISBN-10:   1-4165-9909-6

"T.B. Blues" by Jimmie Rodgers and Raymond E. Hall
Copyright © 1931 by Peer International Corporation.
Copyright renewed.
International copyright secured. Used by permission. All rights reserved.

Photo on p. 234 courtesy of Herald-Examiner Collection/Los Angeles Public Library

Acknowledgments

A true "without whom" to Denise Roy for her peerless guidance, intelligence and insight, and for her warm generosity. I am also so grateful to Paul Cirone and Molly Friedrich for their support. Warmest thanks, too, to the wonderful Kelly Welsh at Simon & Schuster for all her hard work, as well as Kate Ankofski and Jonathan Evans—and to Sarah Hochman for deeply appreciated help in the homestretch. And with a special debt to the remarkable Dan Conaway, for wisdom and kindness above and beyond.

Immense gratitude to Philip and Patricia Abbott, the two people I admire most in the world, to Josh, Julie & Kevin, Ralph and Janet Nase, Kiki and Brody, the muse-like Alison Quinn, Darcy Lockman, Jeff, Ruth & Steve Nase, the Nichols and the Gaylord family (with an extra nod to Dave for his last-minute assistance).

Finally, a special thanks to Patrick Millikin, Sara Gran and Vicki Hendricks, for a very, very memorable night in Phoenix.

Dedication

For Josh, because words dont ever fit
even what they are trying to say at

Bury Me Deep

Part One

Thrill parties every night over on Hussel Street. That tiny house, why, it's 600 square feet of percolating, Wurlitzering sin. Those girls with their young skin, tight and glamorous, their rimy lungs and scratchy voices, one cheek flush and c'mon boys and the other, so accommodating, even with lil' wrists and ankles stripped to pearly bone by sickness. They lay there on their daybed, men all standing over round, fingering pocket chains and hands curled about gin bottle necks. The girls lay there on plump pillows piled high with soft fringes twirling between delicate fingers, their lips wet with syrups, tonics, sticky with balms, their faces freshly powdered, arching up, waiting to be attended to by men, our men, the city's men. What do you do about girls like that?

OCTOBER 1930

He was a kind husband. You couldn't say he wasn't kind.

He found her a rooming house and paid up three months, all he could manage and still make his passage to Mazatlán, where he would take up a steady post, his first in three years, with the Ogden-Nequam Mining Company, for whom he would drain fluid thick, yellow as pale honey from miners' lungs.

He purchased for her, on credit (who wouldn't give credit to a doctor, even one in a suit shiny from wear), a tea set and a small Philco radio for her long evenings, sitting in the worn rose chair writing letters to him, missing him so.

He purchased for her a pair of kidskin gloves and tie shoes and a soft cloche hat the deep green of pine needles.

He took her on strolls around the neighborhood so they might look for the one hundred varieties of cactus promised in the pamphlet given to them at the Autopia Motor Court, where they'd spent their first two nights after the long drive from California. He found the cholla and the saguaro and the bisnaga, which had saved the life of many a thirsty traveler who, beaten down by the sun, cut off the spiky top and mashed the pulp within.

He helped her fill out all the papers to begin her new job, which he had found for her. She would start Monday as a filing clerk and stenographer at the Werden Clinic. She passed the typing test and the dictation test and Dr. Milroy, the director, who was very tall and wore tinted spectacles and smelled sweetly of aniseeds, hired her right then and there, taking her small hand between his palms deep as serving dishes, as softly worn as the leather pew Bibles passed through three generations' hands in the First Methodist Church of Grand Rapids, and said, "My dear Mrs. Seeley, welcome to our little desert hideaway. We are so glad you will be joining us. I have assured your husband you will be happy here. The entire Werden community welcomes you to its bosom."

On Sunday night, late, he packed his suitcase for his long trip, first to Nogales, then Estación Dimas, then ninety miles on muleback to Tayoltita. The mining company didn't care about revoked medical licenses. They were eager to have him. But, with her, he had always been clear: where he was going was no place for a woman. He would have to go alone.

When he was finished packing, he sat her down on the bed and spoke softly to her for some time, spoke softly of his grief in leaving her but with solemn, gravely worded promises that he would return in the spring, would return by Easter, arms filled with lilies, and with all past troubles behind them.

And on Monday morning at seven o'clock her husband, having made all these arrangements, walked her to the trolley and kissed her discreetly on the cheek, his chin crushing her new hat, and headed himself to the train depot, one battered suitcase in hand. As she watched him through the trolley window, as she watched him, slope-shouldered in that ancient brown suit, hat too tight, gait slow and lurching, she thought, *Who is that poor man, walking so beaten, face gray, eyes struck blank? Who is that sad fellow? My goodness, what a life must he lead to be so broken and alone!*

THE DOCTORS AT THE CLINIC were all kind as could be, and all seemed concerned that she felt comfortable and safe in her rooming house. They left a cactus blossom on her desk as a welcome gift and offered her a tour of the State Capitol, pointing proudly to its copper dome, which could be viewed from the clinic's third-floor windows. Right away, Dr. Milroy and his wife began inviting her to Sunday dinner and she heard again about the one hundred varieties of cactus she might see around town and she heard that no other place in the world is blessed with so many days of sunshine and she heard how, as she must know, the desert is God's great health-giving laboratory. Then, at the end of the evening, Mrs. Milroy always sent her home with a dish steaming over with creamed corn casserole, a knot of pork, sweet carrots in honey glaze.

"You're nothing but a whisper of a girl. But you'll need something on your bones for when you start your family. When Dr. Seeley comes back, you know he'll be ready for a son. Am I right?"

She smiled, she always smiled. Dr. Seeley hadn't talked of sons, of children since before the first monthlong stretch at St. Bartholomew's narcotics ward. They'd never talked much of babies, even as she was sure when she married three years, seven months back that she'd be near the third time large with child by now, like all the girls she knew.

IT WAS FRIDAY, her fifth day at the clinic, and she had seen Nurse Louise stalking the halls more than once, stalking them, a lioness. A long-limbed girl with a thick brush of dark red hair crowning a pale, pie face, painted-on brows thin as kidsilk and a tilting Scotch nose. When she walked, her hips slung and her chest bobbed up round apples and the men on the ward took notice—my, how could they not? She was not beautiful, but she had a bristling, crackling energy about her and it was like she was always winking at you and nodding her head as if saying, always, even when stacking X-rays, *C'mon, sweet face, c'mon.*

And now here was Nurse Louise dropping herself, hard, in the chair across from Marion in the luncheon room. She smelled like licorice and talcum powder.

"That's for beans, kid," she said, jabbing her thumb dismissively at Marion's jelly sandwich. "Have a hunk of my brown bread. Ginny—that's my roommate—swabbed it up good with plum butter. Tell me that ain't the stuff."

And Marion took the wedge offered her and it smelled like Mother's kitchen even if Mother never made any bread but white or sometimes milk-and-water bread. And the plum butter, well, that stung sweet in her mouth since she hadn't had much but bean soup since Dr. Seeley left her, left her all alone five days past.

"What's your name, answer me now with your cakehole plug full," she said, laughing. "I'm Louise Mercer. I've been here going on a year now, so I guess there's not much I don't know. I'm happy to show you all the dials and knobs and pulleys, if you like. So nothing crashes down on that slippery blond head of yours."

"Well, I'm Marion. Marion Seeley," she finally got out, eyeing a dab of butter still smeared on her thumb.

"Go on, Marion." Louise smiled, nodding toward the pearly butter. "We don't believe, none of us, in wasting fine things."

SUDDENLY, she was under Louise's red-tipped wing and everything became easier. She learned the best place to hang her hat and coat so they didn't smell of disinfectant, the trolley route that'd get her home seven minutes faster and two blocks closer to boot and that you should punch the clock before you even set your purse down each morning.

Each day, they ate lunch together and Louise gave her the what's what on everyone at the clinic. The doctors no longer seemed half so frightening once Louise had told her about the one who was always pinching nurses' behinds, and the one who tipped his bill in his office all day long, the one who never even gave a pretty penny to the St. Ursula's Annual Blind Children Drive and the one who had ended up here on account of losing his medical license in the state of Missouri for operating a still in his office.

Louise always brought treats—small cakes, a glass canister of baked beans with brown sugar, a sack of jelly nougats, a crimson jar of pickled beets. Wanting to return the favor, Marion brought in her mother's sturdy currant jelly and, later in the week, steamed bread she had spent all evening making in the kitchen of the rooming house. Neither could eat it. Louise crossed her eyes like Ben Turpin.

"It's for the birds, kid," she said. "But a girl as pretty as you, what could it matter?"

Marion was embarrassed, mostly because she thought she was a very good homemaker and Dr. Seeley had dined on her food for years with never a complaint. He always smiled and said, "Very good, Marion. Very fine, indeed."

"You come by our place," Louise said. "You should try my creamed onions. You'll think your tongue ran across a cloud."

What might a cloud taste like, she wondered. Like Mother's snow pudding made for birthdays and Sunday summer suppers. No, no, like dew, like rain gathering on the edge of your winter muffler, brushing against your lips.

THAT NIGHT, Marion took the streetcar to Louise's duplex on Hussel Street, not two miles away. As she approached the house, she could hear female voices pitching delightedly at each other. Swinging open the front door, Louise yanked her inside, the first time Marion had seen her out of her nurse's starchy whites. The housedress she wore was very plain, but cut tight across her chest, and when she walked it all twisted into glamorous shapes.

The place was as small as her own room at Mrs. Gower's, only with an accordion wall that separated the living and sleeping quarters and it had a kind of pullman kitchen. There must have been cracked walls and chipped ceiling tiles and water stains, but you didn't notice these things because there was an abundance of feminine enchantment. *Never seen anything like it, except maybe in that Greta Garbo picture Dr. Seeley took me to where Garbo lived in a harem and her bedroom all overhung with filmy scarves of twisting, winding, billowy loveliness through which chimes tinkled, oh, like such bird songs from far-off heavens. Ev'ry time you saw the long, looping chimes the piano player tinkle-tinkled those keys and you felt your heart lift and tickle you under your chin like you'd do a baby in a high chair and laugh giddily at how wonderful it all was.*

"Sit and entertain Ginny, Marion, doll," Louise said, waving a long arm over at a blond thing reclining on the settee with the claw feet. "I already burned the casserole and am out a dollar sixty-five."

Marion looked across the room at the blond thing called Ginny, wrapped in intermittent muslin.

"Grab a cush, darling," she rasped, her mouth candied over like she'd just eaten a cherry mash. On her chest rested an India rubber hot-water bottle. Her teensy pink fingers tapped across it in time to the radio.

Seating herself in a wobbly chair beside her, Marion smiled and asked Ginny if she was feeling poorly.

"Comme-ci, comme-ça," she said. "Don't you love ole Al Jolson? He makes you laugh and cry at the same time." Up close, Marion marveled at how tiny the girl was, like a yellow feather.

"Ginny's a lung-er," Louise said briskly from the kitchenette, like saying she had blue eyes, which Ginny did, china blue. With the whiteness of her skin and how small she was, a little doll was all you could think of. "Was out of town for two weeks last year, they tried to put her in a Bugville. You know, those camps?"

"I'm sorry," Marion said to Ginny, who just kept grinning. "My, aren't I. I've had some health troubles too, but nowhere near as bad."

"You look it a bit," Ginny said. "I might say, you look a little of the lunger yourself."

Marion knew she did, knew she had a wisp of that drawn look, that pulled look. As a teenager, they'd drained her lungs and she'd twice stayed a month or more in hospital wards. For these reasons, and others, she could not go with Dr. Seeley to Mexico. He would not permit it. *My darling wife, I cannot bear the thought of you, of your dainty ways and your face so like an angel in these dark parts. All those days on muleback, journey by mailboat, bayoneted soldiers. Why, when I think of it! One fellow here, an engineer, brought his wife. A burro ran into her and tore her kneecap off. That is nothing. I do not dare share with you what I see because I would not risk, not for anything, tainting you.*

"Good thing Dr. Milroy han't spotted your Golden Stamp," Ginny said, and Marion's hand flew up to her neck, the spot the doctors effused to a gapy pucker a dozen years past. It had not returned. For years, so many years, in moments quiet and nervous, her hand would go there, her fingertips searching for a return, something gathering beneath the skin.

"Tuber-cu-lo-sis, my dear," Louise said, dropping her voice low—this was her Dr. Milroy imitation and it was a good one, Louise stretching her whole face long and lanternly like Dr. Milroy was right there. "It is a disease of depletion. A disease in which vital energies are continuously exhausted at a rate no replenishment can match. A vermin eating away at our most vital organs, those which allow us to breathe, to breathe and thus to live."

"My family," Ginny threw in, "they got the Christian Science. Who needs them."

"Do not be afraid, my dear," Louise went on, winking over at Marion. "Never has a nurse of mine succumbed. As my mentor, the renowned Dr. Harry Ellington Brook, has said, germs are mere scavengers, feeding their gullets on waste, septic matter long dead or dying. Now pick up those sputum cups, pick them all up. They will do you no harm."

"Before my lungs gave," Ginny said, craning her neck out toward Marion, who tried to lean forward in the chair beside her,

"I had a proper job." She reached out, her forearm white to almost blue and delicate as a teacup handle, and touched Marion's wrist, as if to make sure she was playing close attention, as if to make sure Louise's antics were not drawing Marion away.

"Ginny has had many vocations," Louise said, shaking out place mats and setting them on a card table that sat just behind Ginny.

"I once taught elocution," Ginny said, squirming into ram-rod-straight posture, "and poise. At the Miss Venable Charm School in St. Louis, Missouri."

"She was very popular," Louise asserted.

"I'm sure you were," Marion said, although she couldn't picture silky Ginny, her bosom in danger of sliding out from under her inconstant buttons, standing in front of a classroom, ruler in hand.

"Well, the girls enjoyed me on account I was young and I had been on the stage and had traveled beyond the four stoplights of our grand thoroughfare."

"She was a star of the stage," Louise assured Marion, straight-faced but a smirk nestling there somewhere.

"I never said I was a star." Ginny flounced. "I never said that but once to get a job here. And it worked, my lovely Irish rose." Marion wasn't sure who was the Irish rose, she or Louise.

"It worked enough to get her in bloomers and pointy shoes at the Crimson Cavalcade at the Hotel Dunlop downtown."

"Is that a very grand establishment?" Marion asked.

"So grand you can only get in with a referral."

"My."

"And two bits."

"And the referral usually means whispering 'sarsaparilla' through a sliding peephole," Louise said, then clanged her ladle against a pot lid and whistled. "Soup's on, kiddos."

Lifting her golden head from the cushion with a sly smile, Ginny tucked her hands under the edges of the muslin and stretched her arms, spreading the muslin wide, showing long ribbons of blaring music notes stitched in Turkey red floss. The hot-water bottle glugged to the floor.

CRIMSON CAVALCADE. Just the name painted such plush-throated images in Marion's head. She had never known women who had been to such places. She had certainly never known women who worked in them. Back home, when her brother had his troubles, he'd taken to killing his sad evenings in a little place called the Silver Tug Club, or so she found out when her father and Dr. Seeley went looking for him after he'd not shown up for dinner or work at the insurance office in nigh on four days. Dr. Seeley explained to her that such places were really just gentlemen's clubs but that gentlemen, not like her father but other types, sometimes liked to sit back after a long workday and have a post-prandial beverage with other gentlemen and smoke a cigar and talk over current events, and there was nothing really wrong with that, was there, and shouldn't she know her brother's had hard times enough, what with losing his bank job in '27 and losing his wife to a railroad man in '28?

THERE WAS HASH with a glistening egg on top and chow chow crackling with vinegar, and there were pickled peaches with some kind of delicious glaze on them that made Marion's mouth go hot. The girls all sat around the pocket-sized card table, tilting despite three matchbooks under one leg.

Louise ate eagerly, sopping up egg with puffy dinner rolls

and chatting away at Ginny, who almost never stopped giggling and who never seemed to lift fork or spoon, only her glass.

As they talked, Marion's eyes found their way through the pink-lit enchantment around her. So different from any home she had ever been in, so different from her room at Mrs. Gower's, with its bare walls (save the Currier & Ives calendar) and heavy curtains faded from the sun. There, she had nowhere to look except the rippled mirror above her washstand.

Here, her eyes bounced off everything. The gleaming stand mixer on the kitchen counter that still had store tags on it, a Silvertone cathedral radio, an amber decanter with cordial glasses, a portable Carryola Master phonograph, a silver-plated ice bucket into which someone, Louise, she'd guessed, had dumped peppermint candies of the kind they kept in the children's ward at the clinic.

Random, she thought, to have such a high-tone radio but only a rickety card table on which to eat. And over there, a Hotpoint samovar that stood eighteen inches tall and must have held twelve cups of coffee, all for two girls, yet only one easy chair with thin velvet worn through to the spongy netting beneath.

"We met at a clinic in Denver," Louise was saying, although Marion hadn't asked. She poured a long syrupy slug of something terribly sweet and beguiling into their glasses, something tasting of plums and covering Marion's mouth as if she were swallowing big gummy tablespoons of warm honey.

"I did Ginny's X-rays," Louise said. "Looked like someone spattered her chest with birdshot."

"I'd come from a year in Illinois," Ginny said, pronouncing the *s* with a smiling slur. "The winters clogged me up but good. I was headed west when I got very poorly in Denver and had run out of coin withal."

"We got on like a house afire and I decided I needed a change of scene. When she was hale enough, I cracked open my piggy bank and bought us two tickets out of Dodge. And what better place than this, a place in which one is expected, nearly required to rise up from one's own ruins. Renewal from one's own ashes."

"You got to haul your ashes," Ginny said. "Haul 'em but good."

"Starting anew," Marion said, thinking about Dr. Seeley, thinking about the promises he had made of new starts.

"Lou-Lou's always been an absolute peach," Ginny said, more seriously now, shaking her head fiercely. "She works double shifts when things get tight. I'm a drag on her."

Marion nodded in sympathy.

"Fuh," Louise said, waving her hand in the air, "what else should I spend my dime on? Even if I get hitched again, my insides are tied up good. Might as well throw mama sugar on this yellow chick."

"Tied up?" Marion said, her face feeling so glowy, the conversation going so fast. Was she really understanding? "You mean you can't have children?"

A thread of nerve whipped across Ginny's face as she looked at Marion.

Louise tilted back in her chair and you could feel a swell of plain-eyed sorrow pass across her, turning her into the suffering Gaelic mother of yore, like the brown-tinted portrait of Dr. Seeley's beloved mother, anchored on the fireplace ledge of their home, when a home was still something they had.

"They scraped me so bad when I lost my boy," Louise said quietly. "After that, it all went to ruin with me and Frank."

Marion had heard Louise was married but hadn't known if it was true, or what had happened to Mr. Mercer if it was. Louise's long, ruddy fingers were bare.

Ginny slid from her chair and collapsed herself on Louise's lap, arm around her long neck. "Oh, Lou-Lou, don't. Don't let's fall down that mine shaft."

And Louise, in a second, squiggled out a smile and squeezed little Ginny tight. "You're right, Gin-Gin. We have Marion here. We have our wonderful new girl Marion and, not only that, we have Golden Glow parfaits!"

These parfaits, they were beautiful, shivering golden cloud in fine-stemmed glasses. Marion scarcely wanted to dip her spoon and disturb it, but she did and the taste on her tongue was like summer lemons dipped in sugar.

Marion asked her what it all was, her voice starting to do funny things, the words slipping around in her mouth and the *s*'s stretching out. Her temples throbbing hotly, she began to feel certain that the plum juice they had been drinking was very likely wine.

Louise replied that the parfaits were so simple, lemon junket, milk, an egg white, sugar, stewed apricots.

Marion told them both she'd never had dessert except on special Sundays, and on her honeymoon.

And then Marion found herself telling them, as they sat across from her, eager-eyed and rapt, how she left home the first time on her wedding night, three weeks past her nineteenth birthday, and that honeymoon trip was the first time she'd ever set foot in the lobby of a fine hotel (the Palace Hotel in Cincinnati, she still remembered her hand on the rail at the foot of the walnut and marble staircase, looking up), the first time she'd dined in a restaurant (turtle soup, an encarmined roast beef and maraschino ice cream for dessert, served in a chilled dish of sterling silver that tinkled like a bell when her spoon hit it), watched Gilbert Roland make love to Norma Talmadge in a motion picture, or seen a motion picture at all, the first time she'd seen a stage show (*The*

Cameo Girl), or put on roller skates, or spotted a lady smoking on the street.

"First for other things too, don't I guess," Louise said, her smile filled with mischief. Ginny laughed and squeezed Marion's hand, which made her feel cared for.

"The only first on Louise's honeymoon," Ginny said, still clinging to Marion, swinging her arm, fingers interlaced, "was putting her real name on the hotel register."

"That ain't true," Louise said, twisting her lips like butter-scotch hokum. "I didn't sign the register at all. The bum still had desertion charges outstanding courtesy of the old battle-ax down in Sacramento."

And she and Ginny laughed together, a giddy, earthy, delight-ful laugh, and Marion laughed too. She laughed too and it was all so grown-up. She'd never met any women so young yet so grown-up. So beautiful and no husbands around or downy babies, and if it weren't for the tubercular rack that ripped through Ginny's laugh as it further unpeeled, everything would seem too perfect for words.

SOON, MARION WAS COMING for supper two or three nights a week. It was too much fun. They would play cards, look through *Screen World*, it didn't matter.

There were often new treats to be had, new ones all the time. Once, Marion noticed the big samovar was gone. "Louise cleaned it with bleach and nearly killed us all," Ginny said. "I made her pawn it for *that*." She pointed to a satin nickel roll-around ciga-rette box with a red handle. Marion, charmed, lifted the handle and noticed no cigarettes inside. "Who has dough enough for more than one pack at a time?" Louise shrugged.

One night, Louise made Marion take all the pins from her

long, springy hair and they sheared six inches off, giving her a
shingle bob and declaring, save the blond hair, Marion looked all
the world like Sylvia Sidney. They told her she was now ready for
one of their parties, which, they said, were very famous. What
kind of parties were they, Marion wondered. And who would
come? Who did these girls know?

AND SOON ENOUGH, shimmering pictures in the distance as-
sembled themselves and it was all there before your eyes.

"Marion, can you hop on the streetcar quick as a wink? Ride a
mile and smile the while, dontcha know. Promise me you will."

It was a Tuesday night, nearly eight o'clock and the first time
Marion had ever received a telephone call at the rooming house.
She told Louise she had work to do, a sheaf of case files, fist thick,
her fingers sore, her forearms tingling even as she spoke. She
never seemed to get any faster, always taking work home. Her fingers just didn't move that way. They fluttered, danced—they
didn't, as the other office girls', march in tight formation, march
with the *clack, clack, clack* of industry, of invading armies, of
Progress.

"Don't be a killjoy, Meems. You're off the clock. Your fingers
should be tickling the ears of handsome men, tickling their lobes,
softer than all keys."

Marion felt her face go red as she stood in the rooming-house
hallway. The hallway smelled as always of cabbage, cabbage for
pickling, gusts of vinegar heat wafting through every time Mrs.
Gower came in or out the kitchen door.

"Marion," Louise said, "put on that yellow dress of yours. Mr.
Abner Worth is here, he of Worth Brothers Meat Market, and
the Loomises. Sheriff Healy and his hollow leg. Mr. Worth
brought his hand organ. We told them that you were in your

church choir and now they all want to hear you sing 'After the Roses Have Faded Away.' They've decided to call you the Prairie Canary."

AND AN HOUR LATER, from the rose-hued corner of the girls' living room, she was singing. Surrounded by the red-faced Loomises, she with paper fans for everyone, brought in, inexplicably, from Spokane, Washington, and he with a serape from Tia Juana, a serape now wrapped around little Ginny, who vamped it like Dolores del Rio, Mrs. Loomis dotting her cheek with a jet-black beauty mark, to everyone's delighted approval. Sheriff Healy, still wearing his uniform and tin star, twirled Ginny around like a Russian ballerina. And Marion singing, "The Mansion of Aching Hearts," "My Mexicana Queen," "Sipping Cider Through a Straw" and "In Old Ireland Where the River Kenmare Flows," and Abner Worth spinning his hands, rotating them to unfurl the deep trill of the hand organ. And Mr. Loomis finally crying, crying as Marion warbled, *When you lose your moth-er, you can't buy an-oth-er, If you had all the world and its gold"* and Louise having to drag him down to the sofa, bring his teary head to her bosom, stroke his pink bald head, cooing assurances and reminders that we all love our mothers and it can never be enough.

She would not forget this: Pulling Marion aside in the cramped pullman kitchen, Mr. Worth said, "Another world, my girl, you'd be bright-lighting it at the Palace Theatre in Chicago now. You'd be high stepping it with governors and making Scarface Capone cry in his beer."

Marion, the only one, need you say it, the only one not gurgling bootleg all eve, smiled, sweet and gracious, as she did to the men in her father's church, praising with warm eyes her stirring rendition of "The Old Rugged Cross."

But inside, inside, my, this was fine. Oh, there were other worlds, weren't there? Worlds just beyond her tired fingertips. What she might sink those tips into, soft like clover.

"JUST YOU WATCH OUT FOR THEM, DARLING," Louise whispered as they strode down the clinic's main hall together, Marion's arms filled with patient charts and Louise's with the sputum cups. "The docs ask you to their house for dinner. Trot out the wife. You think it's all copacetic. They're just being grand old dad to you. Next thing you know, they have you knees to flat wood at Old Church of Fair Splinters twice a week plus Thursday night Bible study."

Marion smiled as if she knew what Louise meant and shook her head. "Dr. Milroy has been very kind to me."

"Oh, boy," Louise said, rolling her eyes. "Let's go to the supply room and sneak a smoke, dontcha think? I'll tell you more than you ever wanted to know about all this starch-collar-'n'-high-boots act they're pulling."

Marion did not smoke, but she started going all the time with Louise and she liked how Louise would lift up her long skirt and flash her leg like a can-can dancer, heel propped up high on a supply cart to slide a creased pair of Old Golds from under her garter belt, a ruffle of surprisingly bright orange. Marion had never seen garter elastics in colors like that. It was like the French lady in the pictures Dr. Seeley kept under his talc and his foot powder and the blond strand of baby hair from his brother who died, age six, from diphtheria and his special pills and two francs and a subway token from New York City and his Silver Star.

"These docs, Marion, they do the nastiest things when your eyes shut, or you turn corners, or, God help you, set foot on a stepladder. Keep your wits about you. I got an eyeful of Dr.

Tipton just last week," she whispered, loudly, shaking her match and blowing smoke at Marion.

"What did you see?"

"He was doing something for that pretty redheaded lunger, the one with enough wind left in her sails to blow for a doctor with a snug wallet and a way with the soft solder."

"Oh, Louise, are you sure?" Marion said. Dr. Tipton was nearly forty years old with grown children and a wife famous for her church hats and ladylike ways. But then again, Louise seemed to know everything that went on at the clinic, and sometimes it seemed like the doctors made special efforts to ensure she was well treated. You never saw Louise carrying bedpans or on laundry duty.

"Sure as summer rain, dolly girl," Louise said, flicking tobacco off her lower lip like Warner Baxter. Then she gave Marion a long look and shook her head. "You're lucky you met me."

NIGHTS, SHE'D THINK about Dr. Seeley leaving her here, even as there was no helping it, even as he was not to blame, could never be to blame, her devoted husband going on four years but seemed both longer and much shorter, much shorter. Sometimes wondering who this man was they'd spent so much time apart, so much time in hospital wards, in clinics, in such places. In her head, thinking of him, it was no longer that elegant doctor, a dozen years her senior, with the kind voice, so soft, soft like the soft, gentle pads of his long, elegant fingers. Instead, it was the picture of herself walking down long, milky hospital corridors, seeing him at the other end, seeing him turning the corner to face her, dark-ringed eyes and he smoothing that long forelock and fighting off his shame and she wishing he would not feel it, did not deserve to feel it. Whose fault, after all?

Lying in bed now, she thought of him as if on a holy mission to heal and provide salvation, conjuring vivid images of him in deep-riven Mexican mines, primitive climes where Aztec rites still held sway, like she'd seen in the pictures, like she'd seen in the magazines she peeked at while at the five-and-dime when she was very small. When she let herself, after those first rough days at the clinic, hours spent fingers pressing into typewriter ribbon, carbon stuck, ink pressed under her nails, nails torn tugging, doctors stern in white coats intoning in her ear, intoning about patients waiting and her incompetence—nights after days spent in this head-aching, body-aching fashion, she'd permit herself exactly sixty seconds of anger at her husband, of hating him even. Her husband who couldn't keep his shaking hands off the morphia canisters, all for that gluey, glazed descent into the plush velvet, making his voice slow like an old man, flush-faced and pin-eyed, just like the hollow-chested patients at the veterans hospital in Grand Rapids. Oh, Dr. Seeley—Everett. Everett. Was it worth it? Was it that wondrous a thing?

HE'D BEEN GONE, the doctor had, two months, including even her birthday, Christmas and New Year's Eve now coming upon, and if it weren't for Louise and Ginny, she'd have spent it sobbing over piecework in her cold room like some kind of lost lady in a melodrama, lungs coated with coal soot or prairie dust while her husband fought in the Argonne, in Manila Bay, at San Juan Hill. But Louise and Ginny had big New Year's Eve plans that involved a friend of theirs, one Jibs McNeary, bringing a crate full of tin-pan noisemakers, horns with blower tips, table bangers and jaunty foil hats, the latest stack of race records piled high in the arms of Mr. Scott, fresh off a sales trip through honeysuckled towns all through the South and pink champagne from Canada drunk gushingly and splashing sweetly over upturned faces gay with pleasure, red with heat, sparkling with the endless confetti purchased by the Santa sackful from the five-and-dime.

Most of all, they were glad because their friend Gentleman Joe Lanigan, gone since before Thanksgiving on a business trip back east, would be back for the party and there would be toasts and music and merriment marking his triumphant return.

Gentleman Joe was the girls' favorite among all the men, the one they never talked about without smiling rosy cheeked and making side jokes and winking and tickling each other even, if it was late and the girls were feeling silly.

"Don't feel left out, Marion. You'll meet him soon enough and you'll love him just as much as we do."

"We'd never have met any of our friends without his kind-nesses."

"He brings ukuleles and big jars of cocktail onions and mara-schino cherries."

"All kinds of crazy stuff."

"He calls himself the Greater Downtown Benevolence Com-mittee."

"He's the welcome wagon!" Ginny said, voice tumbling giddily.

"He's the big-brother type," Louise said, her hand on Mari-on's arm. "We all need big brothers, don't we, now?"

NEW YEAR'S EVE CAME and the crowd was just as big as the girls said, the house burning up at near 90 degrees and the men stripping down to shirtsleeves.

Someone had brought a big chrome cocktail shaker shaped like a bell, which Louise swung like a town crier when she mixed the cocktails.

Marion limited herself to one small glass of blackberry cordial, which Jibs's mother made herself with beaten loaf sugar and stored in her cellar.

Everyone was dancing and the music was rushing through her body even when she stood still.

Suddenly, there was a big whoop and Marion thought it must be midnight even as she knew the electric wall clock had struck eleven no more than ten minutes before.

But no, it was all because of the Big Arrival. There was a swirl of looping bodies, everyone in the room but Marion caught in some kind of cyclone, sucking them toward the opening door creaking with their weight as they crushed against it.

The top of his hat, she saw that first and would always remember it. It had a teardrop crease in the center and it was burgundy, the first time she'd ever seen a man in a burgundy hat.

She was standing in the corner of the room and they were all around him and oohing and cooing and cuddling and backslapping, "How the hell you been, Joe?" "Oh, Joe, we thought we'd never see that pretty mug again," "Joe, wait till I tell you about the new plot up for sale on Banville. It's a sweet deal," "My dear, Joe, that's the biggest bottle of hooch I've seen since Ma died."

And finally, tall bottles, cans of herring and silver anchovies, a crate of pearly oysters, a tilting pile of tin hand clackers, a few sliding away from the tangle and clattering to the floor, and there he was. There he was. And Marion would remember it just like that, like everyone falling away, a package unwrapped just for her. How could she not? A motion picture actor, that's what he looked like, with that burgundy felt hat and his broad-shouldered topcoat and shoes shining like church floors on Easter. A smile like a swinging gate and smelling strong of sweet tobacco and slivered almonds and wind and travel and far-off places. When he took the hat off, his hair, blond and bright, shone nearly pink under the overhanging paper lantern, and Marion felt herself inhale fast and her eyes unfocus.

"Who's the peach?" he was saying, and before she knew it he'd swept her up into his overcoat and the lapel rustling up, crushing her nose, pressing into her mouth, which was somehow open.

Peering up over his coat collar, she could see his eyes dancing, his bemused smile.

"That's Marion," she heard someone, Ginny, say, and everyone started singing, *"Mary, Mary's the girl for me, Mary, and I married soon will be."*

She felt a hand on her wrist, cold and strong, and she was yanked from the soft cocoon.

"But, Joe," Louise was saying, and it was her hand Marion had felt, and now Louise flung her sidewise. "We haven't wrapped her for you yet."

And then Ginny popped a cork and it hit Mr. Gergen, the Westclox salesman, in the eye, but he didn't seem to notice. Everyone swarmed forward with their empty glasses and Louise wriggled behind Joe Lanigan to take his coat, running her hand down on it. "Cashmere, my love?" she asked.

"Vicuna, kiddo," he said with a grin, clapping his hand against her face.

Men didn't do that with Louise, not that Marion had ever seen. Not at the hospital, where they held doors for her and lifted things for her and tipped their hats. They might give lingering looks as she walked by them but they never did any wink and tickle like with so many of the nurses. And the men here, the men who came to her home, as careless as it was here, well, they sure liked to bring her presents, and maybe, maybe, they'd go as far as asking for a cuddle on the corner of the settee.

But not this. Not as Gent Joe was. Not so blithe, not so re-laxed like she was a hatcheck girl, a girl in the elevator to press buttons and take pinches. Marion, even head fuzzy as it was, fuzzy like someone had run a dust rag across the whole world, took notice.

And then the crowd swallowed him again and Louise turned back toward Marion and leaned close, pressing against Marion, her velvety breast shining with spilt champagne, foam dappling.

"Help me, dear," she said, Marion in the crook of her elbow, like a coach talking to his star player, whispering the next play deep in the ear. "Will you help me?"

"What is it, Louise?"

"In here," she said, hitching Marion toward the door and into the hallway.

They were in the narrow bathroom and Louise was propped up on the sink. She was lifting her bristly bronze skirt up over her knees, and this time her garters were garnet colored with silver ribbon curling through.

"What are you doing, Louise?" She wondered if it was femi-nine troubles like Ginny was always having, Ginny who had pains lasting two weeks each month, requiring massages, low lights and a steady supply of something called Cardui Treatment, which came in a green bottle and which she'd spoon into her favorite highball glass. *"Blessed thistle, black haw and goldenseal,"* Ginny would lisp, finger pressed on the bottle label. *"Stops flooding spells, heaviness in the abdomen. Giddiness." Am I less giddy, Marion, am I?* She was not.

Here was Louise slipping her fingers under her ruffling bloomers and pulling out loose pills, one after another, into her other palm still sticky from squeezing lemons for the drinks.

"Can you take these for me, Marion? I don't want Ginny to find them," Louise said. "She thinks whatever I get is all for her.

But I have to pay the rent with something other than my fine bottom."

"Where did they come from, Louise?" Marion asked. Her husband's face flashed before her eyes. He was the first person to show her such pills, without meaning to, tucked in his trouser cuffs, on their honeymoon trip from Grand Rapids to St. Louis. When she lifted his suit from the trunk, pressing her hand into the knife pleats, the pills scattered all over the floor of the train car and his gasp was loud and pained.

"Mr. Lanigan, of course," Louise said. "Isn't he kind?"

"Louise, what are you doing with . . . with narcotics?"

"Oh, Marion, don't pull a face with me. They're just medicine. You know how the other fellows, Mr. Gergen and Mr. Scott and Mr. Worth, all bring us notions? Even Sheriff Healy once brought us a marble bust with a bullet in it from that big raid at the Dempsey Hotel. I sold it for four dollars. Why, Mr. Worth brought us the baby lamb just last Sunday. They all bring us the things they sell. Well, Mr. Lanigan, he sells medicines. And he knows Ginny's in such terrible, terrible pain and so he brings me little treasures. And I dole them out one by one. But, Marion, Ginny loves pills of any kind, she's not particular, she just loves them such a darn lot and I've tried to hide them but don't you know she finds them, the little minx."

Marion looked at her in the tiny bathroom, Louise all legs and hot breath atop the sink, her damp hands dotted with pills, eyes on her so anxiously.

"But you said something about paying your rent."

"If I were to buy her medicine, all of it, my darling, I couldn't rub together two dimes for rent. I couldn't, Marion. Don't you know it? Sure, I could pawn the radio. Do you want me to pawn Mr. Loomis's lovely radio, Marion? Mr. Loomis was so happy to give us that radio."

Mr. Loomis had been awfully pleased to give them the Silvertone cathedral radio. Marion had heard the story many times, including from Mr. Loomis himself, who spoke breathlessly about how he'd had it wheeled in on a dolly while the girls were at Sunday services (that's what he said, though she had never heard of either Louise or Ginny attending church), and when they came home, there it was in the living room, trilling Eddie Cantor singing, "Potatoes are Cheaper, Tomatoes Are Cheaper, Now's the Time to Fall in Love."

So Marion slipped the pills into the pocket of her dress, but Louise said that was not near good enough and she wrapped the pills in a handkerchief for Marion and told her to tuck them in her step-ins. Marion felt her face go red and she would not do it and Louise laughed and laughed and laughed. They strode back to the party arm in arm and Louise was still laughing and so beautiful.

Opening the door to the room—the door was vibrating with music, with music so frenetic, that "Tiger Rag" song they'd played five times before, and when the door opened it was like a blast of moist heat in the face, all the energy of so many in such small spaces and the men with collars sprung loose and the women with no shoes.

Mrs. Loomis was waving around the girls' tiny Colt pistol and shouting she'd blow everyone to pieces at midnight and one of the other women screamed.

"Aw, hold your hokum, that ain't nothing but a cig lighter," someone groaned, but Louise said that wasn't true and tried to stop Mrs. Loomis, who was spinning the pistol around her finger, dancing some kind of crazy jig.

And there was Ginny pouring champagne into the oysters on a big silver platter and then walking around with one in each hand to tilt in someone's mouth.

It was the most exciting thing Marion had ever seen.

But she'd had enough spirits and she liked her head steadier and she found her way to a corner of the room by the window and she curled herself up over there and watched everything and turned down lunging offers to dance with smiles, even as Ginny shook her head and murmured, "Marion, there's not enough girls to go around. Take your turn around before we wilt."

So she did one turn with Mr. Gergen, his hands like hamhocks slapping against her, the smell of gin and pickles gusting from his mouth, and when he finally released her, he hurled her right into the chest of Joe Lanigan, who was standing, amused, by the accordion wall, a bottle of Triple XXX root beer in his hand.

She backed up quickly but not before he'd reached forward and lifted, with one finger, a wayward curl from her forehead.

"He likes Marion," she heard one of them whisper in the background behind sweated palm.

It happened so fast she almost missed it because Mr. Worth had his arm around her waist for his turn.

She was being twirled, she was being twirled, and it was like she was a spindle top.

And then Joe Lanigan, he turned to her. He turned to her and focused on her and she felt as small as a baby doll rocking in the corner. She thought if she opened her mouth baby goos would come out. So she didn't say anything. And he folded his arms and looked at her and nodded and she knew he knew everything. About the starch in her underthings, the Isabey powder she passed up and down each leg after bathing and about the baby doll rocking in the corner. He knew it all.

LATER, THE ORDER OF THINGS, she wouldn't be able to piece it together. Not because of the charging liquor but because of everything else, the whole gypsy tumult of it. Later, what she would remember most were flashes, flickers like when the film's running off projection reels. Herself, hand holding a champagne glass, the champagne sloshing over her pink fingers:

. . . pinches my nose, Mr. Lanigan.

. . . they all say that, who doesn't like a pinch, and call me Joe, call me Joe, Mrs. Seeley, Mrs. Seeley you don't seem like any doctor's wife I ever knew and I've known them all.

. . . you've known them all, how is that?

. . . well, Mrs. Seeley, I own some stores, you see.

. . . he owns a dozen stores, Marion—that was Louise, suddenly there—*Marion, he's Valiant Drugs where you buy your lemon soap, isn't that something? Where you buy your witch hazel and your talc and your tooth powder.*

. . . what else do you buy at my stores, Mrs. Seeley? Is that where you buy the sweet magnolia in your hair, the sweet magnolia I will smell on my shirt collar tomorrow, on my cuffs and collars and in my dreams when I dream of you tonight?

Monday, Louise looked pale and pinched.

"My head, Marion, it's two cotton balls wadded with spit," she groaned. "Two days and still hanging heavy as my granddad's long johns." She had a compress on her head like Barney Google in the comic pages.

Marion gave her a cup of weak tea with geranium. She had so many questions about the party but didn't know how to ask them, which words to use.

"You're the shiny penny. Why couldn't I keep temperance like you? Bet you could dance a Virginia reel and still keep that liverwurst down." Louise peeped out from underneath the compress. "Listen, Meems, did I by any chance give you something to hold for me the other night, or did I just dream it?"

Marion nodded quickly, fingering the handkerchief of pills in her pocket.

"Well, that's fine," Louise said, smiling broadly. "That's fine. Do you have them here?"

Marion plucked them from her pocket and handed them to Louise, who smiled like Christmas morning.

They went to her locker and Louise put the pills in the heel of her spare shoe.

"Ginny, she likes to take pills, pills like that?"

"Well, don't she. She suffers mightily, Marion, and who would hold a little peace against her?"

"Not I," she said, twisting her ring around her finger. "My husband, he . . ."

"Oh, I'm sure, as a doctor, he sees such things all the time. I'm sure he understands that in these gloomy days one must pass out glimmers where one may. Isn't that so, Marion?"

"He does understand that," Marion agreed, thinking of her husband, hand covering his face, covering it from her as he lay on his hospital bed, sat on the bench in the county jail, walked in from five days missing, eyes hooded from her, not bearing to touch her. "Yes, he does."

THE DARK SPOT on his brain. That was how Dr. Seeley explained it to her long ago. It was like a dark spot, pulsing. He said were it not for the dark spot the size of a thumbprint, a baby plum, he would be living the life of the man he so clearly was. Intelligent, stalwart, respectable. The town doctor, the trusted citizen. The doting husband. The kindly father.

The dark spot, shaped, perhaps, like a crooked star, a pinwheel, a circle fan.

What it was, exactly, he could not explain, even to her, even as he cried in her arms in hospital wards in three states. It was his private curse.

He had not even known of its presence until age twenty-nine when, while seated in the audience of the Savoy Theatre in Wilkes-Barre, Pennsylvania, a large eave of plaster ceiling fell upon him, upon his leg and hip, and twenty other audience members. The picture was called *A Love Sundae,* he always remembered that.

He was in the hospital for four days and, a young doctor himself, he knew his injuries were far from critical. But his body, the way it moved, never felt the same again. And the medicine they gave him, why, it was a wonder, shuttling his body to Kubla Khan, and there was nothing else like it. Nothing at all. He tried. There was nothing.

Shaking hands, some stolen medicine found in his automobile, that little girl's jaw set wrong. He knew he had to stop. But he could not. That was when he became aware of the dark spot. Its pulsing points, the way it lived in his brain. The spot, it was there, and you couldn't cut it out or wipe it away. It was there and changed everything.

MR. JOE LANIGAN had many reasons to be at the clinic. His pharmacies, three within city limits, brought him into business with Werden and they knew him well. He was there in Dr. Milroy's office and there was no reason to be surprised, to be struck. Marion heard his voice first, the big quality of it, like he was on a stage or in a pulpit.

". . . that's the stuff. That's the future right there. All the doctors back east are using it. Just back myself and that's what they all said. Chicago. Cleveland. Philadelphia. Boston. Even New York City."

Dr. Milroy stuttered a reply Marion couldn't make out and then it was Joe Lanigan again.

". . . ammonium chloride with codeine and, if the cough is loose, the heroin of terpin hydrate. Call me old-fashioned, Doctor, but you can use those ultraviolet contraptions till we're all moon men and it won't shake the rug without some fine chemical assistance."

They talked some and Marion stood by the door with her legs trembling and she felt silly about herself, she a grown woman with legs trembling from some big-voiced man. But what could she tell her body? Nothing. Her body knew things she didn't and it shook like a spring toy and then the door began to open and she saw him there and he saw her.

"Why, Mrs. Seeley, my New Year's baby," he said, his eyes dancing, his body, cloaked in brush-soft flannel, still and easy.

She said hello, Mr. Lanigan, and nearly curtsied, seeing him as she had, three days before, under a sugared skein of girl-pink champagne, under the heavy weight of parlor heat, thick on their skins, thick with their own energies, own high spirits. And now here like this, in the cool, bleachy hallways of the blasted-brick clinic, didn't it look so inoculated? Yet it was a pox, vermin in every sweating pore, sputum lining every crevice no matter how swabbed and brush-scoured it was.

"You tend to all the lungers? God's work," he said serenely, so upright, so upright in this place, at this time, amid no popping corks.

She said it was not quite tending and explained her job in ways that didn't include days filled with her ear to the Dictaphone, with listening to doctors droning on wax cylinders, with stamping ink onto forms with small boxes enfolding smaller boxes enfolding smaller boxes still. She explained it quickly and simply and he nodded, as though listening, as though listening and caring. He asked her about how Dr. Milroy treated her, did he make her work long hours, did he make sure she got home safely, and how did her coworkers treat her, had they made her feel at home here?

Then he invited her to lunch. He said he had some questions about Mrs. Lanigan's care and hoped she might offer her thoughts, you see, his wife was ill, very ill.

She supposed she had known he had a wife. They all had wives. But hearing him speak of her made something twitch under her skin and her fingers sought, quietly, the effusion scar on her neck, the Golden Stamp, as Ginny called it.

"Well, Mrs. Seeley, will you?" he asked again.

What could be wrong about having lunch with a man who wanted help in matters concerning his wife's health? Surely anyone would approve, would think it proper, kind even.

THE BRIGHTLY LIT dining room of McBewley's stretched before her, with crisp white tablecloths and freshly cut petunias and sweet baskets of crumbly breads that came with little glass tumblers small as thimbles of seedy jam that slid on her fingers and under her nails, and she would taste it for hours back at the clinic just flicking secretly her hand along her lower lip, along her part-open mouth.

They served tea in steaming pots dotted with cornflowers and the sandwiches came on porcelain plates and there were tall glasses of tea and crisp-cut lemon wedges.

And Joe Lanigan sat across from her and the table was small and even leaning back, as he tended to do to grant her proper distance, even then his leg crossing still sometimes grazed her skirt. But he paid no notice and talked seriously, gravely, with solemnity, about his dear wife struck down not by lung evils but by kidney ailments and other private disorders, and now confined to bed. Confined to bed now near three years.

Many a doctor had recommended he send her to a clinic for full-time care but he'd have none of it. As long as he could manage a nurse in the home, he would keep her there, keep her with him and their two children, ages seven and nine, who needed a mother, even if that mother seldom left her darkened room, air always thick with camphor and eucalyptus. As long as he could work dawn to dusk making a success of his stores, he would keep her there—wasn't that the right thing, God's will? Didn't she agree?

WHEN HE LOOKED AT HER, she could feel it like his finger, the tip of his finger, was tickling the lace bristles on her underthings. Like it was flicking up and down down there. And she didn't know where she got this idea because nothing like that had ever happened to her. No man's fingers there, not like that, light and teasing and slow. Not like Dr. Seeley, whom she only remembered ever touching her underthings as if they were delicate pages of an ancient screed, beginning on their wedding night when he had to coax her for hours with patting strokes or nothing ever would have happened at all, scared as she was that his plan—any man's plan—was to rip her in two. That's what her church friend Evangeline, who'd married at seventeen and left school, said it was like. Marion saw her at the Sunday social two weeks after the wedding where Vangy had worn her mother's heavy dress, weighed five pounds. She and Vangy carried their plates slick with watermelon juice from the tables and snuck down to the Willow Run Creek and Vangy had said, *Oh, Marion, wait long as you can. I'm riven in two and I never knew from such pain like a hot poker stuck. Each time like wire sticking in me. Don't relent till you can't wait for a baby a*

moment longer. Once I get two children I'm turning face to the wall in
bed each night and just he try and make me lay still for him one more
time. Just he try.

Mr. Lanigan, Gent Joe, took her to lunch twice more that
week. They spoke again, and at length, of his poor wife, buffered in cotton balls, glossed with ointments, wrapped tight like a
swaddled baby, eyes glazed over with narcotics. And then, as they
shook their napkins of crumbs and settled into tea at the end of
the third lunch, he looked across the table and said, "And, Mrs.
Seeley, how is your Dr. Seeley? How does he come to be so far
from your side?"

Marion had been lifting her teacup and as the words struck
her ear, for they did strike and with some force, the handle slid
round her finger and slid from the crook her fingers made and
cracked in two perfect pieces on the table. A chip flew in Marion's
eye and her lashes rustled against and a spot of blood flecked up
and starred her brow.

It was all so terrible, with the crash and clatter and Joe Lanigan rushing round to assist her and the waitress walking her, more
than half blind, to the ladies' parlor to flood her eye under the
sink, head cracking the sink twice, water running everywhere,
even down her uniform, sopping her chest and trickling deep between her breasts and riveting down to her belly.

(For hours afterward, with each blink she'd think the porcelain pock was still there, still there and scraping, ridging her eye
with each flutter.)

Riding from the tearoom in his motorcar, her hair slipping
from beneath her scarf, she told him she couldn't, no, *couldn't*
come to lunch again on Monday. And, far more, she would not be
able to take up his recent invitation to attend, as his new friend,

the birthday revels of one Ephraim Solway, a fellow Knight, in the banquet room of the El Royale Hotel.

She could not fathom what had come over her that had let it go and go and go. Sitting in restaurants together, legs sweeping against legs, hand on her back, the center of it, fingertips there, as she seated herself. It was dreadful. It was unforgivable at the core. In her head, she began formulating a letter to Dr. Seeley. (How was it now she could only think of him as "Dr. Seeley"? The longer he was away, the more impossible to name that looming absence "Everett," much less some coo-cooing term, as she might let slip from her lips in their sweetest times, their private afternoons, he pressing his face gentle into her hair and calling her his darling, his dimple-cheeked dearest. When were those times?)

Yes, she told herself, she would write Dr. Seeley directly, chronicle the whole series of luncheons, and make him understand she'd stumbled—foolishly, yes, but she was young and all by herself and in a strange place for so long—into something improper and found her way out quickly, before a single observer could disapprove.

Oh, Dr. Seeley, you alone in fierce surroundings, tending nobly to the ruined lungs of sad-eyed Cornish miners, their own days trapped under bauxite, silver, manganese miles thick, nights spent brining their grief in sugarcane liquor. Oh, Dr. Seeley, your sacrifices so great and your soul beating off the dark furies inside you, that depthless, dooming taste for the needle and its bloom? Your sufferings so immense, and here I sit in comparative comfort and ease, defaming our marriage by degrees.

By the time Joe Lanigan had driven her, hand to wounded eye, back to the clinic, it was all she could do to fight off a heavy sob in her chest. As if he knew it, Mr. Lanigan was more the gentleman than ever, treating her with the delicacy and gentility he might his starch-gloved grandmother.

But when he'd delivered her to the front door, he touched her arm lightly, which he ought not to have, fingers sliding down her arm to her hand. And he turned her toward him and spoke quietly, solemnly, far too close to her twitching face, tears gluing on her lashes still. And he said this, and it was like a claw hammer to her heart:

"For all the world, Mrs. Seeley, I'd not leave your side. Were you my wife, for all the world, I'd not lose my way from you. I'd not abandon you to the world. Not in such hard times, not in any time. I'd not leave you out there in the dark middle, not you with that angel's face, that beating chest, the pulse in your wrist I can feel even now. I'd not leave your side, Mrs. Seeley. I'd like to meet the man who could."

That night, under covers and eyes still twitching, flickering back into her head, she dared think of a world where she, barely out from behind her father's coats, would have fumbled her way to the likes of Joe Lanigan rather than her husband, brushing middle age even at thirty-five. Dr. Everett Seeley, with each passing year more like some gaunt returning soldier from far-off battles, those once-gallant features half ruined, those dark-ringed eyes and blue-edged cheekbones and the slow shuffle and the smell of his shirts on the ironing board. Dr. Seeley, so noble, so kind, but slipping from her with every passing second since they met. All he was was what was almost gone. The only thing that truly remained was the very thing that stripped their pockets clean twice a year since they'd married and finally sent him miles away, leaving her here, lovelier than ever and ripe for picking.

Oh, Joe Lanigan, you've found yourself a fellow sinner—how did

you know it? Was it on my face like a witch's mark? Or was it some-
thing vibrating in my eyes, something that said I am yours, I am yours.

MARION WAITED. She waited and Joe Lanigan did not call
again the next day, nor the following. And the weekend came, and
there was Saturday, the day of the planned birthday gala for Mr.
Ephraim Solway at the El Royale Hotel, to which he had invited
her and she had firmly, frantically declined.

At noon, collar itching and feeling squirmy and hot, she
walked to the Pay'n Takit to buy laundry starch. On the way out,
head heavy with thoughts, the bent ceiling fan stirring dust and
rustling moth flies, she saw a wire canister by the register filled
with chocolate nougatines wrapped in sticking waxed paper. Her
hand clasped over one like a crow's claw, she walked out of the
store and onto the street, tearing off the wrapper and tucking it
into her mouth and letting it sit there, strips of the wax still sticking to it, powdering her tongue, taking just enough of the pleasure away to send her back to the store, mouth clotted, to buy a
second and pay for both, even as it would mean, for her at least,
for the way she judged herself, no new shampoo for the week and
she'd have a bologna sandwich for supper.

At one o'clock, she carried her laundry basket across the street
to the Maddens, who let Mrs. Gower's boarders use their electric
washing machine if they brought their own soap flakes and put
change in the kitty. Marion had grown up washing with a board
and wringer, big kettle and bluing—it took a day or more. But
then she was washing for the whole family and now she was just
washing her own two work dresses, her nightgown, her underthings, her sheets and bath towel, which Mrs. Gower was supposed to launder but did not.

The hours stretched, arched, curled back, and Marion stood

in the Gowers' backyard where her dresses hung, paper dolls fluttering, and she stood and didn't move and her head was filled with sorrow and it wasn't the right kind of sorrow. She stood, the air barely moving, the sky muddy with late-afternoon muddiness, that dread feeling of stillness, which suggests no movement again, ever.

At seven o'clock, the appointed hour, Marion on the edge of her bed thinking, *This would have been the time, were I to have been so wayward, or less wayward (for doing without knowing why, that must be happiness).*

Somehow, still, she was awaiting his knock, could picture the door opening, his camel's-hair-coat, hair-oil-glistening arrival, he like a man from a motion picture, on Kay Francis's arm, towering over with broad shoulders and her hand slipping eagerly through the crook of his solid arm, he with a smile like Fredric March, like Robert Montgomery, like any of them. He was like any of them. All of them. Bright and shiny like polished dress shoes.

So it was a long hour after that, radio playing, rasping out *"Far away near Havana shores there lives a girl, whom I call dancing Cuban Pearl,"* and Marion darning, like her crook-handed mother, stockings fuzzed with wear. She might have gone to the girls' place on Hussel Street. Louise always said it was an open invitation and that Saturdays were always a scream, they made sure of it.

But then there it was, like an air horn blast. Eight o'clock, or three minutes past, the sharp knock and frog-jawed Mrs. Gower, robe pulled across low-slung chest, saying, "A Mr. Lanigan should want you on the telephone, Mrs. Seeley. Told him I shan't expect you to take calls this late but he said mightn't I try. Couldn't barely hear him. Sounds like he's telephoning from a train station, or a rodeo."

Marion's breath fast, her hand nearly damp on the mouthpiece, fingers pressed on the thrumming ringer box. "Mr. Lanigan?"

Was that his voice amid the crunching sounds of the festivities, glasses tinkling, dishes clapping against each other, chairs skidding, a trombone drawling, but most of all waves of laughter, men and women laughing together?

"Mrs. Seeley . . . I know you had declined me, but I do believe you have the wrong impression . . . should come . . . respectable celebration in honor of a fine civic leader and Mr. Solway himself would so appreciate your presence . . . might you consider attending? . . . You might take a trolley car down and I would meet you and escort you . . ."

THE TWO YOUNG MEN next to her on the trolley, both wheezing corn liquor, kept rustling her, each time apologizing, hat doffing, but still so caught up in their drunken stories that they'd inevitably fall to it again, one of them even jabbing her straight in the bosom.

Don't I deserve it, Marion thought. Her knees shaking, her heart vibrating like a tug spring, she cursed herself for not hesitating fifteen seconds before putting on her one fine dress, daffodil colored and ironed to shininess, borrowing trolley fare from no less than bristle-lipped Mrs. Gower ("It was my brother, Mrs. Gower. He needs me to wire him train fare home to see our dear mother."). And now, heading alone to a downtown hotel to see a man she had no business seeing. No business seeing at all except the business of ruin. She felt her stomach flip three times, and could barely wait to get there.

No one was waiting for her at the trolley stop. She could see the El Royale from where she stood and then she was walking there. She wondered, as she kept her eyes on the hotel, which sprawled a full city block and had a front canopy of gold, if this awfulness in her was new, a spell cast, or something inside her that he had stoked or merely touched and watched enfold in her.

But then, walking alone into the cavernous Thunderbird Dining Room, a sea of dark suits and mustaches, cigar smoke and preening, she felt everything inside her held so tight for a week or more release itself. She saw only a handful of women, their dresses like glowing paint streaks—poppy, turquoise, parrot green. They were young like her, but their dresses dipped low, showing shiny flesh, and their eyes were fringed with dark lashes and their cheeks were like berries bursting, crinkly hair marcelled, and it was all very, very wrong that she should be here, and one man, a stout patrician type with a bulging pocket-watched vest, he had his hands clambering down a girl's lightly clad, shimmery gold back nearly toward her behind and then, definitely, there. The music hammered at her and the floors felt sodden with champagne and maybe it wasn't so different from Louise and Ginny's and yet it was. It was. It was because that was their party and this was not. This was not. It was something else and it felt a little bit like these girls had, stiff-faced and cold-eyed, punched a clock.

Then, from the corner of her eye, something: a swath of dress the color of crème de menthe and it was a dress she knew, as Mrs. Loomis had worn it on New Year's Eve, and it fit so snug across her swelling chest that the trim kept tearing. But it didn't look like Mrs. Loomis, not the way the dress was hanging, swinging.

Her eye followed the dress, followed its peacock spread, trailed it as it spanned and tucked and then settled behind the large gray shoulder of a man she recognized as one of the doctors at the clinic, Dr. Jellbye, Dr. Jellieck, Dr. Jellineck . . . and then he turned and behind him Marion could see that bristle of deep red hair and then Louise's kohl-rimmed eyes, jittery with pleasure.

"It's my prairie canary," came a voice slipping rough in her ear, startling Marion, making her flinch. But it was only Mr. Gergen, the Westclox salesman, and he took Marion's arm in his sausage fingers and plucked her from the crush and as he did said, "Joe Irish is looking for you, bunny rabbit." And she felt overwrought and angry and she said, "I don't know who you mean. And you may tell him I have gone."

But Marion's voice seemed to get swallowed up by Mr. Gergen and his big double-breasted suit jacket and then, like a game of Pass the Parcel, she was fast in the arms of Gent Joe himself, tuxedo black as India ink, and she looked up at his eyes, his eyes smiling, his face doing smiling things as if there were never any such thing as shame in this world, and she caught his eyes and she said, in a voice that surprised her, "Mr. Lanigan, you will remove me from this place," a strong, spiky voice like Louise telling a noisy patient, "I suppose you know you're disturbing the entire ward, Mr. Milksop."

He did as she said. He removed her with great speed.

Then they were in front of the hotel and the cold pinpricking her and he putting his tuxedo jacket around her.

"These are not the kinds of places I can . . ."

He pulled his jacket tighter around her and said, mournfully like those Irish can do, "I shouldn't have asked you to come. But I saw no other way. You had closed the door on me. But I was wrong. Of course I was wrong. I should have realized this was no place for you. That's a lie, Mrs. Seeley. I knew this was no place for you. And yet."

He said he'd take her home in his motorcar and she didn't like it but could think of no other way. The trolleys ran an hour apart this time of night.

In his car, she sat far against the door, feeling suddenly like he'd seen her without her clothing. She felt like, in coming, she'd shown him everything. She knew she had. And now she must retreat.

The sedan was filled with him, he was so large a presence, so tall and with that hair thick like a layer cake, and the way he talked, which was big, like the best salesman, filled with tricks of tone and turns of phrase—there was this way he had of always reminding you how important and marvelous what was happening to you just then was.

"And that El Royale Hotel, I've invested a substantial amount in it, it will be colossal. Did you know, they put circulating ice water in every room and automatic cooled air that changes every three minutes? I timed it. But listen to me sitting here talking nonsense about circulating water and I get these moments with you and it's a thing of glory, just like this, this is all I wanted, Mrs. Seeley, and I just didn't know how else to make it happen."

He drove three miles past Mrs. Gower's house, would not stop pressing until she turned and let a snarl loose like none she knew was in her.

"What kind of husband," she said, "with an invalid wife at home no less, spends his evenings like this, Mr. Lanigan?"

"What kind of husband is your Dr. Seeley," he replied, rough as a razor strap, "leaving his wife behind and packing off to savage Mexico?"

And that was a terrible thing for a man to say, for anyone to say, what did he know of her husband's sorrows and burdens, and Marion felt it like a hot iron to her chest and she hated Joe Lanigan, she did.

IN BED THAT NIGHT, face greasy with cold cream, she recalled the way, after apologizing and apologizing once more for his harsh words, for his poor behavior, he opened the car door and doffed his hat and followed her to the front door and his head, the top of it, brushed the porch lamp and his hair shot through with light and his face so grave, long shadows meeting beneath his chin. "I wish you could see, Mrs. Seeley, what this is. This thing that has happened, that is happening still, that cannot be stopped from happening. I wish you could see what this is."

"I know what it is, Mr. Lanigan," she'd said, clipped and abrupt, shutting the door behind her.

THEN NOTHING FOR DAYS and Marion, head down in work and evenings spent writing a long letter to Mazatlán:

> *Dr. Seeley, please do not forget me here. My lungs breathe*
> *free and clear, couldn't I come to you at last? I know you*
> *said it would not be right to have babies until you had*
> *beat this thing, but you have and now I have babies to*
> *give and everything else too. All the dark snarls in my*
> *head are gone and I can be the wife I . . .*

Each day the idea of another evening spent in her room was near too much to bear. And so she threw herself into the girls' mad embrace and was so grateful for it.

A midweek supper at Louise and Ginny's, Louise trying out a new dish she'd created called February Surprise and it was canned cream of celery soup and egg noodles with baking-powder biscuits on top and everyone agreed it was wretched and Ginny tried to throw it out the window and there was screaming laughter. Marion was so glad she'd come.

Even still, seeing Louise, she found herself worrying about the party at the El Royale Hotel. Had it been Louise, and had

Louise seen her? Somehow, she had come to persuade herself that she had misseen, as distressed as she was.

But then Ginny, breaking a fever and feeling sour, said, "Marion, do you think it's nice that Louise leaves me alone so often? I wonder if she'll go out on the town this weekend, like she did last. I had to entertain myself with Chubby Parker and Pie Plant Pete on the radio instead."

"Poor little baby," Louise said, singsong. "Did you need me to wash your hair, Princess Virginia?"

And then Ginny broke the onion face and did laugh and Marion said, almost a whisper, "Where did you go, Louise?"

"Birthday party." Louise smiled, lifting Ginny's ankles off the sofa, and settled herself beneath them, squeezing Ginny's pink-slippered feet.

"And my, did she tie one on." Ginny rolled her eyes. "Came home near three o'clock and drank bicarbonate all Sunday."

"I'd've just as soon stayed in Saturday night, but someone was rattling like a diamondback."

"So I drove you out, that it? Drove you to ruin."

"Something like, kitten."

Marion almost spoke up but didn't. To say anything would be to admit she was at the party and that she could not do. She could say nothing, not even to her new, her dearest friends. She would have to live with her shame, but she didn't need to share it with others. Never that.

LATER, LOUISE MADE MARION a bed of the settee, muslin tucked tight.

"You are a lonely girl," she said. "We won't let you be lonely."

Marion smiled.

"It's funny," Louise whispered, head tilted confidingly. "For Ginny, men are only to play with."

"But not for you?" Marion whispered back.

"Not for me," Louise said, shaking her head. "Sometimes one gets under my skin and *poppoppop* like a needle."

"Yes, that's what it's like," Marion admitted, in spite of herself. "That's just what it's like, *poppoppop*."

DR. SEELEY, *you must understand my plight. I am in peril. I am nearly lost.*

FRIDAY STRETCHED LONG at the clinic. Six new patients were admitted, papers needed to be put in order for the state inspection on Monday, and two nurses had been dismissed the day before (Louise heard tell and shared with Marion they were caught in the east utility room with a male patient and a jar of corn liquor, not a stitch on and he with hands on them both).

The day never broke and Marion's stockings itched and her back had a mean twist three notches long and Mr. Joe Lanigan had forgotten her forever, hadn't he, and Marion had never finished the letter to Dr. Seeley and had torn the half-finished draft into pieces and hidden them in the toe of one of her wedding shoes because she was afraid if she threw it in the wastepaper basket Mrs. Gower might find it.

On the streetcar home, she set her handbag, heavy with the medical histories she had not finished, across her lap so that she might slip her hand underneath and between the buttons on her skirt and scratch her legs, tickling unbearably underneath her stockings, worn and no new funds from Mexico for three weeks. Under her bag, her fingertips found her thighs and she chanced only a few deep scores before lifting her hand away. The man opposite her, standing, looming, hat on, close-set eyes and toothpick prancing between lips, he looked like he could see and there was a nasty flicker in his eyes and something curling, raw, in his lips. Marion's face fell hot with shame.

TWO HOURS LATER, after a starchy supper with Mrs. Gower and the other two boarders, unmarried girls glum with no dates that night, after helping with the dishes and mouth top still burning with macaroni custard, Marion retired to her room and turned on the radio and opened the window as high as it would go and sat listening to *The Misadventures of Si and Elmer* and knew she should be doing the work she had brought home, or working on the cross-stitch on the handkerchiefs she would send to her mother for her birthday. But she sat by the window and sat until near nine o'clock and that was when she saw the flash of Joe Lanigan's oyster-white topcoat under the streetlamp below.

Later, she would try to tell herself the story of that hour as if it were a fairy tale: the knight climbed up the tower clasped in three centuries of black ivy and he cut through the ivy with a mighty sword and found the fair maiden and she was his.

Later, she would see that hour as if it were a motion picture: the leading man, so handsome, and the leading lady, bathed in white light, and he moving toward her and she toward him, jittery and lovely. And they embraced like in all the pictures, and it was filled with all the things—magic, longing—that picture kisses are filled with. And the darkness on the edges spiraled toward the center and swallowed the screen black.

Later, she would recall again and again the events of that hour while coverlet to chin in her bed approaching three o'clock and hidden under the hood of late-night melancholic dark where everything means so much and everything is so raw and tender and open and it would be like this, like this:

He stood in the doorway, his hat in his hand, and he said, "Mrs. Seeley, you are an honorable woman. I would not for all the world's fortune test your honor. But you must see there are things I have to say to you. Will you let me come inside?"

But she would not. How could she, into her room, the room the good doctor had secured for her. The thought of him in that small space, with only one rose chair, one chair and a bed.

He reached across the threshold and his eyes were on her and wouldn't let go. His hand went out and she jumped back as though he were made of fire, and wasn't he?

"Mrs. Seeley, might you step outside with me, then? Might you walk with me a little?"

But she would not. To be seen on the street with a man, this man, a man all knew was married, with a stricken wife and—

"Mrs. Seeley, what if you were to take a drive with me? There are things I wish to tell you. Private things."

She said she would not, but he stood there still. He looked so weary and the things that touched her about him flew forward for her. She liked to think of herself as the kind of person in whom another person might confide. This is what she told herself even as she knew the things he would say would unravel her. She knew that and she agreed anyway. She agreed and soon enough she was in his Packard, the two of them rumbling down the dark streets, turning corners and not speaking and continuing to go forward until they broke free of the snarls of houses and the dots of street-lamps and into the desert.

And he pulled the car on the side of the road and turned to her. She tried to keep her eyes straight ahead, fixed on the velvety black. But of course she could not. And she waited for a speech from him, a declaration, a confession. Maybe, maybe a sad story about the weight of illness in his house and how it twisted his heart and nearly broke him.

But no speech came.

He reached out to her and took her hand.

Then he asked her to move closer to him.

She would not.

Then he moved closer to her and she could feel him everywhere, his linen coat pressed against her. He whispered something in her ear, but she could not hear it, because his hands had started their way, ways she knew they would find, under her dress and buttonholes gaping and the weight of him and she could stop herself no longer. It was all too much. It was all the kinds of things that had never happened to her and now that they were happening she would not stop it. As she felt herself slide flat against the car seat, as she found herself gripping tight the fine linen of his coat in her hands, lashes fluttering against his face and the roughness of his cheek good and hard on hers, very good. It was then she realized what he'd said, what he'd whispered in her ear.

Marion Seeley, you are mine.

THAT WAS HOW IT BEGAN. And the biggest surprise was that there were no tears, no tears at all for her, that night or the following day. And on Tuesday night, when he arrived again at her door, it happened all over again, this time slow and stretched fine and lovely as blown glass, and then he left and when he did he took her close to his chest and kissed her with great force and told her that he had waited life long for something to mean half as much.

"*WHEN IT RAINED DOWN sorrow it rained all over me. 'Cause my body rattles like a train on that old SP. I've got the T.B. blues. . . .*"

This is what the man with the Adam's apple thick-knotted in his long neck was singing in Ginny's ear, plucking at a banjo.

"You need a har-monica, Floyd," Ginny was saying. "That's the way they do it in the colored joints."

"What do you know from colored joints, Gin-Gin," Louise said, running the carpet sweeper by them, trying to pick up this Floyd's cigarette ashes and the crumbs from the oyster crackers he had brought in a big tin all the way from Green Bay, Wisconsin.

"Why's Marion standing there in the doorway like the Fuller brush man?" Ginny chirped.

They all looked at Marion, who had just arrived and only stepped a few feet into the room.

"I'd buy a Fuller brush from her anytime," Floyd said, then dropped his long black-rimmed fingernails across the banjo strings. "*I've been fighting like a lion, looks like I'm going to lose . . .*"

He did not seem to recall her, but Marion had met Floyd at least twice at the clinic, where he'd come, sick as a dog, from taking gold cyanide given to him by some doctor in Montana.

"Mims looks like she saw a ghost," Ginny said, talking over Floyd's snoring croon.

"*. . . 'cause there ain't nobody ever whipped those Fuller brush blues.*"

"Likely she wasn't expecting such a crowd," someone said, and it was Joe Lanigan, standing by the pullman kitchen, suit jacket off and suspenders twisted, smoking.

Marion stepped in finally, her head jumbled. What was he doing here? This man who had pledged such momentous words to her not two days earlier, now standing in the home of other women in the morning hours as if a dandy bachelor in a red-light bordello?

"We had a late-night gala," Louise said, tugging at carpet with the sweeper, even as Joe Lanigan was dropping fresh ashes from his cigarette. "Maybe you read about it in the society pages of the morning paper."

Knowing Joe Lanigan was a regular guest here, was in fact how she had met him, did not change the fumbling horror of the moment. Joe Lanigan here, like this, at 11:00 a.m. on a Saturday morning. Was this how it was and would continue to be?

Not twelve hours before, on the telephone in Mrs. Gower's dark hallway, whispering into the dark slot of the mouthpiece, *I cannot see you tonight, Mr. Lanigan. I cannot leave here at this hour. You should not ask me to. You know, oh, you know, it's not for not wanting. The wanting is a burning in me. I am all wanting.*

Talking like a French novel, cover creased, in her brother's dresser drawer. How could such words slip from Marion Seeley's lips? And she had naughtier words than that, that was certain. She offered them to Joe Lanigan's curving, shaving-oil-scented ear, offered them in fast torrents, florid as *The Sheik*, which Marion's schoolmates read behind sewing machines in Home Economics, but with words one hundred times as raw. Where did she come to know these words? Had he given them to her secretly in the night as she slept?

"Gent Joe here came over going on midnight," Louise said, flopping down next to Ginny, who curled up against her, sucking on an oyster cracker, blond curls springing and whirling about.

"We were in our bedclothes counting sheep," said Ginny, poking a bare toe, painted violent purple, at Floyd, who, prompted, started again.

"Lord, but that graveyard is a lonesome place. They put you on your back, throw that mud down in your face. I've got the T.B. blues...."

"We really tied one on." Louise yawned. "When did Floyd get here? I don't even remember. Suddenly, he was here."

"Like a fairy sprite," Ginny chirped.

Marion's eyes were still on Joe Lanigan, who was now smiling lightly at her. She did not smile in return.

"Marion, don't you like Gent Joe?" Ginny cooed, stretching her toes out.

Louise looked over at Marion. "Yes, Marion, for goodness' sake, sit down. You're like Sister Abigail over there."

"My good gal's trying to make a fool out of me," Floyd sang. *"Trying to make me believe I don't got that old T.B."*

"He's back to the beginning again," Ginny announced.

"I will sit down," Marion said abruptly. A party, that was all. A party that went on too long, as their parties often did. They never stopped them. They never cared to.

"You should have invited that bright thing last night," Floyd said. "She could have brought her brushes. I'd've bought several myself."

Sitting closer now, Marion could smell the alcohol wafting from him, from all of them.

"We would have, had we known," Louise said, looking harder at Marion now. "There was not time enough to issue the engraved invitations." Something seemed queer in Louise's tone, but Marion couldn't stay on it, couldn't focus. Her thoughts kept caroming back to Joe. When she declined him the night before, she had pictured him wandering despondently in the sickly hallways of his sick house, not here, not here like this. Was it possible he was not her tortured swain?

"Mrs. Seeley is not that sort of woman," Joe Lanigan said, moving toward them, leaving his perch by the kitchenette. His speaking, moving, broke some awful pressure, scissored it clean. But it also tied new knots.

"Marion likes to have fun," Louise asserted, straightening up slightly. "She's always ready for high times."

"There is a difference, Louise, that may be subtle for you but is actually legions wide and fathoms deep," Joe said. "Mrs. Seeley may be alone in these parts, left to fend in our wilderness, but she retains her proper bearing, her breeding, her fine womanly ways. She does not degenerate, she is evolved. She does not come here and let herself be transformed into a backward thing. She is Mrs. Seeley from a good family, good and proper still."

Ginny plucked one of Floyd's banjo strings with her outstretched finger. "Well," she said, feigning to scratch her underarm, "guess I'd better twist myself a banana."

Louise's face was tight, but Marion was too distracted to pause over it. Instead, Marion felt herself unspool inside and it was lovely and she wanted to touch Joe Lanigan's arm, lightly, as she wanted to smile to him and even curl herself at his feet.

He knew her, he knew her, he knew even as he dallied and caroused and sauntered through red rooms everywhere. He might let spangles and sin cover his upturned face so handsome, but in his heart . . . In his heart . . .

"What are Ginny and I, then, Joe?" said Louise, mouth just a shade hard. "Some Friday-night taxi dancers?"

"I wasn't speaking of you, Louise. Nor Virginia. I was speaking of Mrs. Seeley, whom we have made uncomfortable, which is the last thing I would want." He reached for his jacket slung over the back of a chair and put it on.

"Aren't *we* talking high tone," Louise started.

"Don't fluster, Louise," Ginny piped. "Gent Joe is just brushing his boots clean on our bosoms to flatter our lady. What's the harm? Sing us some more, Floyd. Sing us out of our hungover blues."

"This one's dedicated to my stalwart former employer, King

Copper," Floyd said, "for whom I toiled the smelter, 1924 until they took my breath away." With great flourish, he raised his arm and dropped it down fast like a jackhammer on the strings, peeling into a frenzied jazz number.

"That's the stuff," Ginny said, and she leapt up from the sofa as if the picture of health and commenced dancing. Marion had never seen her move a hundredth as fast. Her legs kept twisting around each other and kicking backward as she spun so fast, Marion was sure she'd collapse, but Floyd only played faster and faster and Louise was finally laughing. Looking over at Marion, she said, "Get a load of that jig trot. She made us four bits on that once when we were broke outside Albuquerque."

And Marion looked up at Ginny's face, steaming red, and stone-cold ecstatic, like Saint Bernadette.

MARION STAYED and Joe Lanigan kept his suit jacket on, even as Floyd, three slugs into the new round of drinking, stripped down to his undershirt and suspenders and threw Ginny round the room.

Louise dragged out a big punch bowl and filled it with gin, black pepper and a can of consommé.

Marion could feel Joe Lanigan standing behind her chair, but she did not look back.

"Lou-Lou, don't we got some tomato juice to toss in there?" Ginny said, breathless, still dancing.

"Mrs. Seeley, would you like a glass?" Joe Lanigan was saying, and he set one hand on Marion's shoulder and the tremble through her body, well, she felt the floorboards might crack.

"No thank you," she said.

"Mims is a two-finger girl," Ginny said, finally stopping long enough to run for a can of tomato juice and slinging it into the bowl. "She'll do two fingers of sherry. Two fingers of champagne. Maybe two fingers of crème de menthe if you push it. But never more than two fingers a night." She cocked the bottom of the can for one more glug and added, grin broad, "Just you try to get more than two fingers in her, Joe Lanigan."

"Tut-tut," Louise said, grabbing the can from Ginny. "That's enough."

"It makes my head hurt," Marion explained, now the only one sitting. She felt surrounded.

"That's 'cause you've been drinking bad hooch, doll," Floyd said, taking a glass from Louise's hand. "Try the new medicine, doctor approved."

"Which doc?" Ginny said.

"Why, Doc Joe," Floyd said.

Joe walked around Marion's chair and looked down at her, folding his arms across his chest. "Mrs. Seeley, I know you don't generally partake, but it might do you some good. And you're among friends."

"How's she look, Doc?" Floyd said.

Marion let him meet her eyes. She felt like the killjoy. The church girl at the beer blast. She wasn't sure what to do. She showed him everything in her face and let him decide.

"Hmm, the patient looks pale," he said, and his hand reached out and touched her chin, tilted it up. And everyone saw. But it seemed so natural and no one said a word. "One might even say consumptive. She likely needs to go home and rest."

"Eh," Floyd said, waving his hand dismissively. "How about a second opinion?" He strode over, skin as white as his undershirt only bluer, carrying a fresh glass. "Dr. Floyd prescribes an immediate transfusion."

"She should go home," Joe repeated. "No good can come from this. She is a delicate thing."

"Guess we're a couple of log-splitters," Louise said, rolling her eyes. "Marion, don't let these gees tell you you can't have fun. You might be a taxi dancer yet."

"I don't wish to go home," Marion blurted out. "I don't wish to. I will have a glass. I will."

"How about five fingers?" Floyd said, eyebrows mast high.

"Five fingers full," Ginny hiccupped from behind her.

And Marion took a sip.

HE GAVE HER her first taste and it set her teeth on edge. He'd slugged it with long shots of sugar to cut the grain sting and it swelled in her mouth, a gritty cotton-candy swirl, then a rush of heat sending tears to her squinting eyes (*My, did he love that, laughing, calling her baby snooks*). Her belly warm and loose and everything turning, stretching, she reached for his hands, wanted them, urgently, on her. She'd never taken a man's hands like that, placed them on her, on her thighs so his fingers fell between. Those soft, peppermint-oiled, half-moon-nailed hands that'd find their way in there, in everywhere, as the hooch bloomed, just bloomed.

IT WAS AN HOUR LATER, maybe two, and Joe Lanigan had his arms around her and they were outside, a hot gust twining her skirt between her legs and he pointing to his car, and Marion held on tight because she was spinning, like she was doing the jig trot in her head.

And before she knew it, they were in his car, all leather and chrome, and the backseat big and the leather soft and his hands on her stockings, her only good pair, and his hands between her legs and it was raining softly outside, the first time in weeks, wasn't it, and then she felt his whiskers prickling along her stomach and thighs and then she felt the rocking start and then she felt and then there was all feeling and the rain, like a *t-pit, t-pit, t-pit* and . . .

MONDAY, THE CLINIC, Marion sat at her desk, still blurry-headed, no sleep, long hours spent writing and unwriting Dr. Seeley and reading his latest correspondence over and over again, its skeiny pages tattooed blue with India ink:

> *My dearest Marion, I am heartsick to hear of your loneliness. There is a song the natives sing at night, when drinking. It is called "La Golondrina" and it is all about a wandering swallow caught in storm and wind, so far from home.* También yo estoy en la región perdida, ¡Oh, Cielo Santo! y sin poder volar . . . *It is the most beautiful of all songs, Marion.*
>
> *Marion, do not doubt my shame in leaving you as I have. My father, your father, these are men. I wish to be men such as these. My desire and commitment to take care of you was the most noble of my life—a life I have time and again thrown away. I intend to restore that part of myself strong enough, and good enough to be worthy of you. But to do so I must confront my own weaknesses and I must cure myself of them. I am working on just this with more diligence than ever in my life. What I mean to say is this: I have not touched the stuff, Marion, I swear to you, I haven't had one taste.*

Oh, what did she care, what did she care . . . Reading it now, the tenth time in so many missives . . . how much could it mean, this man who'd plucked her from her sawmill Midwest town, who'd danced with her at her church social and spoke of a cottage on a river and tousle-locked children and all that a committed young doctor could give . . .

It meant nothing.

And now, in her swivel chair, working, trying to do her work.

In her head, it was like this:

You turn your heel and press the ball of your foot, feel the quiver there. Because when he looks at you, you feel it five different places, places you did not know about, like a violin string vibrating. Like a string vibrating hot under your fingertips. A trickle hot now in the small of your back slipping from knot to knot on your spine. And most of all of course in that place where your cotton underthings meet, pressing against the metal of the garter, down to where the garter tugs mercilessly, as if gnawing the wool tops of your stocking itching, rubbing you raw, metal clasp cold, stockings rough, slashing strands of cold sweat, the friction unbearable and there and there again and the typewriter keys clapping, tapping, 4 DAYS FROTHY MUCUS SPUTUM, SOME NOCTURIA, MORPHINE, BROMIDES AND HYPNOTICS ADMINISTERED AS NEEDED. DIGITALIS LEAVES, GRAM 0.1, 3X/DAY, *even as you feel everything twisting, churning, rubbing. Enough to make you sick and you're smiling, you realize you can feel it on your hot-cold face.* DR. WARNER ATTENDING, SCHED. UV RM. 2X/WK. *Oh, to put him out of the head, to put him in a drawer and shut the drawer, she pictures herself*—clap clap clap *keys*—*putting the thinking of Joe Lanigan in the cardboard-bottomed drawer of her dresser and shutting it and shutting it and then the thinking of him gone and her legs stop trembling and and and . . .*

LOUISE WAS CHATTERING away in the lunchroom yet again, chattering in such dipping lovely lyrical ways and Marion didn't have to listen too closely and she could just let it hop along, brush up against her, keep her distracted.

"Oh, she's a fine one, did you see her with no girdle swinging her stuff around? No sale here, swivel hips."

Then:

"That orderly, he wants some of her honeypot, but I ask you, has he two dimes to spark? Orderlies, they can make time with chambermaids, factory girls. This is America, Marion, doll. Stars bursting."

Then:

"Oh, Marion, did you see that? Myra. She's always giving me the fisheye. She thinks I cost her friend Fern a job. And she's right."

Marion glanced over at Myra, a broad-faced country girl known for good spirits and a clear, sunny whistle that the patients loved.

The look she was giving Louise twisted that face into something rigid and brow-beetled.

"What did you do, Louise," Marion asked, trying to focus, trying not to slip back away.

"That two-faced crackpot Dr. Milroy . . . I had to go back east to see my ma last fall. Was gone for nine days. Just nine days. Two days coming and going. And while I'm gone, he had no one to run the new X-ray machine. I'd gone for special training to learn and it cost me forty dollars. So I'm gone not three days and Dr. Milroy decides to show this other nurse, this claptrap Fern, how to use the machine to make X-ray pictures. He told everyone, 'She's from a farming town and is familiar with equipment.' What, tractors? So I come back and they don't want to pay me the extra four bits a week anymore."

"That doesn't seem fair. Nor safe," Marion said. "Those machines can be dangerous."

"You don't have to tell me, buttercup. But I showed them," Louise said, grinning. She leaned forward. "First chance, I went into the X-ray Department right before her shift and turned the voltage up real high. The next day, darling Fern uses it and near burns a hole right through some poor clod."

Marion looked up at Louise, wondered if she could be serious.

Louise grinned, red-lipped like a baby caught with hands in the jam jar. "Well, shouldn't she pay for being such a louse, such a nasty little s.o.b.? Myra best keep her talons short. She causes trouble, wait and see. Wait and see what I got cooking."

Marion thought, *Why, she's just playing, she always plays.* Besides, there was Joe Lanigan to think of. Joe Lanigan.

She wanted to share it all with Louise, but she really couldn't, could she. What might Louise think? For Louise, bad behavior was coming by for supper with empty hands, or not paying mind to Ginny, so clearly itching to play Tiddly Chase or Chinese checkers. Sins were looking down long noses at unmarried girls while carrying on with parlormaids on the sly.

"So do tell where you and Joe Lanigan stole off to on Saturday, my little nightingale," Louise said, over hoecakes she'd brought for them.

"We went for a drive," said Marion, fingers to her mouth. She felt like everyone could see it on her, Louise most of all. Like the one time, the only time, seven years old and being fresh, she sassed her father and he made her stand under the cherry tree at the foot of their lawn with a writing slate hung round her neck that said, I DO NOT FEAR OUR MAKER.

"I thought you went the way of the Parker baby, but Ginny has a slyer eye," Louise said, smiling the whole time. "She says to me, 'Marion plays the prairie flower but she's got a hot mitt on Gent Joe.'"

Marion could feel her chin shake. "He needed someone to talk to. You know, his wife is so ill." This was true. Joe had talked about his wife, at length and in ways that made Marion feel he had sorrows deeper than her own.

"They do hot-air treatments," Marion went on. "When it's bad, her lips, they . . ." Here, telling her, he had touched his fingers to his mouth, embarrassed. "They taste of urine."

He told her too that when his wife came to realize this herself, kisses stopped forever. Her humiliation was so great. She was dirty, she said. Dirty and foul.

Before she fell sick, he'd admitted, he'd never seen her lily-white bride flesh, even in low lamplight, curtains heavy across every window. He'd not seen an inch of it, only felt it, tense and wincing, under his hand, under two coverlets, under the grave dead dark of long winter nights.

Now he saw that flesh and it was pushed full with air, with sick, with awful inner squalls of illness. It was like touching the thin, skeiny membrane of a newborn birdling.

"Is that how it is," Louise said to Marion now, nodding, eyes fastened hard. But she seemed to be, could she be, finding a giggle in all this.

"She has the Bright's," Marion said. "She's infirm." *Marion, you must understand,* he had told her, fingers on the ties that held her dress together, *I cannot help myself. You are all I have that is not dead. Dying or dead. Dying and dead.*

"Is that what they're calling it now? You don't have to tell me about Mrs. Lanigan, Marion," Louise said. "The three months I worked for her were the closest I've come to San Q."

"You worked for her? You were her nurse?"

"When I first blew into town. It didn't last. She's no bed o' roses and that's how come I always felt so for dear Joe. Can't be pretty in that household. We try to keep his spirits up. Seems like you're doing the same."

"I never knew that," Marion said, wondering why Louise had never mentioned it before, or Joe.

"Three months, best," Louise said, waving her hand. "I got my better job and enough cabbage to pull Ginny from cooch dancing downtown. Just in the nick too. She was Camille up there on the stage and not enough meat on her chops to waggle anything but bones."

WITHIN A WEEK, Marion began to think of it as a kind of demonic possession. At her desk, on the streetcar, at Mrs. Gower's roasting dinner table and especially at night in bed, her body twitching. In private moments in late night hours, she thought demons may have set in and taken her body and she might require an exorcism to be free.

Joe Lanigan. Mr. Joseph Lanigan. Entrepreneur. Beloved husband and father. Man about town. Friar. Knight of Columbus. Member, Chamber of Commerce. Lector at St. Mary's Basilica. Gentleman Joe.

"If I cannot see you at your room, I don't see any other way," he said. He had telephoned Marion at the clinic. Mrs. Curtwin, Dr. Milroy's secretary, was not pleased that Marion was receiving calls at work. Marion had to speak quietly, discreetly into the receiver. She felt as though the woman could hear everything.

"Mrs. Gower, she . . . It wouldn't look . . ."

"I think you should come here, Marion."

"To your home?" Marion's voice turned rushed. The secretary's eyes were fastened on her.

"Write down this address."

She did. But she already knew where he lived, in that fine Victorian house on Lynbrook Street, three stories on a sloping hill and a large porch that curled around it.

She determined not to go. She said to herself, *This is it, Marion, your sin is great but you can save yourself from worse sins still.*

BUT STEPPING on that streetcar she did not go home. Instead, she took the streetcar to his grand house on Lynbrook Street. She just had to, like it was a fever. It was a fever.

A nurse in white collar and apron answered the door and Marion said what he had told her to say.

"I'm from the clinic. I have brought Mr. Lanigan the late orders for immediate processing." And, palms wet, she showed her the accordion file she had brought.

"This way, miss," the nurse said, no expression. The house was dark, with shushing drapes drawn and thick-fringed brocaded chairs. Marion could smell mercury and rubbing alcohol.

"Right through that door," the nurse said, gesturing down the hallway. Then she lifted a tray of medicine and rubber tubing she had set on a hallway table and silently ascended the towering staircase of carved walnut.

As Marion walked, she could feel the woman's, the wife's, Mrs. Lanigan's, presence. Could feel the weight of her in her sickroom above. The house carried no sound.

She paused in front of the heavy door to which she had been directed. She paused, and nearly lost her nerve. But it was too late and Joe Lanigan, in shirtsleeves and smoking a cigar, opened it. Oh, the look he gave her, didn't it say such things to her. She felt like he could move her as if by invisible strings. He had such ways, you see.

It was his study, all mahogany and green leather with gold braid. The window behind the desk was draped and she saw the long tufted davenport and knew she was meant for it, that she would in moments be pinned there, one foot on the floor, and that he would have her, and he did.

Afterward, her body rubbed to roughness, to blood-pocked flushy ruin, she fastened garters with shuddery hands and watched him, standing now, leaning against the front of his desk, cover his face with his hands like he might cry. He did not cry and she was glad he did not, but she couldn't guess what was in his heart. She never could.

For a moment, she felt he might finally have been struck by the ponderousness of their joint sin, here only a foot of plaster and wood separating him from his enfeebled wife one floor above.

"Oh, Marion," he said. "Look what I have done."

But when he pulled his hands from his face, she saw no grief at all, no trace of stricken remorse.

"I have made you a whore," he said, and he couldn't stop his smile. Saw no need to.

For her part, looking into her own battered heart, she could summon no anger, nor even fresh guilt. She believed that in his mind, which she now saw as disturbed in some way, the consequence of years of feeling lost and unmoored, like a widower with a wife, in his mind, he was giving her his highest praise. Her legs still damp, she reckoned this terrible revelation: she was strangely gratified. She had pleased him. Wasn't that, in some odd way, wondrous?

This man, he has shamed me twice over, once by treating me like a whore and once more by showing me I am one.

I am a sinner, Dr. Seeley. What's more, I grew to love my sin.

No one had told Joe Lanigan that she was a flower, a doll, an ornament of finely spun glass, something to rest on a mantelpiece. Somehow no one had told him he couldn't fondle her, twist her filmy skin, grab her with his rough Irish hands and throw her on a bed and do just awful, awful things to her.

You are Pandora, Joe Lanigan had said. *You came to town with that beautiful little box I had to, had to open.* As if it were her. As if she were the one. Was she?

She wondered if she'd showed him, without knowing it, that she could be treated like he treated her. *What had she shown him, and had she shown it to Dr. Seeley and had he not seen? Or, oh no, had he understood and been frightened and such the more cause of his private habits, so destructive to them all? Things too horrible to know.*

But Joe did not bother with talk of sin. He never missed Sunday Mass and he saw no predicament, said the one had not to do with the other and there was a gospel of hedonism and she might follow it, but she with her Dutch ways, with her grim church and its coldnesses and not the hot, bloodied breath of Catholicism, she knew not where to turn except to pray and pray and pray to turn her back into a doll, or a flower, something inviolate on a shelf, never touched.

"Marion's got a new beau," came Louise's whisper across the table in the lunchroom that Monday. A prickling toothed thing dragged up from Marion's knees to her chest.

"What did you say, Louise?"

"Oh, you just have that dreamy-eyed look, your little rosebud mouth all aquiver and eyes so loose they'll go cross."

Marion tried to smile. Louise, fingertips tapping on the waxed paper of Marion's balogna sandwich, watched.

"Let me guess, Fair Mare, the Vagabond Lover climbs up Mrs. Gower's trellis and into your window each night at the stroke of twelve. Marion's beau would be no less gallant."

"Oh no, Louise," Marion said, watching as Louise rotated the sandwich, eyeing the pink meat suspiciously, then slid it back to Marion. "I was up late writing to Dr. Seeley."

Louise grinned, picking up the fat apple she had brought. "Such a dutiful wife," she said, extending her long arm, the apple glowing like some royal citrine.

"Have a taste, Fair Mare, do share."

Marion started to speak—

"Or is your rosebud mouth too small?" Louise added, eyes cracking. It was like a saber lain before. It was a saber, a gauntlet, somehow. Marion saw it glinting. You could not miss it. Marion saw it but did not know why it had been lain there.

Part Two

I told Mrs. Seeley to keep her distance from those two. But Marion, she liked their lively ways.

Everyone knew about Louise Mercer, like what happened at the Dempsey Hotel. How someone called the law because there was a ruckus and there she was in the fifth-floor corridor going on two o'clock in the morning, only one shoe on, and they brought her in and they let her go because some calls were made. She had friends. The right kinds, it seems. And all her friends have wives.

And that Mr. Lanigan. He's one of those. All those big fellas strutting around with fancy waistcoats and running the town. Well, he's an Elk. A Grand Knight with the Knights of Columbus. He sits on the Chamber of Commerce, handing out favors. If he weren't a papist, he might be mayor.

All those comers, every June they send their wives eighty miles straight up into the mountains. The Hassayampa Mountain Club, they call it. Then, back here in town, they make hay all summer long. The office girls. Girls that work in the shops. And the nurses. Always the nurses. And there was talk of Marion being Mr. Lanigan's summer gal, only it was still spring. I didn't talk of it, but others did.

See, I walk in the Lord's path of kindness, and I figure I'll tell Marion that there's buzzing in the air and she might do best to keep her quarter, to walk in churchly ways. After all, she is a married woman and, the way it sounds, those girls are running a regular operation there. Wild parties and who knows what. Those girls have no starch in their pleats, do you know what I mean to say? When Louise Mercer walks, there's nothing that stays still. And the other one, one hears tell, she haint stood upright since Hoover took oath and sunk us all.

But Marion, she don't care to listen. Like I said, she liked their lively ways.

—Mrs. Ina Curtwin
Secretary to Dr. Milroy, Werden Clinic
Interview, *Statesman Courier*

It had been only a month, thirty-four days. Yet Marion could no longer remember the before of it. Her body, she would rest her hands on it and it was changed. The face in the mirror, hers yet not the face that had been there before.

Her fingers on the calendar, so glad that the blood had come, would go to church twice that week for the blood, had gone twice last week asking for it.

Fingertips on the calendar, she saw forty-six days before Dr. Seeley might come for Easter.

IT WAS IN THIS MODE, this reckless mode, that she, fevered head to toe, laid herself open. Would that she had her head about her, she would not have let him talk her, breathless and confused, into stealing away to the third-floor supply room at the clinic, three oxygen canisters rolling, rolling endlessly across the long floor as her legs curled and curved about him.

That evening, she had gone after work to Diamond's department store intending to purchase the straw, grosgrain-ribboned hat of taffy pink in the front window with the five dollars Joe Lanigan had given her, twisting the bill between her breasts, saying, "Here's a little candy, Marion. Show me something." Once she arrived, however, she found herself in the undergarments department, lips tearing between her teeth, softly fingering lingerie. The salesgirl slipped the shirred ribbon garters and peach crepe de chine step-ins into a slim box of deep blue. Jostling on the streetcar, she tucked her hand in the bag and rested it on the top of the box the whole ride.

But he did not appear that night and apologized the next day, on the telephone, as she covered her face with her hand, elbow resting on the typewriter. What's more, he could not see her to-night either. Why could she not manage two days without, and what would she do if Dr. Seeley arrived, if money held and he forbore, and arrived in town now just over five weeks away.

That night, he with a daughter's birthday dinner and she off to Louise and Ginny's and Louise was going to henna her hair and Ginny decided that Marion should go platinum.

"Oh no, Ginny, Dr. Milroy wouldn't like it and I don't think it suits me."

But Ginny, lips gleaming, was jiggling soap flakes into a footed dish tingling with peroxide and teary ammonia.

"Have a cocktail, Marion," Louise said. "So's you won't notice while Ginny burns you like morning toast."

An hour later, they were rubbing her head with a soft towel, one on either side of her, and when she looked into the waved mirror, it was like a swirling puff of cotton edged in bright silver. Trying, she could barely see herself from six months ago, the long thick sandy mane she had to soak in castor oil. Now she saw this twirling silver pinwheel. Who did she think she was, and Ginny twisting a tube of violet lipstick and dragging it across Marion's lips dizzily, her happy breath on Marion's face?

"What did you do to our fair girl?" A voice rang out from the front door, and wouldn't you know it was Joe Lanigan there, carrying a creamy wedge of birthday cake.

"Joe!" Ginny squealed, and Louise ran over to take his coat.

Marion stood, shaking her hair, which felt unreal to her, like someone else's silk trimming.

"Don't she look like Joan Bennett?" Louise said, taking the cake wedge from him and lifting it to her outstretched tongue for a taste. "Isn't she a dream?"

"It was my idea, I'll have you mark it," Ginny piped up.

Joe Lanigan, he was looking at Marion and she felt her neck

still wet from the sink. She felt the front of her shirt clinging to her and she felt his eyes on her. It did things to her.

"Do you like the new Marion?" Louise said.

"I like all Marions, old and new," Joe said, running his icing-edged hand along his mouth. "And I like how many Marions there are. And how many you have to give," he said, winking at this last bit.

"Look at Gent Joe getting an eyeful," Marion heard Ginny say.

"So you like what we proffer, Joe," and this was Louise. But Marion could only focus on Joe. She felt her skin raise up under his eyes. And she knew she was in trouble.

By the time he had walked over to her, her legs were quivering, vibrating—all with Louise and Ginny seeing everything. Knowing for certain what they may have only guessed before.

"Marion," he was saying, and he was putting his hand in her hair and then he was right up against her.

"Maybe they want to be alone, Lou-Lou," she could hear Ginny say, giggling.

"I don't suppose they mind either way," said Louise, as Joe Lanigan was pressing Marion into the small bedroom, pressing her against the shutter doors, skin pinching, his hand flat on her wet front, "but I'd just as soon play Parcheesi."

"The hell you would," Ginny was saying. "Wouldn't you like to see Marion's pretty skin?"

"I don't need to watch that to see Marion's pretty skin, Ginny."

"What, dear heart, might you be suggesting, and please pass the peanuts, I got terrible hungry, just like that."

From one of the girls' twin beds beneath her, springs squeaking, Marion could hear them play Parcheesi, the dice clattering.

"I'm eating your pawn, Lou-Lou."

"Eat away, little brute. Show me your teeth, and your tongue."

An hour later, maybe more, floating in and out of sleep on Louise's bed, the peroxide tingling in her nose, her head, she could hear Louise talking, or thought she could, through the door.

"Remember, Gent Joe, remember. Remember, because I surely do. Watch the way my gums move up and down and up and down. When I have the inclination, I just can't stop talking."

And he, and she could hear the laughter in his voice, keen and sharp, and she could feel it jigsaw in her stomach as if his hands were back on her: "How could I forget, Louise? I wouldn't want to. We all marvel at that gorgeous mouth of yours, don't we? It's worth all the noise it makes."

"Don't play. You got enough to play with."

"That I do."

Then Marion shook her head and felt a swell of the ammonia all through her head and there were no more voices, no voices except her own, recalling her own past words to Dr. Seeley, *Remember me. Do not abandon me here. Remember me.*

What could her letters to Dr. Seeley say now after so many days of this? *Dr. Seeley, I have let this man in, this smiling gentleman, and the things he has done to me, could I list them for you? Could I share the time he pulled the ribbons from my dress and wrapped them tight round my baby wrists? Could I share the time he rubbed me raw, my face flat on the Oriental carpet of his drawing room, my face speckled red, knees strawberried raw, and not one curl of regret as he ruined me, Dr. Seeley, over and over again? Is this something I can share with you, Dr. Seeley, and have you forgive me still? Especially after your own sorrows and the ways in which I have punished you for them, for your private weakness? For some things*

*there can be no forgiveness, nor even words. Some things are meant
only to be fevers in the brain.*

"YOU KNEW ABOUT Mr. Lanigan and me," Marion said later,
hours later, as Ginny played with her hair.

"Oh, Marion." Louise smiled. "Oh, Marion."

"You acted the goodly virgin, Marion," Ginny said. "And all
the time you were playing the hots with our Gent Joe."

Marion felt her face rush red. "You know it wasn't like that,"
she said, shaking her head away.

Ginny laughed and leaned back. She was rolling and unrolling something in her hand. Something green. She rolled the bills
tight and fashioned a horn and blew into it.

"It's all clover. Joe left behind something for us too," Ginny
said, winking.

"You figured it all," Marion said, still dazed.

"We knew, Marion," Louise said. "Of course we knew." And
she smiled again and there was something flickering in her eyes,
gentle or not, but flickering, and Marion, Ginny's fingers tangling
in her hair, tried to read the thing in Louise's eyes, tried to understand it. But she could not. She could not. There was no way to
see.

IT WAS A BALANCE. A surprising and quite fragile and quite
beautiful balance of all the elements, and it felt so delicate that
Marion knew it could not last. But for a few weeks, it did. Louise
and Ginny held Marion fast to their chests when Joe Lanigan
spent nights away to parts unknown, or even in his own home-
stead. And Joe Lanigan continued to take Marion for long drives
into dark corners outside of town where he whispered tender

things and placed his hands on her in ways that she couldn't bear because the bearing was so sweet. But it was all like the pressure before a crackling summer storm, strangely still air knocking curtains ever so lightly against the window screens and the sky turning colors slowly, simmering from blue to brown to violet and you knew it was going to break, and break in ways for which there was no preparing.

It was within days that it all turned, as if in a second. Marion could even point to the exact moment that this man for whom she had broken herself to pieces and built herself anew, a platinum pleasure doll, showed her, showed her he had begun to grow a little bit bored.

"Aren't you coming by, Joe? Mrs. Gower will be at her choir practice and I could make you supper."

"I'd like to, Marion, I would. You know I'd like to see you all the time. It's just this lodge function. They need me."

And the next day hearing, from Louise, about the raucous smoker at the Silhouette Club where the men brought in ten burly-q dancers for the night, paid them each twenty-five dollars to dance on tabletops and *Oh, Marion, Mr. Trask told me, you know, he is a member of the lodge, he said, confidentially, more than one of those girls stripped down to her birthday suit and jumped into the big punch bowls. The janitors spent hours picking up spangles, sequins, fluttery feathers.* And she could see, in her head, Joe Lanigan, in some back room, in some side hallway, mouth pressed against sugared, sticky skin, oh, she knew, she knew it. She could taste it herself.

"And Mr. Lanigan," Marion said, looking at her fingernails, pale and freshly torn from a night spent teeth to nub. "He was there."

His eyes never stopped moving. What would it take to make his eyes stop moving?

What had she imagined? She as a desert Rapunzel preening in her tower, Joe Lanigan, fingers buried in her long locks, grappling to reach her, to rescue her, to save her and in so doing be saved? Oh, she couldn't have possibly thought this. There was no time. It was all too fast.

"Don't be jealous, kitten," Louise said. "That's how he is. It's his way. It doesn't mean he cares for you any less."

How could it not mean that? she said to herself, and Louise, as if mind reading, said, "You've an awful lot to learn, Marion. I do wish I could have saved you from learning."

It was kind of her to say, but Marion did not want to hear Louise being kind. Louise always knowing so much more, about Joe Lanigan, about everything. "I don't care what he does," Marion said, chin up, like Lillian Gish playing prideful.

"Of course you don't." Louise smiled. "But do remember, Ginny and I, we are true to you. We're always true."

Thinking of Joe in that smoker, mouth covered with sequins, a filthy image, she could think of nothing else. She in the same company with those girls, those dancing girls. In a voice automatic like a thing possessed, she said, "I must live with it. If I were stronger, I would make myself stop. I would, Louise."

"No one's telling you to stop, Marion."

THE FOLLOWING DAY, Marion looked in vain for Louise, peering down every hallway at the clinic. Where was Louise, her swishing, fishtailing walk?

"She had to catch a night train," Ginny told her. "Her brother got pegged in Calico on a vag charge. She didn't even know he was out this far west. Last time she saw him was in St. Louis right after the Crash."

Marion hadn't even known Louise had a brother. She knew about vag charges, though. Dr. Seeley had three to his name, the last in Leimert Park, Los Angeles, not fourteen months before. Marion thought him gone forever, but he was only on the junk. On the junk, that was how the policeman put it, as if she would know what it meant, which she did.

"Is she going to post bail?" Marion asked.

Ginny nodded. "Don't I know it. We were at Slanty's at the crack of dawn pawning all our honey. Everything but our sweet lil six-shooter and the Silvertone. I made her promise me that. He's blood, sure, but I worked hard for that radio. And the pistol, well, Joe Lanigan gave us that after a suitor with a bad case of the rapes got itchy for Louise and tried to squeeze in our bedroom window. It's good to be heeled. Did the doc leave you heeled, Miss Silk?"

Once, when Dr. Seeley had gone to the hospital for ten days in Victorville, he left her with a flare gun. Marion hid it under the bed, afraid to look at it, and when the doctor got out, he sold it for the thing he sold everything for.

"How can I help, Ginny?" Marion said, trying not to think of Ginny doing as she did sometimes, pretending to twirl the gun like Annie Oakley and shoot the cigarette out of Floyd's mouth. "Do you have everything you need while she's gone?"

"Do I ever. She wants you to keep an eye on me, but that's how she is. She knows what's best, but if she's gone, who needs best?"

"But, Ginny, you don't want Louise to have to worry about you too."

"She *should* worry about me. I count more than her lousy brother, goes off with sailors, gets lockjaw, always in some scrape."

⤜◎ ◎⤏

THERE HAD BEEN something in Ginny's face. It was an avid insolent look, even a defiant one, and Marion thought of it more than once throughout the day. After work, she took the street-car to the girls' place. Ginny didn't answer the door, but it wasn't locked and Marion went inside, ylang-ylang and jasmine flooding her nostrils and mouth and bright clothes strewn everywhere, even an errant peacock feather on the sofa trembling from the draft. On the coffee table was a bottle of Auntie Sheba's Lung Syrup and a highball glass red-bottomed with the remnants of its glossy charms.

Marion poked her head in the bedroom, which, pocket-sized as it was, was in similar disarray, a long red strand drizzling from a bottle that read Heering Crème de Cerise oozed from the head to the foot of Ginny's bed and Louise's was stacked high with pho-nograph records flung from their sleeves, empty jars of cold cream, a corset that could've wrapped around Ginny three times.

But no Ginny.

Marion could think of no way to reach Louise and it made her nervous to think of telling her. She thought of telephoning Joe Lanigan, thought he could help her, but she did not know what she might say if someone else answered the telephone. She sat down on the divan and tried to concentrate. It took her a long time to think of Mr. Loomis, and she was glad to see his name in the address book Louise kept in a wall nook in the kitchen.

She telephoned from the soda fountain three blocks away.

"Oh, sounds like Ginny's on a tear," Mr. Loomis said, called away from a winning poker hand by his anxious wife.

Marion could hear Mrs. Loomis in the background, crying

out, "She's like a trapped bird. It'll be like the last time, smashing windows all through town."

"Get, get, angel mine." Mr. Loomis shushed his wife, who was always dancing the sharp edge of hysteria. "Get-get."

"Louise will be panicked," Marion said, fingertips edging along her teeth. She could picture Louise in some far-off county jail laying down bill after bill, her home emptying itself for the pawnshop, pearly bit by pearly bit.

"Don't worry, Mrs. Seeley," Mr. Loomis assured her. "I bet she's back with her old pals, those chickadees working the Hotel Dunlop."

Marion recalled Louise saying Ginny used to work there, high-kicking it bare-legged to great acclaim.

And one night, one night at a party, Mr. Loomis had pulled Marion aside, sweaty-faced and brined, told her about the night he first met Ginny nearly two years back, about how he'd made his way, by virtue of sheer salesman charm, backstage at the Crimson Cavalcade. The showgirls all had red blotches smack in the center of their powdery cheeks, like baby dolls. Their ruffled panties, deep red and deeper violet, were trimmed with gold-flecked ribbons that dangled from them, slipping about between their half-gartered thighs.

There was Ginny, he said, curled daintily in their frilly center, like a doll's doll, painted and trimmed and with a pink O for a mouth, an O open for all kinds of pleasures and now for the heavy bottle of moon passing among the dolls' bright-gloved hands.

"My, that's fine," Ginny had said, not even noticing Mr. Loomis. "That's mule for moon baying."

Ginny had lived so many hundreds of lives, had she not?

"She doesn't much care for alone," Mr. Loomis said now. "Louise is her everything, you see. With her gone, she will find fluffy feathers elsewhere to plush her lil nest."

It reminded Marion of something. Something seen, half in sleep, many weeks before. She had stayed the night with the girls, curling up on the sofa under Ginny's muslin, a garment no doubt laced with heavy sickness but also popping whimsy, and awoke unsure of the time, staggering, blurry, to the sliver of a bathroom, and as she did, passing the girls' bedroom. The accordion wall gaping slightly and the tableau like a gold-leaf painting. No, like a soft-wash painting on the wall of a pink-walled powder room in an elegant hotel, fairy nymphs at rest on a bed of clover. Ginny's curving, marble-white thigh slung and Louise's arm slid between Ginny's bent leg, dimpled knee, and Louise only stockings, garters sapphire blue and her fingers spanning Ginny's bitty doll breasts, lifting with anxious breaths.

Later, she would swear she'd dreamt it.

It was a purer love than Marion had ever known.

AND SO MARION WENT HOME. She went home and tried not to fret about Ginny and hoped in fact she was with friends who would take care of her. And at nigh on five o'clock in the morning, Joe Lanigan had found his way in through Mrs. Gower's back door and up to Marion's room and he crawled in beside her with a gust of applejack and confetti crinkling from his hair, seeping from his suit. *A friend's anniversary celebration,* he whispered, *and all I wanted was to get here, Marion, for I know I've been negligent and I so wanted to give you something new.* And with that his fingertips were on her lips and—

—*I wish I could help myself with you, Marion,* he said, then she could feel him shake his head on the pillow. *That is a lie. I don't even wish it, not for a moment. I just want to do things to you,* he said, and he rubbed something on her lips, her gums. And it was buzzing, and everything was buzzing. She tried to reach her fingers to her mouth, but there was nothing there, nothing there, it was like her hand would go straight through.

What is that, she asked. *What is that,* but it came out funny, and her heart was thudding and he began to do things, such things, and she did not stop him or ask any more questions.

MORNING, BEFORE WORK, coming on seven o'clock, Marion, cotton-headed and raw and sick with herself, took the streetcar to Hussel Street.

The house in even more disarray than the day before, Marion slipped on a throw pillow torn seam to seam on the floor, its feathers fluttering in the air like a chicken coop—and was that wax beans crushed into the carpet, she wondered. And what of the empty jug of Cheracol cough syrup nestled upright on the corner of the divan, like a child's stuffed bear?

She found herself pausing before peering into the bedroom—what might she see? But before she worked up the nerve, she heard something like water lapping and the bathroom door was partially open and she called out, "Ginny?"

There was a familiar twitter. *"Then she met a sailor man named Popeye the Skipper."*

Marion tentatively placed three fingers on the door, the steam glazing her face, the warble vibrating wetly, *"When she was mean, boy how he used to whip her."*

Marion looked down at Ginny, eyes closed, naked as the Kewpie doll she had tucked in her arms, sinking in a half tub of water.

"Ship ahoy," she crooned. *"Ah, ship ahoy."*

"Ginny," Marion said. "What goes on?"

Her eyes fluttered open, her red mouth smeary.

"It is the she herself," she said, and the warble was gone and the voice was hissing, it was a keening hiss.

"It's Marion," she said, realizing her own hands were clasped to the doorframe, clasped tightly. "Ginny, are you all right?"

"It is the she herself. Why are you not in Calico, or something like it?" Ginny's eyes, normally so baby-bird blue, crackled roughly.

"Ginny, it's Marion," Marion repeated, as if talking to a blind woman. "Louise is in Calico."

Ginny tilted herself and a splash of water flew from the tub and caught Marion, ice-cold on the leg.

"I figured you was with her. I figured you was off with her," she said, slanty-faced, that sheet-white face, blue in the temples. "I might do anything when it's like this. I've done things. You can't guess what you'd do until you've done it. Just you see what I can do."

It was such a strange thing to say and Marion felt struck. "What do you mean, Ginny? You were the one who told me where Louise went. I've been looking for you. I was worried about you." She had never seen her like this, never once. She remembered Louise once saying things, meaning things (*Marion, Ginny is prone to dark moods. She must be watched. She must be kept bubbling, mustn't be allowed to sink, sink*).

Ginny's eyes began to slowly soften and she squirmed in the tub. "Oh, Marion, well, I am glad. I am glad. You're my friend, aren't you, Meems? Aren't you? You don't leave me to sawdust, do you?"

"No, Ginny, no," Marion said, finally stepping forward, shaking off her strange words. "Ginny, that water is like ice. You must come out."

"I had a nosebleed and I thought it might help," she squeaked.

Marion turned to reach for a towel hanging on a hook, but found it sticky, and before she could do more, Ginny let out a long scissoring hack straight from her ambered lungs.

Swinging around, Marion looked down to see Ginny, spread forsakenly, long strands of blood lashing down her face.

"Ginny," Marion said, and could say no more.

"Don't fret." The minx grinned, breath wheezing from her like when putting your ear to a seashell. She covered her nose and mouth with a bone white hand and grinned more widely. "Don't fret."

"OH, MARION, I am sorry for that mess Ginny sunk you in," Louise said on Monday morning, her eyes feathered with red.

"It was all fine," Marion said, placing her hand on Louise's. "It truly was. I tucked her under every coverlet in the house and the hot-water bottle to boot."

Louise rolled her eyes, wringing her kerchief and sniffling. "Well, let me tell you, she was in a bath all weekend, a pickle bath, that's what's what. I just hope that's the worst of what she started up."

"Oh, Louise."

"I should have had you come over. I should have had you stay with her."

"Louise, you—"

"By morning she was barking like a dog. Like a coal-mining dog with consumption."

And Marion could see the worry painted all over Louise's face, across her ruddy cheeks.

"And don't get me started on that brother of mine," she groaned. "Cost me four bills and then skipped town with a merchant marine."

⚜

HER MAD WEEKEND behind her, Ginny skidded hard into a toffee-sludged, lung-clotted collapse and her face within days became edged with blue death. Blue rimed lips stretched across teeth, oh, it was not pretty.

Louise was frantic and finally hocked the Silvertone radio, but it was not nearly enough. Finding Marion at her desk at the clinic, she leaned against the doorframe and gave a cold look.

"Your lover man is ducking me like I was the bill collector, Marion."

Marion saw anger and a gaunt fear twinning dangerously in her eyes. "I guess he's occupied with business. He has that new store opening on the south side."

"Well, *I* have some business for him. I need some lettuce or some packets of pink or anything else he can sling my way, or else my girl's going to break a set of ribs, hacking like a piner miner."

"He has been hard to reach in recent days," Marion lied. She had been hot cheek to his thigh not ten hours before. She wondered why he could not help the girls. She believed he would if he knew, really knew. She must make him know. But he had only just returned to her after days of gallivanting sideways. What if he slipped loose again?

"Gent Joe's old vanishing act," Louise said, clacking her fingers, jittery and white, on the doorframe. "Word is, he's papering a shopgirl downtown with Alexander Hamiltons."

Marion looked up from her stack of patient records.

"I am sorry, Meems. You know I am. But it's true."

"There's always gossip about Joe," she said. Inwardly, she considered that Louise might be lying. But then there was the thing: the smell on Joe, on Joe's wrist cuffs, frantic perfume and woman scents, and it was on his hands and other places and she had pretended not to notice. Because she did not want to know. And she did not want to look at the fact that knowing might not change anything. Not for her.

"I'm just saying, give a poke, Meems," Louise said, clucking Marion roughly under the chin. "It's not just about our radio and our chrome toaster. It's rent and medicine and food on the plate."

Marion nodded, but she was still thinking of shopgirls and nurses and office girls and could not focus.

"Marion, we need to take care of things," Louise said, and she tugged Marion's ear. "You gotta get off the dime. We need to keep our Mr. Lanigan local."

That evening, Marion wrote a letter to Dr. Seeley in which she stated that her cough had returned, and some of her women's troubles, and might he send an extra five dollars next time? She sealed the letter and walked to the mailbox to post it before she could change her mind. When the slot shut, she thought she might begin to cry, but she did not.

She would ask Joe for money for the girls. She would ask him. But not yet. Not while it seemed he might be flickering away, like some beautiful mirage.

MARION, *do you know what it means to be willing to do anything?* Louise had asked her that once, one night, so late, both nestled side by side, face to glowing radio, singing. *I'm just a lonely romancer, Right at the end of my rope, Though I've had your answer, I can't give up hope,* and that was when Louise, eyes heavy with happy-tired and fingers tapping on the burning green dial, asked, *Marion, do you know what it means to be willing to do anything?*

I do, Marion thought. *That I know. That I know. I didn't once. I know it now.*

And so much worse to suspect, privately, when all alone with thoughts, that he wasn't worth it. Not even close.

Then again, maybe that's what lies at its center.

He is nothing and yet still.

THE GIRLS COULD TALK of little but how to get their pawned radio back. Ginny was small as a dormouse on the sofa, a handkerchief to her face, but her spirits were still high, rabid even.

Louise, worry-browed, was mixing up a home cough brew, glugging in ammonia and chloroform boosted from the clinic.

"Don't we got any glad stuff at all, beanpole?" Ginny mewled. "Better yet, how 'bout a li'l yen-shee suey?"

"Ask Marion," Louise said. "Marion, have you talked to our Doc Joe?"

"I haven't seen him yet," Marion said, truthfully.

Louise's eyebrows knitted together and Marion felt her heart pinch a little. She would talk to Joe. She would.

"I know you're trying your darnedest, doll," Louise said, touching her arm gently while, with the other, she stirred the pot with a wooden spoon. "We'll make do."

"We gotta be creative," croaked Ginny, raising her legs in the air and doing wee kicks. "Like 'fore Gent Joe came along. We got on before him."

"It was a lot more work," Louise said.

Suddenly, Ginny said, "Have you ever done it for money, Marion?" and she was smiling and there was a shine on her lips, a shine gleaming and Marion felt her stomach flip. "It's a cash register waiting to ring, ring, ring."

"Look at her," Louise said, thumb hooked back at Ginny. "Wouldn't billfolds go fat ready for her?"

The two of them, so casual, Marion couldn't speak. Were they truly asking this?

Ginny sliding around in her silk pajamas, arching her back and twisting feline in her favorite china blue lounging pajamas with long white lilies tipped in green twisting down the front, bought in San Francisco's famous Chinatown by Mr. Burton Haskell, who owned Haskell's Dry Goods and who had been such a good friend to the girls until transferred, tragically, to Oklahoma City.

Louise nodded her head in Ginny's direction and said, "We can trot out that little slip of a thing again, Marion."

And there was Ginny, fingers overspread, splayed across the dragon embroidered thickly, fierce red tongue vaulting between her bosoms.

A twitch in her brow, Marion felt like she was staring at one of those trick drawings where it looks like nothing but fancy women gossiping but then you stand back and see the face of the devil himself, begrimed and thick-lipped and dreadful.

She looked over at Ginny, who had started up a new cough that looked like it might make her face split.

"You never do such things," Marion said softly, even as her hand set on the space the posh radio had sat. "You never do."

"Fine coin she'd get with that," Louise sighed, eyes on the thread of blood that had begun issuing from Ginny's bluing lips.

Marion rushed to Ginny's side and let her curl up against her, white hands clawing.

"She won't put any food in her either," Louise said, shaking her head.

Ginny held her hack back, punching her chest with her hands. "I'll not eat," she said, and her voice was stern, like a minister in a pulpit. Then softer: "I'm trying something," she said.

"They say she'd best get lots of fresh air and lots of food," Louise said. "So she stays in here and doesn't eat."

Ginny burrowed into Marion's lap, tassels whipping round, twisting, "I bet they'd still spread bills for me. I got talents you'd cry over."

"Don't I know it. I'm crying now," Louise said, stone faced. "Marion, don't fall for her fairy dance. Let's you and me settle. Won't you rub my shoulders like before?" Louise sat down on the floor beneath them, dragging a pillow beneath her.

"Come here, Meemsie," she went on. "Come here, Marion. You're like a little buttercup over there."

Marion slid away from Ginny's stiff blue hands and huddled onto the floor beside Louise.

"Sit quiet with me and let me play with those goldilocks," she said. "You're so sweet. My, your face is warm." And Louise's hands, light and soft, played in Marion's hair and along her downy cheek.

Marion wanted to comfort her, but it was Louise who comforted, she surely did. Something old and lovely fanned before Marion's eyes, herself as a young girl, three or four, curled in her mama's lap, her mama feeding her sugar lumps off sticky fingers. She could taste them. *Oh, Mamy, darling thing.*

"Isn't it sad, Marion, to have no bosoms at all?" Ginny said, looking down at them from her perch on the sofa.

Marion looked up and saw it. It was something happening in Ginny's face, a spectral thing. A flattening. Her face snapped flat like an Indian head.

"You've such small, lovely tulips," Ginny went on, in the strangest high tone, like ice tapping on windows, "but I've not even that."

Then there was a tug of the ribbon on her silky bed jacket—ta-da!—and Ginny's baby-soft skin, only two rosy nipples like the blushing dots painted on a porcelain doll cheek. "I dab them with rouge, for effect," she said, lifting a small rouge pot from the side table.

Marion felt her mouth open, then close.

"But Louise has enough tomato for both of us," Ginny said, laughing, or looking like she was laughing but it was just the look of a laugh. She curled a puny finger into the rouge pot.

"We'll get the funds," Louise said, ignoring Ginny, twisting Marion's nose with a grin. "We always do."

But Marion was still looking at the icy blond thing on the sofa, at Ginny, whose fingers danced light and pretty along her own chest, swirling the rouge in strange patterns as she whistled soft to soothe them all.

AT WORK AGAIN, walking down long clinic hallways, spinning carbon paper and willowy onionskin around the feed roll, jamming keys under fingernails, taking long dictations, crying in the ladies' room, tearing tissue into long curls around her fingers.

What glamour might I cast, she wondered, to embed needs under this man's skin, make him crave me so deep like the deepness of something that goes through the blood, goes through the blood and bursts soft or swells hard in the brain?

A new hairstyle. A violet dress like the one in the window at Heckscher's, the one she could not afford any more than the plain shirtwaist one at S. H. Kress & Co. Underthings, could it be more underthings, not so genteel, like her peach lace dainties—no, more like the canary yellow sparking out from under Louise's dress as she slid from Ginny's spindly arms to slip over to Marion to take her into her strong arms, "Mimsies, come to sup, I made a jellied ham roll just for you."

Was that what was needed? she wondered. Because that she

would do. And try as she might she had no thought of toasters or grocer bills or rent money for her girls. She could not make herself think of it.

"I DON'T MEAN to leave you forlorn, my darling girl," Joe Lanigan said. "I don't mean to break so many engagements."

She nodded, she nodded and held on to him, fingers curled around his lapel as he stood in the clinic's main office, waiting to speak with Dr. Milroy.

Anyone might have come in, but she had seen him and he was there and she had him for a moment.

He made as if to dance with her, spinning her slightly.

"You're the apple of my eye," he crooned, as he was looking through the large glass windows at the new nursing students gushing by. "You're the cherry in my pie, the angel in the sky."

But even as he said it, the eyes were darting, pupils hopping like Mexican jumping beans, taking in the willowy blondes, the crackling brunettes, the freckle-dancing redheads in their starched whites, just through the glass.

The corridor, filled with girls—she saw suddenly how it appeared to him. How it was like the grandest candy counter in the finest department store in town. A candy counter packed fat with brassy blond nougats and licorice-whip brunettes and auburn twists of taffy with round cinnamon-button cheeks, honey-faced brickle with sweet dimpled legs powder sweet as marshmallow, jellied lips of every color, with mouths red and glossy and waiting for him. He need only drop his pennies on the counter and take his pick. And pick and pick. Candy Man.

What candy could she tuck in her own wet palm to keep his lips sugared?

This was no way for a strapping man of thirty-five, handsome-faced, broad of chest, fast of grin, strong of heart, to live, night after lonely night in the airless mahogany and velvet house his wife had chosen eight years before and which was now the most expensive gingerbread-trimmed sickbed the town had ever seen. This was no way to live when each evening the streets filled with burbling office girls and waitresses, librarians and students, dancers and school-teachers, all bright-eyed and twitchy-tailed, little canaries with Jean Harlow puffs of hair, cheeping and twittering to him, "Come and get it!"

Part Three

She was so lovely. Like a doll on a high shelf in a nursery. You wanted to reach up and touch the pearly wax cheek. You wanted to put your fingers on the curling brush of long eyelashes. Feel them against your finger. She was so lovely. And she wanted to be my friend. A doctor's wife. I told her I was from way up in the high country by Fool Hollow, which is famous for its walleye and all kinds of panfish. She said she had a friend, a Mr. Joseph Lanigan, who loved fishing, was mad for fishing. I said I bet he's never seen one of our red-breasted breams and she said he surely had not. 'You must tell Mr. Lanigan about it,' her voice so fast upon me, high and excited. 'I'll arrange it. You'll both come over for coffee. No, no, for dinner. I'll make Mexican eggs and we'll sit at the table and you'll tell him about red-breasted breams. He'll be so glad. Won't that be fine?' And I said it would and wouldn't it be nice to meet Marion's husband, who was a physician. And I'd never been invited to a doctor's home before and wouldn't that be something. Of course, it didn't happen that way at all. I never did visit Marion's home nor meet Dr. Seeley. But that's later. At the time, oh, was I excited, and I went home straight that night to darn the holes in my best stockings and try to bleach out the old lace on my Sunday dress. After my toilette that night I looked at my long hair hanging to my waist in the mirror and wished I had a smart bob like Marion and then I'd have my hair marcelled like her and look like Constance Bennett. My, wouldn't that be something?

—Elsie Nettle, R.N.
Interview, June 21, 1931
Det. Thomas Tolliver

"Marion, who is that new nurse at the clinic? The one with the dark hair."

"Elsie?"

"Elsie," Joe Lanigan said, as if giving the name a taste, rolling it along his tongue. "Elsie. Well, she's a fine girl, isn't she?"

"She's very nice. A good girl."

"Do you like her?"

"I don't know her very well, but she seems very sweet. From a good family."

"Well, maybe you should bring her by Louise's."

"Oh, Joe, I don't think . . ."

"It's the right thing to do, Marion. Make her feel at home."

Elsie Nettle, just nineteen years old and at the clinic one week.

Not three days before, Dr. Milroy had made much the same request. "Mrs. Seeley," he said, one dry hand on her shoulder, a new turn since Marion's hair went white as powdered sugar. "Since you are no longer the youngest lamb, might we call upon you to play shepherd to our newest member of the flock? She is a young girl from the mountains and new to the big city, such as it is."

Dr. Sweet, standing next to Dr. Milroy, nodded in big-grin assent. He liked to stride past Marion in the corridors and swing his stethoscope so it hit Marion's hip or backside.

"I'd like to help," Marion said. "Nurse Mercer was such a friend to me when I began."

"Nurse Mercer." Dr. Sweet rolled banjo eyes at Dr. Milroy. "That is love's labor lost."

"Now, Jasper," Dr. Milroy said coolly, and turned back to Marion and smiled. "Nurse Mercer . . . Well, I'd much prefer your help in these matters. With such a young girl."

Marion did not know what to say, but she had seen such winking and nonsense about Louise before and sometimes Louise did too and sometimes it seemed to fluster her, made her look over at Marion as if to see if Marion saw too and how Marion took it. There was always tittle-tattle, though, about the unmarried nurses. That was the way it was and Marion never bothered with it, never did.

"I am glad to offer any guidance I can," Marion said, not meeting Dr. Sweet's preening gaze, not participating in his foot-bouncing, chest-fluffing show.

She would guide this girl, her eyes big and dark, like a forest doe, and show her the things she knew. The nurses, after all, did not like to help. The nurses viewed new girls, especially ones as young as Elsie, the youngest by six years, as nothing but trouble, Louise most of all.

"I don't fall for her line," Louise muttered. "No one's that green. Says she never even heard a radio till last week Sunday."

"But she's darling," Marion replied. "If one of the doctors says a word, she jumps three feet from fright."

"They cut our hours on account they can pay her less," Louise said. "Who do they think they're fooling?"

Elsie Nettle, though, was dear, and Marion found that she liked to help, liked to be a friend. She showed her all the hidden corners of the clinic, where to catch a lungful of fresh air out the back, the best route home to the Millicente Boarding House for Young Women on Pettington Street.

And now here was Joe Lanigan, wanting to join the party.

How did he even know there was a new nurse, and was this about the darting something in his eyes, the thing that looked like sorrow if Joe Lanigan knew sorrow from the next girl-fed folly?

"See what you can do, Mrs. Seeley," he said, finger dancing along her stomach, making little patterns that sent sweet breaths up her throat. "Let's see about our Elsie Nettle."

MARION HAD JUST washed her hair and it smelled like flowers and she knew Joe would like it. She had pressed her good dress and tried to pleat over the spot where the threads had started to pull away from each other.

When she walked to the trolley stop a dusty breeze kicked up her skirt and she thought about seeing Joe for the first time in six days, even if it was with little Elsie Nettle.

She ran her wrist under her nose and smelled rose milk and she knew Joe would like that too. It made her think of his finger-tips tracing along her hip, his face pressed against her thighs, saying she smelled of violets, and she had laughed and said did he know what violets smelled like and he smiled and said yes, *like this,* and she could feel the flush all up her body, like a desert gust, a soft carpet unrolling, the sharp bones of a radiator shuddering, something, something.

But here was Elsie, waiting at the streetcar stop in a lavender dress and dark curls hanging all down her back and the hesitant smile of a young girl because it was what she was. You could near see the dew beading on her dark eyelashes.

They exchanged sprightly greetings and walked arm in arm to the Celestial Chow House. Elsie asked where Dr. Seeley was and Marion explained, very quickly, that he had a temporary post so far away but was due to visit for Easter, and that she missed him so, but goodness wasn't it a warm evening and wouldn't a tall glass of tea be heaven?

HE WAS THERE when they arrived, talking with some other men in shirtsleeves and jackets off, and Marion could tell from the red pitch to his face that he had been drinking.

"Mrs. Seeley, my, aren't you pretty as a picture," he said, sweeping her under his arm, pressing her to his chest. She could smell the booze on him.

But he straightened out and bowed toward Elsie and took her

hand and kissed it with great delicacy, like he was performing on a stage.

Elsie could scarcely face him, so shy and stuttering, and they all sat, and Joe had already ordered. Waiters in pale gold manda-rin coats kept bringing out steaming dishes with heavy silver lids, and it was egg flower soup and pineapple spareribs and egg foo yong and everything with a glossy sheen about it. Marion had not eaten so much since her wedding day, and she couldn't help but think about how long she and the girls could live on just the cost of this one frilly meal.

She had not told Louise about her evening plans. She had in fact openly lied, claiming she had to stay home and complete her transcriptions. The way Louise talked about Elsie Nettle, the way Joe Lanigan was dodging her—Marion knew she shouldn't be doing this, knew it was stirring things up that were already unset-tled and dire. But Joe, but Joe . . . There were things he wanted and she felt so long past saying no to anything.

Joe ordered Sue Sin tea for everyone, even when Elsie spoke of wanting to try oolong, and that's when Marion knew the Sue Sin was spiked, but she was sure Elsie wouldn't know and she thought the poor girl must be wondering why her cheeks burned so hot and why her words kept coming out in long taffy twists. By the time the salt almonds and fortune cakes came, Marion snatched the girl's teacup away and Joe saw her do it and winked at her.

She had to admit that it was all very gay, though, and Joe paid them each so much attention, but Marion even more. He told jokes and funny stories about the pharmacy customers, the whin-ing toothachers and nervous mamas and the blossom-nosed lawyer with the clove breath, and then he kept saying he was going to order more food and Marion and Elsie kept laughing and holding their stomachs and begging him to stop, and he would twirl his hand in the air, threatening to summon the wait-ers, and the girls would shake their heads wildly and make him promise, no more food, no more food.

Marion could see that Elsie was having such a time and that she was admiring of Joe Lanigan. As the last plates were cleared, he reached out his stiff white napkin and put it to her cheek where the faintest dot of orange glaze rested, and Marion watched as he ran his fingers, thumb along her cherried lower lip, and grinned at her. Elsie turned five colors deeper and Marion put her hat on and said it was time to go.

Joe laughed that Marion was stricter than a schoolmarm, wasn't she, and surely they had time for a drive in his automo-bile, all three of them catching a whisper of breeze, wouldn't that be a wonderful way to digest and round off the wonderful evening?

Elsie supposed it would and Marion looked at Joe, who only laughed, and when they pushed together in the front seat of his car she could feel Elsie's excitement radiating off of her, almost a burning thing, and she did not know how it made her feel.

JOE WAS DRIVING THEM WESTWARD, toward the thin ribbon of river and the promise of moving air, but before he reached the far end of town, he made two sharp turns and they ended up on Hussel Street and the girls' bungalow.

"Mr. Lanigan," Marion said, "I wonder what you have in mind."

"I'm just going to make a quick stop to Nurse Mercer. I promised to deliver some medicine for her roommate."

"Isn't that a kindness," Marion said to Elsie, an edge slipping into her voice in spite of herself. "Owns four pharmacies and still makes his own deliveries."

"My, you're starting to sound like Nurse Mercer herself," Joe said, grinning, as he shut off the car.

"That is very kind." Elsie beamed, oblivious, and Marion tried to keep her head. She knew this was not a good idea. She knew without knowing all the reasons why Louise and Ginny would not like this. It was something she felt, a pressure in her throat.

"You two can stay here," Joe assured them. "I won't tell them they're missing our fun little party."

He was inside for a moment when Louise's russet head suddenly popped up along the car's passenger window, making Marion nearly jump from her seat.

"What's doing, kids?" Louise piped, reaching through the window and embracing Marion, tugging at her curls.

Marion looked for signs of ire, signs of anything, but Louise just grinned at her, at them both, Elsie nearly bouncing in her seat, having such fun.

Trying for a smile light as air, Marion said, "You know Elsie, the new nurse and new to town."

"And she's getting the special top-o'-the-line Joe Lanigan tour," Louise said, reaching past Marion and pinching Elsie's blushy cheek as if they were old chums.

"Hello," Elsie said, smiling.

"Hello yourself, puss." Louise grinned.

"Mr. Lanigan gave you your medicine?" Elsie said.

"That he did, whip-poor-will. That he did. Soon enough," she said, "he'll be giving you yours."

TEN MINUTES LATER, in the car, Joe was laying his hand on Elsie, very light, and Elsie looked over at Marion and Marion did not know what to do, so she just began chattering to Elsie even as she saw Joe Lanigan's hand on Elsie's leg, just resting there, just resting. Marion could very nearly feel the fluttery heat coming off Elsie. Oh, the poor thing could hardly manage it. She had no idea what was happening, but her head felt funny and maybe it was all the tea?

All the while Joe was talking gaily about the new houses being built on the northeast corner of town. Now it was nothing but desert dust, but in two years it would be filled with families and businesses and prosperity. Marion could not truly listen, Elsie's face so close to hers, so confused and unsure, her blushful face near bursting, cherry beamed. Marion wanted to soothe her, whisper tangled assurances in her ear, but how could she when she was hand-holding her into such a dark, abominable breach.

It was three miles or so from town when Joe stopped the automobile in a dim patch of cleared field. The night air grit-gleaming the plundered left-behinds—brown glass shards, foil and rusty rinds of Sterno tin, a hobo camp ransacked, burned flat.

"Marion, I'm going to show Elsie where the new store will be once these houses go up. Would you like to walk a ways with us and see it as well?"

"Oh, I don't think so, Joe," she said, and she felt her head shake back and forth hard. "But if you're longer than five minutes I shall scream." As she said this, something pressed, rose up in her throat and she made Joe meet her eyes and feel it. He did feel it, but he was so hard to surprise.

"She's afraid of rattlesnakes," Joe confided to Elsie, whose hand he took as Marion moved to let her past.

Elsie looked back at her as Joe escorted her into the brush.

She looked back at Marion with a face darling as a puny chick and she was biting that petal-pink lip of hers and her eyes were filled with heat and fear. Marion could almost hear her little pullet heart beating.

IN THE CAR, Marion sat and touched the worn spot on her dress and thought of any number of things. The time, age thirteen, she rubbed her cheeks with beet juice before school and Mrs. Pace called her a Magdalen and made her stand with her dress over her head in the yard. The way the wallpaper gaped in the Carson City rooming house where she and Dr. Seeley had resided for three months while he awaited the final judgment of another state licensing board. The time Louise's fingers danced along little points of hair at Marion's ears, temples and the middle of the forehead and said, *These are the five points of Venus, Marion, did you know?* And Ginny piped up, *I think you forgot one.*

Had it been five minutes? She was not sure, but she thought suddenly of Elsie's downy cheek trembling and she hated herself, she hated herself.

She opened the car door and got out, slamming it as thunderously as she could, and made to start walking, made to start running.

At that moment, they came out of the brush, urgent as a shot, and the chick had one hand on her skirt, rustling it down, and the other on her face, which was scarlet. Her giggling was not soft and had no rhythm. It trailed, jangling, and was filled with a giddy panic.

His eyes shone. His gait was jaunty and light.

When he got to the car, Joe Lanigan kissed Marion flush on the mouth. She knew why. He kissed her because he was proud.

THEY DROPPED ELSIE OFF at her boardinghouse and the girl shivered up the front steps and Marion could only imagine what thoughts might seize her the night through—she didn't even need to imagine, she knew. During the ride home, she had seen how Elsie's right leg could not stop trembling. It rattled so. She knew what the girl's shaking leg meant, shaking like a pinion and her stocking damp and her face, if you looked closely, it was like there was a gash across it, like a hook caught in her mouth and dragged round. Not a real gash, but a secret mark, a deep score, from five to ten minutes she would never forget.

Joe Lanigan could scarcely wait until he found a secluded street not three blocks away to pull over under a pair of bottle trees and throw Marion's skirt into the air, and he didn't bother with himself and instead used his hand on her so fast, his fingers and knuckles, not rough but nearly so. It was so frantic and then he shuddered love thoughts to her and she told herself that what she had done, allowed to be done, helped to make done, might be enough for a long while, might have purchased for her months of love unfettered by deviance. But she knew it wasn't so. She had only raised the stakes, hadn't she?

"THESE GIRLS I can balance five to a finger, Marion," he told her, "because none of them matter, so many cigarettes snuffed out."

"I can't fathom that, Joe," she said, picturing one's heart rent in so many pieces, diced clean to spread widely. She wanted to leave his car and walk up to her room and sleep for a thousand years.

He became serious and his expression was so solemn. "I am sorry, Marion," he said, looking down at his hands, "because I know your morality may not be large enough to accommodate my weakness. It is a weakness. It is that."

He was pale and it was the gravest she had ever seen him. "It's one thing, Marion. It's one thing," he said. "I am more than that."

It reminded her of something. A moment. Behind the police station in Indianapolis, Dr. Seeley, fingertips still inky and shirt browned and wrinkled, that dark forelock fallen across his brow and his arm too heavy to lift it, to sweep it back.

"One thing, Marion," Joe was saying now. "One thing isn't a man."

She looked at him and said, softly, "Oh, but it is."

In bed that night, Marion thought about Joe Lanigan and his weakness and then about Dr. Seeley and his. These men and their weaknesses. Could they not restrain them at all?

But then she thought about her own: here a man with a way of smiling so and doffing hat and tilting head just so. These accumulations of gesture and a tender word or two and then she pliant on any bed, seat cushion, what have you? Well, if that wasn't a weakness, what was?

I am filled with shame. Love me yet, Doctor.

Part Four

Whether I loved you who shall say?
Whether I drifted down your way
In the endless River of Chance and Change,
And you woke the strange
Unknown longings that have no names,
But burn us all in their hidden flames,
    Who shall say?

  . . .

But, whether you love me, who shall say,
Or whether you, drifting down my way
In the great sad River of Chance and Change,
With your looks so weary and words so strange,
Lit my soul from some hidden flame
To a passionate longing without a name,
    Who shall say? . . .

—From "The Teak Forest,"
by Laurence Hope,
Pen name of Adela Florence Nicolson (1865–1904)

They had asked her to come and play cards. She didn't know
what Joe Lanigan had given them for the kitty the previous night
while she sat on tenterhooks in his automobile with Elsie Nettle,
but whether it was pills or money or both, Ginny sounded gay,
calling from the neighbors' telephone, breathless and cheery,

and Marion was relieved. All worries seemed to be forgotten in the giddiness that so overswept the girls as they planned their evening.

Hurrying about Mrs. Gower's kitchen, Marion made bread-and-jelly pudding and wrapped it in a thick kitchen towel. On the streetcar it sat in her lap, hot and sweating, and when she arrived, her dress was wet and the evening air was barely air at all.

Ginny answered the door, a rare thing, especially now that she was so poorly. She had three curlers in her hair and eyes rimmed with kohl and a deep rouge on her lips.

"We decided this is Monte Carlo night, Mims, and you shall be the Duchess Estrella from Hungary and tonight you risk losing the crown jewels and your mountainous duchy on the Rhine—" The cough started then and Marion reached across to hold Ginny's arms and they were like kindling bits.

"Did you get the money, Louise?" Marion whispered to Louise after helping Ginny to the sofa.

Louise, who did not appear adorned for Monte Carlo night and looked queasy, sticky, jumbled, said, "No, Marion. Can you imagine. Joe Lanigan gave up neither gold nor grain. Only a jug of the slickery white. He is nearly useless as a sugar daddy, wouldn't you say?"

Her face was pulled and there were heavy things in her eyes and Marion felt those things tugging at her too, and she placed her hand on Louise's arm and Louise's eyes filled for a moment and then she turned back to the stove, where a pan with sauerkraut was simmering.

"Marion," Ginny's voice creaked from the sofa. "Marion, none of them came by at all this week. None of them. Not Mr. Worth, nor Mr. McNeary, nor Sheriff Healy, nor Mr. Loomis. Not even Floyd of the mine-black hands. And yet we're still here." Eyes jumpy and eyebrows doing strange, twittery things, she looked over at Louise. "But they'll be back next week, don't doubt it. With the finest corn and an RCA Victor Electrola with swank Oriental trimmings like Mr. Loomis showed us in the catalog. In the meantime, who needs 'em? I'm entertainment to burn."

"This is a sorrowful world," Louise said, and she began pouring from the jug of gin. "One needs victuals. That's what's needed."

The sadness of Louise was spurring things in Ginny, disturbances and peculiar energies that were making her manic to amuse, and these energies were making Louise nerved up and drinking more, and finally Marion surrendered to the witchy electricities and took a glass too because it seemed the only way.

"God made man frail as a bubble," Ginny sang, *"God made love, love made trouble."* She pressed one hand to her chest like Sister Aimee. *"God made the vine—then is it a sin,"* she asked, lifting her glass, *"that man made wine to drown trouble in?"*

It was a heavy effort on all parts, but within the hour, the mood was lifting, and the close air of the house filled with sweaty laughter and a glistening on Louise's cheeks from the stovetop, the gin, Marion's ministrations, twisting her friend's hair into curls drawn tight with vitamin oil and looking like motion-picture flappers. "Oh, Marion," Louise said, smiling, "your hands are like butterflies."

Ginny, trying to help, singing and frolicking, kept having to plunge her face fast into her skittery kerchief with each grinding hack, and Louise kept shushing her away and Ginny would run to the open window and cough out into the night air. Her energy was all wrong and Marion could feel it but didn't know what to do about it.

On one such circuit, Ginny, now stripped down to bloomers, ran to the bathroom sink and dunked her head under cold water, then circled back, flouncing on the settee, jamming one skinny leg between the girls, seated on the floor beneath her on lumpen pillows, and belted out, "So, tell us about your triple date, toots."

Marion, so loose and slippery from Louise's cooing and their shared girl talk, jolted suddenly to alertness. She had known it would come, but like this? She reached for the jug and poured herself a second glass of the tongue-curling stuff.

"Yes, Marion," Louise said, eyes now on her, saying it in a jolly way, but Marion couldn't believe in the jollity. She tried to. She took a sip and tried to do that. "Did you have a snapping time?"

"Oh," Marion said. "I guess I have become the welcome wagon now."

"Is that what's happened?" Louise said, and her voice was tighter now.

Retreating from her own question quick as a crab, Ginny reached for her pair of finger cymbals, which she kept tucked under a cushion. "Shall I do my Salome dance?" she asked, clicking them over her head.

"No, you shall not," Louise said, head whipping round to Ginny. "You be still, bad girl. And stay seated for a piece and a half. You're on my scolding list." She turned back to Marion, eyes so black, the pupils dilated so wide she looked like a Katzenjammer kid in the Sunday comics. *Oh, she is stewed,* thought Marion.

"All day, Marion, before you arrived, I set to scolding her," Louise said, waving her arm, pointing fingers at Ginny, who had started to giggle. "She's been blasting herself with secret frolics passed to her by our very own milkman."

"He likes to help a sister out, that milkman does." Ginny trilled. "And who knew he had such bonbons and all I had to do was give him a dimple."

"Those kinds of candy will not help your blown-out lungs one bit," Louise said, straightening her back to nurse posture.

"They help my lungs on account of my lungs go poof the minute I blow," Ginny said, tapping her nose with her fingertip. "I can lick anything with this glow I got on."

"Oh, Ginny—," Marion started to say, but Louise, head swiveling back round, shot out, "Elsie Nettle, that wood sprite, that mountain apple-knocker. All angel-face, angel-bottom innocent, Joe Lanigan's favorite variety. Looked to me like you wrapped her up with a fat ribbon for our Gent Joe."

"Wrapped her up?" Marion said, not liking the look on Louise's whirring face. A hot, burring energy, a fitful, angry thing. It didn't seem fair, somehow. Was this Louise's concern, after all? And wasn't it unkind of her to shine a spotlight on Marion's private shame?

"Let's just say it," Louise said, thumping the sofa's edge with open palm. Ginny crawled across the sofa, arms out to her. "Let's not pretend, Marion. I'd love to pretend with you and just play with you like this, as we are, but I look at those bow lips of yours as you lie, lie, lie."

"Don't get yourself in a fit again, Lou-Lou. Don't let's," Ginny said. "You told me to calm myself and here you are."

"We have . . . It's not . . . It's not . . . ," Marion stuttered, but she could feel something ruffling in her, something ruffling and setting off hot feelings of her own. "It's not your affair, Louise. It's not your business."

"Don't you get it, Marion?" Louise snapped, reaching out to grab Marion's wrist, but not before Marion pulled it away and rose to her feet. "Don't you get it? Joe Lanigan is all our business." She paused, then said, razor sharp, "We're all in the business of Joe Lanigan."

"Last night, it wasn't about *you*," Marion blurted. All the while thinking, *It is I who had to eat my pride up, had to have it forced down my throat.* "It's a separate thing we have, Joe and I. And you can't know what goes on with Mr. Lanigan and myself. You don't know anything about what we have shared." She could feel the junipers tingling under her skin. My, it was fine gin her lover had brought them.

Louise jumped up, shaking off Ginny's bluing hands.

"Could you really think that? I wonder, could you? Has he gotten so far between your jerking little virgin legs that you've gone cross-eyed?"

"Don't you say such things, Louise," Marion said, her face hot. She'd never seen Louise so mad, not ever. "I introduced him to Elsie to be nice. That's all I have done."

"You're telling me he doesn't have plans to spread-eagle her, Marion? Don't you know his man ways by now? And she, of all girls. She."

"She? What? What?" Marion asked. "Why are you both against me?"

"Don't you know what she's holding tight, that Elsie Nettle," Ginny said from the sofa, eyes on the reddened edges of her kerchief. "Marion, I hope to goodness you did not know. Because if you knew, if you knew . . ."

"What? What can you mean?" Marion said.

"I wonder how you'd dare," Louise hissed, tongue forking. "I wonder how you'd dare fasten him up with a gal sick through like that."

"Sick?"

"She's got ole joe," Ginny said, pounding her fragile boned forearm down on the sofa. "Nursie Nettle's got the dread syph. Ain't I finally the lucky one in some comparison?"

"I don't believe you," Marion said, Elsie's fairy-pure face looming before her eyes. It was impossible. "She's not got that."

"She's got it, don't you doubt it," Louise said, grabbing again for Marion's wrist, which Marion wrenched free. "Look what you've set us in for."

Marion backed up three steps, feeling like the waif in some handkerchief-twisting melodrama. What had she done to deserve such wrath and deceit?

Louise couldn't stop. "First you start up with him and you don't dally, no, it has to be a love match, a grand passion, Greta Garbo in the drawing room. *Ca-mille,*" she said, throwing her head back grandly. "But you don't see that it's Gent Joe we're talking about. Gent Joe, who lifts every skirt hem in ten square miles. And so Gent Joe doesn't come round so much. You decide you like what he gives you and you gotta get it all the time. So what do you do to keep him? Trot in that sickly nymph all loaded up on Neosalvarsan. Even as you must know she'll empty what's left of Joe Lanigan's pockets and run him through the sick. She's a filthy thing. Myra Jenks told me. She saw her file. Well, you know those mountain rubes and their ways. You brought her in, Marion. You brought her in."

"It's not true," Marion said, with shaking breath. "You haven't any right, Louise Mercer, to go spreading such lies. Lies no doubt spread by Myra, who's a horrible gossip and has had her ire on you for months." She knew it wasn't true. She knew how the nurses were, with their careless tales. And then it came into her head and before she could think about it, she added, "Just like with the machine. Just like you did with that X-ray machine. I didn't forget it."

"Marion!" Ginny started up fast, then her cough disclosed and she could not go on. Her body, though, it was quaking and her eyes pinpointed. She looked ready for something and it was frightening to Marion. Something was not right with her, like Marion's cousin, six years old, stayed with them while suffering through rabbit fever and thought Marion's father a demon and screamed all night.

"You so high and mighty," Louise snarled, face flaming, moving closer toward Marion, finger pointed, the heat coming off her. "Yet when do you turn your hands up at our offers of cakes and candies? You just don't wish to think about how we come by them. The doctor's wife can lay in velvet as she chooses, but where is she when the bill comes? And now things aren't raw enough for us and you bring her in. You bring her in and crowd over the pot. The pot near empty already. That rotting girl."

"I can't know what you mean, Louise. I can't. Elsie's an every-day girl like we are, I am, I don't know what you are, I don't know it now," Marion said, feeling suddenly dizzy, feeling suddenly the prickly junipers bursting before her eyes, making her head quaky. Who were these women? she wondered. Who were they and what was she?

"How," Louise began, then her voice shook apart and she had to pull it together again, breathing deeply. "How . . . *How* do you think we live, Marion?"

Marion could see something tear loose in Louise, something tear loose, and she was so lost and the thing in Louise that Marion knew so well, the tremendous thumping heart and all it held, it was there. It was still there. The rest was panic and noise.

Then something struck Marion urgently, even as she realized she had in some dark, unsaid way known it all along. "Louise," she said, "did you intend to give *me* to Mr. Lanigan? Was that your idea, Louise? Was I your gift? Your payment, past due?"

"No!" Louise said, shaking her head, shaking it so vigorously her dark red curls unspooled. "He *took* you. All I could do was keep it under our roof."

"I think you set me out for him, Louise," Marion said, her head reeling. "How is that not what you accuse me of?"

"You don't see, Marion. How do you suppose we make rent? She . . . ," Louise said, almost a howl, then, pointing to Ginny, ". . . has not worked in sixteen months. She has had to go to County three times. We can't afford a clinic like Werden. We're still paying bills to the last hospital, so behind they smeared me for delinquency. They tried to pin a fence charge on me too for selling our own things. Gifts that were ours to sell. The only shimmer, Marion, the only shimmer we got is the fairy dust Gent Joe has scattered."

And with this last sentence her face fell in on itself, and her shoulders fell too, and it reminded Marion of something she couldn't quite name, something she'd seen on a face once, someone's face, was it her own face? Her own face in the mirror the night Dr. Seeley first did not make it home and the room he had left her in but half paid and she not even knowing for certain if they were still in Nevada or if they'd crossed the border into California. And she with not twelve cents in her battered handbag.

"Oh, Louise," Marion said, moving toward her, and Louise came upon her fast and embraced her, clinging tightly to Marion and saying whispered things Marion could not quite hear. Secret words too lovely to say out loud.

It was as though Marion could see Louise's beating heart laid bare, and she knew then how Louise had taken her as her charge and she herself had treated it too lightly, like a gift easily given when it was not. When it was blood meant. How had she missed that? Had anyone taken such care of her before?

"Louise," Marion said, "I promise, we will get whatever money we need. We will. I will make sure of that. Dr. Seeley is on his way here. He will be here by Easter and he can help us. He will."

Louise didn't say anything, but her hands on Marion were so tight.

"I'm sorry, darling," Louise said. "I'm sorry. I didn't want him to do it. I didn't think it would really happen. I thought you were just silver trimmings for him to eye. And then he won you over, as he does. You were my friend, but there it was. He took you and it worried me. It grieved me. But there it was. You see what he is now. You see we must fasten ourselves to each other. Tie each other post to post. We must."

Neither of them was looking at Ginny, both so wrapped in their girl forgiveness and Marion daubing Louise's tears with thumb and forefinger and Louise vining her arm around Marion's waist and they pressed forehead to forehead. Back somewhere, though, Marion could feel Ginny, could feel her watching, watching like the green tuning eye on the radio, flickering hot.

"We're hitched wagon to wagon for the long haul, aren't we, Meems? Don't you know?" Louise murmured and nuzzled nose against Marion's lips and it turned to kisses and Marion felt a funny flush but before she could think twice, Ginny's voice came crackling out.

"Look at you now, arms all over Louise, after what you've done."

Arms all over, Marion thought. A flash came to her of that private tableau, Ginny's white thigh slung and Louise's arm sliding between bent leg, dimpled knee.

Something quivered in Marion's chest and she pulled fast from Louise's arms, eyes on Ginny, who was like a snapped trolley wire sparking on the pavement.

All that rabid energy that had been rushing through Ginny all night—like before, like before, in the cold bathtub, she drawling, ugly, *I might do anything when it's like this. . . . Just you see what I can do.* Then, seeing her and Louise like that, somehow worse than her and Louise fighting, much worse. And now there she was, like a cornered thing, teeth bared.

"Propping up that polluted nurse for his pleasures," Ginny spat at Marion, voice jumpy and rough. "You're the pretty little leech. Drawing him dry for us. A sharp-toothed little blood-sucker. Must supply Gent Joe with fresh gash. Bring in that slanty little gash. Infecting us all with her, stealing Joe's charms and dancing high kicks while we can't make rent and the wheeze from the lungers' camp, I can hear it from here."

It was the ugliest words she'd ever heard and Marion wanted to cover her ears.

"No, Gin-Gin, it ain't—," Louise started, turning as Ginny rose from the sofa, muslin twining between bare legs.

"She may fool you, Louise, because you are softhearted, but I have long had this prairie flower in my keen sights," said Ginny, and her face had that aspect Marion had seen but once before, like a white sheet pulled taut and eyes slanting to black arrows and mouth but a red line. "Trying to get her dainty hooks in. She's been at it for months. And here I get sicker and she slinks closer, playing the innocent, like I don't know."

"Ginny," Marion said, but she couldn't focus. Ginny's face, torn flat, was like a stranger's, some strange girl you'd see in a high-up window at the state hospital and she'd be tapping at it, tapping at you.

"Ginny, don't you dare," Louise snapped. "Marion isn't doing any such thing. She loves you. No one's doing the things you're . . . No one's doing—"

"Now I know! Now I know!" Ginny crowed, and Louise, as if realizing something, rushed toward Ginny, grabbing her shoulders.

"I wonder who's been filling your ear with tongue oil," Louise said, holding Ginny fast between strong hands. "I wonder. Was it really the milkman who gave—"

Ginny pulled herself free, face coloring with angry blood.

"She's fooled and enticed you, Louise. She has her way, you'll light a shuck with her and leave me to wither. But I will put a stop to it. She's Pandora, come to town with her dirty little box to bring us all to ruin. She's a plague and she has ruined us all."

"No, Ginny," Louise tried again, voice edging into panic, which edged Marion's further still. "Ginny, you're all roostered up and you don't know what you're saying. You're not to do this. You're not to do this."

"Just you wait until Dr. Seeley returns and I give him an earful of what his wife has been up to in his absence."

"Don't you dare, don't you dare speak of such things," Marion said, so hot now she felt like her skin was curling from her. "Don't you dare mention his name."

"Oh, won't he like to hear of what dirty deeds under coverlet with Jack Lanigan. Filthy things, abominations, the stuff of whorehouses. Oh, and won't I add about the pills and tonics and goodness knows. Knowing Joe Lanigan there was a shakerful of snow, wasn't there, Marion? Wouldn't he like to know his dear-heart wife was spending her evenings back flat on heaving mattresses, blowing like Cocaine Lil? Wouldn't he like to know what his wife—"

Marion's hand shot out and slapped Ginny hard in the face.

"You won't say a thing, Ginny, you won't, else you'll hear what I can broadcast, wild tales." And once Marion started, she couldn't stop herself and it came out. It just came out, even as Louise kept pulling on her and Marion tried to wriggle away roughly.

She did not know she was going to say it and never would have thought she would ever say it, but she did.

"I have things I can tell, I have things I can shout to high heavens to shame you," Marion burst out, grabbing Ginny's spindly arm with one hand and with the other jabbing her own chest with her thumb. "You know what they say about you two at the clinic, don't you? Love's labor's lost, that's what they say. Oh, the whispers and winks, and everyone knows how unnatural you two—"

As if in one move, Ginny tore Marion's arm away and, squirming like a silverfish, she reached in the side-table drawer and drew out the girls' famed pistol.

"Oh, sweet Mary, Ginny, put that thing away," Louise said, and it was nearly a wail. "She doesn't mean it, she doesn't mean it."

Marion's heart galloped wildly and the little gun looked so big and Ginny's face so frightening, her veins rising from her arms as she lifted the weapon, cording blue up her neck and to her forehead.

"I will do no such thing. I will not have this, Louise," Ginny said, voice curdling, her cough threatening to overtake her.

Watching her and heart lashing, Marion began backing away, but Ginny was upon her. "Don't you run, Marion Seeley. Don't you dare run from me."

Ginny upon her so fast, Marion felt the back of her head knock against the wall and the pistol pointing straight at her chest. Wriggling away and shoving Ginny, she turned to face Louise, stock-still and white with terror, and Marion heard the sound, the short report, before she could even gasp, and the sound of flesh tearing from her hand. She grabbed desperately at the pistol, singeing hot, and she and Ginny fell to the floor, Marion on top and looking down at twisty little Ginny, that minxing blond thrush, now beneath her, churning under her and spitting and hacking and cursing Marion and cursing her so. "I'll shoot you, Marion Seeley, for what you've done. You will be sorry. I'll shoot that pretty face to pieces."

Both pairs of hands wrapped tight on the burning pistol and Louise shouted something in the background, the second shot came like a bolt in Marion's ears, and her hand felt as if pierced in two and then the gun flew up and there was a third shot.

Ginny's face crumpled like shiny paper and Marion felt her blood screaming and Ginny's face, it turned black, and in an instant it was gone.

Marion felt herself spring backward like a jack-in-the-box and thud against the wall. Lifting her head, she saw Louise, looking down at her, fingers to lower lip. Then Marion's eyes fell to her own hand, her burning hand with gun still wrapped tight. Her other hand torn to pulp, like a bloody keyhole in the center.

"Marion," Louise said, and that was when Marion saw the gaping red ring on Louise's dress, just above the hip.

"Louise, you have been shot." Marion heard her voice say these words.

Looking down at herself, Louise saw the blood, which was blossoming, and then her legs gave out on her and she collapsed to the floor.

JOE LANIGAN was leaning over her and his hand was open and was he going to slap her?

The crack came at her and the burning on her face something fierce.

"Don't hit me, Joe," she murmured. "How'd you get here, Joe?"

"You telephoned me, Marion," he was saying, and he stood back up straight. He still had his hat on, that one with the brim, he said the brim was felted under water by hand, but that couldn't be, could it, and his linen suit was so white, like vanilla ice cream.

Her hand was in her lap, but it was not her hand but the hand of a carnival clown, big and spongy and not hers at all. And the red from it was everywhere.

"I did? I telephoned you, Joe?" Then she remembered wrapping Louise's housecoat around herself and running down the street to the soda fountain, which was closed. The old man mopping the floor saw her and let her in. "I burned myself," she had said, "but my husband is a doctor." The man shrugged and kept mopping.

She went in the booth and whispered, "Mr. Lanigan, it's a dreadful thing. Her face is gone. It's just gone and my hand is hot."

"Mrs. Seeley, what . . ."

"Mr. Lanigan, Louise is lying still but what of Ginny and that elfin face crushed like a cigarette?"

"Marion, where are you?"

"I'm in hell, Mr. Lanigan. You never told me how it felt. You should have, so I'd've known."

Now Joe in his ice-cream suit looked down at her, and wet, oh, her temple felt wet, and reaching up she felt the thin tuft of Ginny-blond hair stuck to her forehead.

"Marion, what, what—"

She tried to tell him but the words were floating from her and she couldn't hold on to them, her blood still rushing so hard, her chest still heaving, and Joe Lanigan's face, his eyes darting, his mind working, trying to piece it together.

"And the gun exploded, and her face went too."

"And Louise?"

"I don't know how. The gun exploded three times. And click-clacked about."

"I see," he said, but how could he? He started to walk toward Louise but stopped several feet before her body, sprawled.

"We were fighting about such dreadful things and they were saying these things about you. These horrid things. And Louise, she . . ."

"What were they saying, Marion?"

"It doesn't matter, for I am lost. I am lost. I shall go to Mexico," she said, even as she said it remembering Dr. Seeley was well on his way up north by now. Two, three days away from here.

"Marion, stand up and let me see your hand," he said, and he helped her to her feet and put his tender hands on hers and she felt certain now he would save her. He would save her.

"You've been shot, Marion," he said. "I can see the bullet."

"Oh, Joe." And she leaned toward him, and then his eyes, she caught sight of them, and they were so dark and lost. *I have thrown him,* she thought. *He does not know what to do.*

He looked down at the floor and saw the gun there. He picked it up delicately, as though it were a wounded sparrow. Together, they looked at it.

"Marion, what have you done?" he said, and she'd never heard such lostness in his voice.

"I was to be killed," she said.

"They were base women," Joe said, still staring at the pistol. "They were degenerate women and I should never have let you traffic with them."

At that moment, she saw the blur out of the corner of her eye, the pale flash of Louise's blood-fronted dress from behind Joe.

"Louise," Marion said, clutching her chest with one hand and reaching out with the other.

Wan as Lazarus, Louise had climbed to her feet.

Joe's eyes seized on Marion's and he half turned and saw Louise, like some forlorn ghost, blazing red hair and flushed chest and advancing upon them and it was all only seconds.

It was the way his arm extended, like he was batting off a fly, but the gun in his hand came with it and the crack from its barrel sizzled in Marion's ears.

Louise slumped to her knees like at a church pew.

Marion and Joe watched her and Marion felt herself go toward her, to lean down and catch her, but the look in Louise's eyes, the awful surprise in them . . .

Her mouth opened as if to speak but then nothing came and Marion saw the smoke rising from the hole in her chest. Then Louise buckled and pitched to the floor.

"I WILL TAKE CARE OF IT, MARION," Joe was saying, as he dragged Ginny's doll-like body across the room. The sight was one Marion knew she would never forget.

"I will repair this," he said, his suit jacket now off, his sleeves rolled up, his forearms pocked with blood. "I will repair this as if it were solely mine to repair."

He had piled the bodies in the corner. They were a heap of worn silk and curls and blood-rimmed sorrow.

"Joe, what can you mean?" Marion managed. "We must explain to the police. Accidents. Accidents. We must explain it."

"No good, Marion, and don't think about it or I will have to shut you up about it," he said, and he lifted the coffee table and moved it off the rug. "Look what you did. Look what you did, Marion. You took a gun to your friends and you've made me share a part and you think the police will understand? But I will take care of it. Because you are a sick, sick thing."

"I am not," Marion said, wrapping the dish towel around her hand tighter. "Why did you shoot Louise?" Her voice edged into a scream. "Why did you shoot her?"

"Marion, you told me they were trying to murder you. Do you think I'm the kind of man who would not protect you from violence?"

"I don't understand, I don't understand," Marion moaned.

"I think you do," he said, and his eyes were cold.

HE ROLLED those girls up in the carpet.

He rolled them up in the carpet like Cleopatra.

Then Mr. Worth came with the Worth Brothers Meat Market truck. When he walked in, his face turned gray. He said some things to Joe and then he looked over at Marion, who sat in the corner still, holding her hand to her chest, looking up and watching them.

"Is she all right?" he asked Joe, and Joe said it didn't matter, and they carried the carpet out like moving day.

"Where are you taking the girls," Marion said suddenly, head jerking up, body rising stiffly. "Where are you taking my girls."

"Marion, look out the window. See if the street is clear," Joe said.

Twitching, her body feeling as if on strings, she made it to the window and floated a finger through the curtains, peering out to a great black nothing.

"When I come back," Joe said, "this place must be cleaned, Marion. It must be cleaned top to bottom."

And she looked up at him in his blood-edged shirtsleeves and one browning strand stretched across the starched shirt.

"It will be clean," she said, and it was her voice, but it was as if someone else were using it, cranking it from her chest like a windup doll. "It will be clean, Mr. Lanigan. It will be virgin pure."

LATER, she would remember nothing of it, but the cleaning went on for hours. Carbolic acid and white vitriol. That house had never been so spotless, Marion's arms red and raw, her wound festering under its wrapping. She could feel the bullet there, small and tight, and her skin puffing around it, cradling it.

Sometime, Joe returned, now in a pearl gray suit and hat, clean-shaven as if on his way to morning church service.

He had found Marion on one of the girls' beds, hand wrapped in the dish towel.

She didn't move when he entered the room, he seemed so funny standing there, almost as if he were picking her up for a date.

He was saying some things.

"Worth and I, we took them away. And Mr. Worth, well, he fixed everything, Marion."

"Mr. Worth," Marion said, and she didn't remember him at all, not even the leg of lamb he once brought or his trilling hand organ. "Did Mr. Worth fix the girls? Did he really?" She felt her body shake and jerk. She wondered if she'd dreamt some or all of the night before. How could Mr. Worth put Ginny's face back together? Mr. Worth, who spent days dressing young beef for the silk stockings in town who could dole out for more than brisket and soupbones. "Are they fine now, Joe? Are they mended? Where are my girls?"

Joe took his hat off, shaking his head. "Marion, Marion," he said, and he walked toward her and rested a hand on her leg. "You know what you did to the girls. The girls are gone. And now he's fixed it so we can take them away."

"Take them away?"

"I had planned that we would take them to the desert and bury them. But after some conversations with Mr. Worth, who is very familiar with those roadways for his businesses, well, he said it was foolhardy. The highway patrol are a constant presence on those roads. The more distance, the better. So we need to get them far away, Marion. Do you see? This is where we need your sweet face."

He sat down on the bed beside her, taking care not to brush against her hand, nor let the bloody dish towel touch his suit. "I am sorry for my coldness before, Marion, you must see. You are mine and I will protect you. You will see what I have done for you. For us both."

He helped her to her feet and guided her to the living room, air heavy with bleach, making her stomach spiral.

ALL SHE COULD THINK of was Louise buried six feet deep in the desert, body weighted with rocks. Ginny's candied mouth open, caught, midcry, and filled brimful with glittering sand.

How could she reckon with this?

In the middle of the room, next to the teetery coffee table, sat two black, silver-latched packing trunks, one very large and one more compact.

"You see, Marion," he said, arm around her, holding her up. "It's all taken care of."

"I don't see," she said, clutching fingers to his lapel. "Are we going on a steamer? Are we running to far-flung lands?" And her head twisted loose, and she began giggling and Joe did not like that one bit.

"Marion," he said, reaching round and grabbing her face in hand. "Marion, you must see what we have done here. You must know what we have done with the girls. Do you see?" Turning her face with one hand, turning it hard, he pointed to the trunks with the other. He pointed to the trunks and Marion would always remember this. His right arm around her neck, hand grooved under her chin like a vise, and left arm pointing, like God himself, down to Earth, down to Adam, down to the black trunks on the unimpeachable floor.

Her girls, her girls. Her girls in those trunks like so much packing. A flash in her head, Louise's long limbs curled at funny angles, crumpled like a magician's assistant inside a magic box. And Ginny like some stretched-thin rag doll twisting round itself.

"Oh, Joe," she said, and she felt her shoulders convulse, but there was nothing in her stomach but gin. "Oh, Joe."

"Listen, Marion," he said, voice stern but gentle. "You must pull yourself together here. I need you to help. You can't fall to pieces on me."

"No, Joe," she said, "I won't."

"Here," he said, taking a packet from his pocket. "Take these."

They were pills and she raised a palm of them to her mouth until he swatted her arm down. "Not all of them, Marion. Not now. One."

She did as she was told, eyes never leaving the trunks. "Joe," she said, tongue dusty with the powdery pill. "Joe, how did you get them in there? How did they fit?"

"Worth took care of everything, Marion. Don't you worry about that. He has," he said, and there was the sparest of pauses, "operated on Louise and made it all work."

Marion felt her knees turn to soft dough and she began to drop to the floor.

"What did I say to you, Marion?" Joe said, pulling her back, raising her shoulders high, turning her to face him and then slapping her twice hard across either cheek. Her head rang. "I have done everything, Marion. And now it is your turn."

HE TOLD HER how it would be. He told her to go home and pack a bag. He told her to telephone the Lightning Delivery Service and have them pick up the trunks and take them to the station and load them on the train and then they would be waiting for her twelve hours later when she arrived in the Southern Pacific Station in downtown Los Angeles. See how he'd rigged it, so she would never even have to touch them? See how he had arranged everything? And she would never have to lay hands on those trunks. Never even have to touch those awful boxes sitting there. Those awful boxes.

"But won't Mr. Worth . . . Won't he . . ."

"He won't say a goddamned word, Marion," Joe said, and it was the first time he had ever cursed before her. "They're *his* trunks. He knows I have enough on him to hang him. Horse meat to hospitals. That's just the start."

She didn't know what that might mean and didn't want to guess. Everything seemed so different with Joe now and yet somehow the same, just with her eyes struck wide, lashed open, there was no hiding. Joe was Joe. And it was a dark thing.

Was this the one who had held her curls between fingers and pressed lips to, tickling stomach, lips on faint down and eyes bewitched?

It was a dark thing.

So she packed her bag and it was all like a dream, fuzzy, ill defined. Later, she recalled running her good hand along the front of her good dress, smoothing its worn cotton.

"WHAT YOU GOT IN HERE, BARBELLS?"

The Lightning Delivery Service men looked at the trunks. One had started raising it onto his dolly and then stopped.

"You joining the circus, angel? Gonna be the Strong Man, or Strong Gal?"

Marion smiled. She surely did. The pills, they were helping. She could feel herself move as if marionette lifted and she recited over and over again Joe's instructions in her head. He told it to her three times and three times he made her repeat it back to him.

"You sure there's not hooch in those trunks?" The other man winked. "'Cause we *would* have to report you for that."

Marion kept her gentle smile and shook her head, filling out the baggage slips. "Oh no, I'm a Christian, gentlemen." She did not know where that line had come from, but she was glad for it. It sounded so sincerely meant. Inside, somewhere under the gauze of the pills, there was a whirring terror, but she could barely hear it, a vague purling somewhere far away. And so she returned to Joe's instructions and recited them with care: "A fellow worker and her friend, well, they packed all their worldly goods in there. They asked me to ship them. They've moved west."

"And left you behind? Damn fools, I'd say."

"They met some men," she enunciated, "and went off with them to Los Angeles."

"Sound like some girls. I'd like to meet those girls."

"That's the kind of girls they are," she said.

"I'll say. Say, this is going to cost a pretty penny."

"I have the funds. They left me the funds." As Joe directed, she showed the men a roll of bills.

"Well, how 'bout that? Those are some girls."

THINGS BEGAN HAPPENING very fast and all the time was collapsing in on itself, softly falling to the center. It had something to do with her head and something to do with the pills and something to do with everything that mattered being gone.

She did not remember taking the streetcar home, but back at Mrs. Gower's, she telephoned the clinic and told the weekend receptionist that she was quite sick and expected she would not be at work on Monday.

"Oh, I am sorry, Marion. You do sound rotten. Not yourself at all," the girl said. "Take care. Hot-water bottle and hot toddy, you know?"

Suddenly, she felt terribly anxious. "I hope Dr. Milroy will not be mad at me for missing work." As the words came from her mouth they sounded so silly to her, so frivolous she nearly laughed.

"Don't worry. Everyone likes you, Marion," the girl said. And Marion replied that she was so glad.

THE PLAN WAS FOR JOE to come to the rooming house at eight o'clock to drive her to the station. She had her head covered with the old cloche hat, as he told her, and she tucked every platinum bit of her hair underneath.

Waiting by the window, she watched her wounded hand and she could smell it and it smelled unclean despite all her ministrations. She took another of Joe's pills and finally saw his Packard pull up at 8:20, leaving them only ten minutes to get to the station.

"You're drunk, Joe," she said as they pulled away from the curb, she with her satchel so heavy and he didn't help not one bit. He was drunk and she couldn't believe it.

But he just laughed and steered the wheel. He began instructing her on what to do. What had made sense earlier made no sense now. She said, again, "But, Joe, why don't we just take the trunks into the desert and bury them? Why don't we just do that? Why must we send them all the way to California? And why must I go too?"

He waved his hand at her, Masonic ring flashing, and she thought he might strike her again, but he was somehow gay. "I told you, baby doll, I told you. The highway patrol'll find the trunks before we can blink and it will all come back to you. This way, it's two girls, two girls *notorious* for their reckless, aberrant ways, out on a tear to Hollywood for a new life of casual debauch. Who wouldn't believe that of them?"

She looked down at the ticket in her hand. MRS. H. MACGREW, it said.

"But why must I go too? Why can't the trunks go without me?"

"You must go to be sure that the trunks are safely in the hands of my associate, Mr. Wilson. He will take care of everything there. What's more, he will bring you to a physician to tend to your wound. It works perfectly, you see, as Los Angeles is a place I have associates and it is a place you have been before. It will swallow this up. Los Angeles is a place that swallows things like this up whole."

He pulled an envelope from his pocket and slid it across the seat to her. "Take this," he said, and she smelled the booze coming off him, from his mouth, his suit, his whole body. There was something in his face too. Something closed and done. "Now, what did I tell you, Marion? What are your instructions?"

"Get off the train at Southern Pacific Station and wait for Mr. Wilson. Mr. Wilson will find me," she said, "by the pansies on my lapel." She fingered the cloth pin on her dress. "Look for a thin man with yellow hair and spectacles and a green gabardine suit. It's just like a motion picture. Like *Mata Hari*. That's what you said. You said I was to be Mata Hari."

"That's right, darling, Mata Hari. That's you," he said, laughing, eyes gaudy with liquor. It was awful, and the look on his face made Marion, even behind the numb the pills cast across her, feel herself die. She died right there. It was all over. It was all over and she knew that once she got on the train, it would be as if all the lights had gone out all over the world.

For twelve hours she sat in her seat on the Golden State Limited and barely lifted her head. The man seated next to her had a large shiny face and big teeth and a pomaded head of hair that shone across the car like a searchlight, and he told her he was going to work in motion pictures and she should too, or did she already, because she looked the spitting image of Constance Talmadge and had anyone ever told her that.

The man talked for a while, and Marion looked out the window, her hand hidden behind her purse, which contained the envelope Joe had given her, and she knew the hand was aching but she couldn't feel it aching. She looked into the black pane.

"Honey, there ain't nothing to see," the man said, and she could feel the wink in his voice. She wondered, suddenly, seeing his grinning reflection in the glass, if this was how Joe Lanigan was, really was at bottom. Was this him?

But it couldn't be. It couldn't be, and she would make him love her once more.

WHEN SHE FINALLY FELL ASLEEP, that was when she could shut out Louise and Ginny no longer. They were there, they were in the seats across from her, lounging nudely like lovely harem girls with jeweled fingers and toes, and they were chattering away at her, and Marion could feel herself wanting to laugh with them and it was lovely and they were back. They were putting arms around each other and Ginny was singing "Cheerful Little Earful" and Marion wanted to reach over and squeeze her little thrush cheek and as she started to, as her fingertips nearly touched that flushed face, before, before . . . *before the face blew to pieces, to shimmery black powder, to nothing. To nothing.*

To pause and think, to think about what had occurred—the savage thing she had, with fumbling hands, wrought—would ruin her. To pause and think of those black boxes jostling in the freight car behind her, to picture the bodies curled round inside—well, one could not allow thoughts to scamper in that direction and yet go on. No. No. She knew in some way it was God's wrath fallen upon her for her sinful ways and worse still her rapture over the sin, her openmouthed hunger for it.

And yet thoughts of Joe Lanigan still came. They wouldn't stop, even now. She couldn't break it. Nothing could break it. She so wanted it broken for good.

IT WAS LIKELY TWELVE HOURS LATER, the spidery hands of the Southern Pacific Station clock told it, but it felt like a minute or a year and she took another pill, noting sadly only eight left and how would she go on without them?

She found a seat under the arrivals-and-departures board, fluffed her crushed pansy pin and awaited the arrival of Mr. Wilson, who would wave a hand and fix everything, Joe Lanigan's gleaming West Coast proxy and her savior.

AN HOUR AND TWENTY-SEVEN MINUTES had passed when she felt the nerve pulsing in her face. Eyes weary from scanning the crowd, wave after wave of blond men in gabardine, nearly all of whom smiled back at her but none of whom answered to Mr. Wilson, though one said he could be President Hoover if she were so inclined.

Oh, he was not coming. She wondered if Joe Lanigan had deceived her and Mr. Wilson would never arrive—if in fact this Mr. Wilson existed at all. She wondered this, but she could not let herself believe it, not now. She couldn't slip down into that murky place. It would swallow her whole.

LOOKING IN THE LADIES' ROOM MIRROR, she felt herself tingling all over. There was a monumentality to the moment. It was so big she was made breathless by it.

Outside, in the bank of telephone booths, she had telephoned Joe Lanigan's house. "I'm sorry, miss, but he is out on business," the nurse said. "We don't expect him until this evening." Marion could picture her, tray in hand, in that silent house, that dark mahogany corridor, that lonely telephone in that lonely house, the metallic smell of illness choking the air.

She knew of no other way to reach Joe.

Joe had made himself impossible to reach.

For one long minute she was sure that the best, the only, the correct thing to do was to walk back to the tracks and throw herself under the next train like some white-necked heroine from a melodrama. She was certain this was the thing she must do. She was certain of it.

Placing a hand to her face, to her quivering chin and jaw, she asked, *Marion, is this the end? Is this the dark pitch at cliff's edge?*

But it was not. It was not. She would not let it be so. She had found herself in dark corners before, not so dark as this, but dark in other ways—*Nights spent lonely as if alone, Dr. Seeley, hollow-eyed and lost, crying to her and skin-popping, and what to prepare her for this, minister's daughter Dutch Reformed pure and Sunday school in her eyes; this was not for her but it was hers and she had to*—she had found her way out before. She would find her way out now. In some ways, she was surprised how fast her blood still ran, how hard her heart still galloped. She was not such a wilting thing. It turned out she was not that thing at all.

Forty dollars remained in the envelope Joe had given her. She had forty dollars with which to save herself.

Her first thought was to abandon the trunks and use her return ticket for the next train home. But the station officials would, of course, find what was inside them and then where would she be, where would she be? It was all too close, it was all right upon her. Those trunks. Those trunks. They were leering, black-hearted things, weren't they? They were so big, she was sure she could see them through the station walls, through the walls of the claims office and right through into their messy centers.

She felt her throat catch, her eyes turn dun in the mirror. She shook her head, shook her thoughts away, juggled them out of chaos into focus.

Oh, God, one can't think like this, one cannot, she determined. She just needed time, she needed distance. She needed to figure things out. To slow down her thoughts, to think things through. She tried to concentrate. If only she had time, time to reach Joe, who would have to account for himself, who would have to make things right.

A picture came to her of the Hotel Munn, a shaggy place on Olive Street where she and Dr. Seeley spent six weeks the previous year, awaiting yet another licensing hearing. But the staff might recognize her.

Then she remembered the place on East Fifth Street, above the Blue Bell sandwich stand. The St. Curtis Hotel. She had gone there once, summoned by the manager to retrieve her husband, who had spent four days lounging in the lobby, ascending the stairs on occasion to take his pleasures with bug-eyed hah-peeners in various rooms whenever, as he said, the poppy fleet came in. The St. Curtis, she would go there. It was not a place where anyone was remembered. No one bothered you there. Not even the manager, who'd only wanted his two bits.

"I HAVE COME for those two trunks."

"Aren't I the happy fella," the baggage claims man said, "because don't they ever weigh a mother-in-law-sized ton and I thought I might have to move 'em to Unclaimed. What you got in them anyway? They sure are stirring up a stink."

Marion smiled brightly. "Oh, I am sorry."

"You know," the man said, eyeing the trunks, "last year, fella up in Montreal, Canada, killed his wife with a claw hammer and shipped her here in a steamer. Ten days en route and stalled in the Plains on account of bad weather. By the time she got here, there wasn't much left inside but some bones and slime. Only figured her out from her teeth. Her skin had slipped off like a moldy peach peel. Baby, did she stink. I'd've taken another shot of the ole mustard they gave me in the Marne over that any day," the man said, handing her the slips to sign. Looking at her face, he added, quickly, "Aw, I'm sorry. I got a big yap. Are you okay, miss? I made you all green, didn't I?"

"I'm all right," she said, fingers delicately to lips. "Just a little travel sick. Will these fit in a taxicab?"

"Between you and me, I think you're better off hiring a truck. I know a fella runs a hand laundry truck between here and Good Samaritan."

"Will you phone him for me?" She showed him all her teeth,

had not smiled so broadly since playing Little Eva at her grammar school drama pageant.

"Consider him on his way. He ain't gonna like that smell any more than me, but slap him some extra green and he can hold his nose the whole way." He paused and looked at the trunks again, and then at Marion. "I *am* supposed to ask, that wouldn't be meat in there, would it? 'Cause it sure stenches like meat."

Marion bit her lip. "I know it's against the rules, but I promised Mama." She had no idea where the lie came from, or how she was spinning it with such bright conviction. "It's just two white-tailed bucks my brother shot up in the mountains. For Mama's Easter dinner." Where did such lies come from and from what place did such reserve glide, smooth as churned butter? Was it the pills? Was it Joe Lanigan's mesmeric speech in her ear? It was as if she had been born to it, and it was so much easier, so much easier to declaim than anything real or true.

"Ham always worked for me," he said, shaking his head. *Mrs. Wilson,* she scrawled on the form he handed her. "You're lucky you remind me of my sister Irene," he said, stamping the form. "Gee, I miss her. She got the lungs bad."

THE KEEP KLEEN LAUNDRY DRIVER, chest wide as a squeezebox, rubbed his chin and tilted his head.

"I know they're quite heavy," Marion said, twisting her handkerchief between her fingers. "But I'm not going far."

"Hell, Fritzie, I'll help you stack 'em on the hand truck," the baggage claims man offered.

Sucking on his teeth, the driver nodded. "Could do it for five bones. You got five bones?"

Marion said she did.

"You sure this is the place for you?" the driver asked when they turned onto East Fifth Street. A building on the corner promised INDIVIDUAL LOCKERS FOR 450 MEN, 20 CENTS.

"Yes, I am," she said, fumbling in her purse for five dollars.

Three doors down she saw the St. Curtis, a sun-beaten awning curling across its narrow façade, iron grills spidering along the windows. Painted just beneath the eaves were the words NOW FULLY FIREPROOF. The Iwaki Cafeteria had replaced the Blue Bell sandwich stand, but the same sign covered the window: GOOD FOOD 5 C.

THE SWEATY MAN at the front desk was leaning over some pocket toy and didn't look up until Marion had cleared her throat three times. His sleeves rolled up, Marion could see a blurry tattoo of a flaming dove and the word FOURSQUARE.

"A room, please."

He looked up, squinting. "Sure about that?"

She nodded, dabbing her neck with a handkerchief.

"I'd warn you the cops did a lady bed toss just last night, but you don't look that sort. Then again, these days, there's all sorts."

"I'm just tired," she said, "and need to rest. You don't need to worry about me."

He squinted at her again, then set down his toy and handed her a pen, spinning the heat-rippled register to face her.

She signed *Mrs. Dove.*

"The gal they rousted, she was tired too. So tired she had to be flat on her back every fifteen minutes for three days straight."

Marion handed the man a dollar.

"I tried to give her Jesus," he said, sliding four dimes toward her, "but she said Jesus broke her heart one too many times. How you like that?"

Marion smiled.

"She rooked us for a dollar and a half, that pinkpants did, but left this behind," he said, picking up the pocket toy, a small tin compact, and displaying it for Marion. One side was a smudgy mirror, the other had a picture of a man in a porkpie hat blowing three rings of smoke. "The gig is you gotta get the cigarette in his mouth," he said, tilting it back and forth, with great delicacy. "It's tougher than it looks."

The Keep Kleen driver wheeled the trunks in for her. After a quick survey of the lobby—the man splayed across the spongy wing chair, hat covering his face, the tins of Doctor Bedlam magnetic powder in each corner, the tiny woman in the red hat with the feather, biting her thumbnail and pacing between the front door and the telephone booth in the back—he said he'd take the trunks upstairs, no charge.

"You be careful now, miss," he said, elbow leaning on the doorjamb, the hotel room nearly too small to hold Marion, the two trunks and him. "This ain't a place to be for long."

She thanked him and assured him her friends would arrive shortly for their trunks.

"Kind of a world," he said, walking away, "leaving women alone in such places."

The sorrow came crashing in, it overtook her. She thought she might drown in it.

She fought it off. She tried to make it unreal. But the trunks seemed to grow larger and turn blacker with each passing minute. Standing there, the smell of dirty linens, pest powders, ammonia and something like wet fur stifling, she felt a deep, bone-curling aloneness she'd never known before. It was a sorrowful thing, but it was something else too. For the first time since gazing up, baby-eyed, into her father's long face, she felt no one at all was looking, no one at all could see. No one could stop her from whatever she might do. And nothing she might do would leave a mark, no one would ever know. She felt drunk with it, braced and grimy and fixing to curl her fists—even as those trunks bloomed larger still.

The trunks, it was true, she could hear them creaking in the hot room, the heat expanding the canvas and pine, stretching the slats. She put her shaking hands on them. That was when the smell first came to her, began to seep into the space. She could feel it climbing up her body, skimming under her clothes, under her fingernails and into her skin. It made her think of the clammy bottom of things, dank and lost and dirt-mouthed. She felt something damp on her ankle. Bending down, she saw the puckering side of one trunk, wet to the touch.

It was all too much. It was so much that it might well have been nothing. She sank to the bed and covered her mouth with the cloth pansy she had unclipped from her dress.

Marion, there are things you are sure you'd never do, Louise had said to her once. *Until you have.*

SHE TRIED TO FORCE HERSELF TO SLEEP, but in her head there were some thoughts and the thoughts filled vivid-to-bursting pressures in her head: Joe Lanigan sleeping off his drunk, thinking he had rid himself of her, some sash weight wrapped round his ankle.

Joe Lanigan, safe in his rich man's bed, thinking she would

surely end up in some doomy prison cell, so love-struck as to never breathe his complicitous name, or so disordered, so hopeless, who would believe her?

"BUT I'M TELLING YOU, he's not home yet, miss." It was that private nurse again.

"You put him on the telephone," Marion said, and it was a voice she'd not known before, a voice filled with iron vibrating, a blade struck to quiver. "You tell him for me, nurse, that he must speak to me, or he won't like what occurs. You tell him that."

"Yes, miss," she replied, voice trembly.

Marion waited, tucked in the lobby's telephone booth, the woman in the red hat giving her a witchy stare and clicking her heels on the floor, tugging up the ends of the threadbare rug, throwing dust into the air. It was quite a show. It was quite a show this crimson-lipped tootsie was giving, and it reminded Marion, achingly, of Ginny. For a moment, she thought, *Oh, I miss Ginny.*

The mind can do what it wants, she thought. It can make anything so.

"Mrs. Seeley." Joe's voice hustled into Marion's ear, and it was his softest, deepest, kindest voice and she found herself wishing he were here, wishing he were still caring for her. "Are you with Mr. Wilson? Has he mended your hand?"

"Mr. Wilson never came, Mr. Lanigan. I had to take care of things on my own. I am trying to fix things, but I . . ." She felt her throat seal around the words. The gaudy red-hatted woman was now tapping her fingers along the glass of the booth, clamoring at Marion to hurry off the telephone. Her face was nearly pressed against the glass, a face from a burlesque handbill, a carnival poster. Marion couldn't speak, couldn't look, couldn't stop shaking.

"I am so sorry, Mrs. Seeley," he said. "Are you at the station?"

"No," Marion whispered, voice pitching high, "I couldn't stay there, don't you see? I am all alone and the trunks, Mr. Lanigan, the trunks are so large and they can't be hidden. Everyone can smell them. Everyone can see them. There's no hiding them."

"Mrs. Seeley, I want you to listen to me—"

"Don't forget me, Mr. Lanigan."

"I would never, Mrs. Seeley. I couldn't. You know I couldn't. Tell me where you are and I will reach Mr. Wilson and make sure he comes to you directly."

Marion felt something crackling in the back of her brain. Joe's voice, the way he was speaking. The promises and now this.

The woman outside the booth was still rapping on the glass, her shiny red nails rattling away. Marion thrust open the booth door and whispered, rough and raw, "I will call the police, ma'am. Don't doubt it. I will call the police else I set my nails to your face."

The woman backed away with a low curse.

"Mrs. Seeley?" Joe was saying.

"Who is this Mr. Wilson?" Marion demanded, face turned back to the mouthpiece.

"He's an associate. He is my California medical supplier. Tell me where you are, Marion."

She began to speak, but then stopped herself. A picture came to her, shimmered before her, of that look on his face when he had dropped her off at the station. That look on his face that almost seemed to say, *I'll not see you again.*

"I don't think I will," Marion blurted. "I don't feel like I will meet Mr. Wilson."

"Marion, listen to me, Marion, my darling . . . I know you are in a dark, obscure place right now. I cannot bear to think of it. Please, Marion, I want you to listen to me and very closely."

"I don't think I will," she said, and hung up before she began to cry. Taking her forehead between her fingers, she told herself she would not submit to despair. She would not.

RETURNING TO HER ROOM, she saw a small card on the floor had been slid under the door in her absence. It read: *Dr. Bell, Room 402. Please see me.*

She stepped back into the hallway and saw a woman with sunken shoulders walking slowly in the other direction.

"Did you leave this card?" she called out. "Do you work for Dr. Bell?"

The woman turned around, spectacles balancing on the bridge of her nose, and jerked her head, gesturing Marion to follow.

Marion, pulling her own door shut behind her, did follow. Somehow it seemed she was to follow. She kept her purse in front of her bad hand and followed.

The room was larger than her own, was in fact two rooms with an adjoining door. The smell of ammonia was even stronger than in her own. A steel cart stood in the middle of the room, packed with smoked bottles and a tray with a tangle of pokey instruments.

Marion could feel her wounded hand throbbing chalk white and monstrous behind her handbag, which barely concealed it. Looking at the forceps and iodine swabs made the wound seem to pucker and dilate and she felt herself wincing.

"Do you know how far along, Mrs. Dove?" the woman asked her.

"Pardon?" How does she know my name? Marion wondered, and then thought of the man at the front desk.

"Do you know how far along you are? You can't be more than six weeks." She was eyeing Marion closely.

"Oh no!" Marion said. "I'm not . . . No, no. Why did you think—"

"Don't worry, Mrs. Dove," she said, fingering the stethoscope, which curled around her hand like a licorice rope. "It's completely discreet, I can promise you."

The woman's eyes were soft, and Marion almost felt like consenting, even though there was nothing to consent to. That was how eager and tender she felt, so ready for some comfort. Any comfort.

"You're Dr. Bell, then?"

"Yes. Listen, Mrs. Dove, it will not take long and then your troubles, which seem so immense at this moment, will be gone."

"But I'm—"

"Times are hard and fifteen dollars will do the job, Mrs. Dove."

"But I am not here for that, ma'am—Doctor," she said. "My troubles are not those troubles. But they are troubles."

And she set her purse down and slipped off her stained glove, strained and pulled to seam tears by her swollen skin.

"Discretion is discretion," Dr. Bell said, taking Marion's hand in hers and turning it slowly for a better look. Metal glinted from the center of her doughy palm. "Three dollars. And you can keep the slug."

BACK IN HER ROOM, Marion was both satisfied with herself and freshly terrified. The baggage claims man, the driver, the desk clerk, the doctor. *How many witnesses must I collect,* she thought. *How many will know? Every hole I dig myself out of brings in another party who may hang me.*

The smell was getting stronger and she knew it was time to decide some things.

She turned off the lamp and the room was quite dark, and

when she pulled the blind on the window, there was no light but the thin band under the door.

When she was very young, six or seven, she was afraid of the dark, afraid of the night world and the world of sleep, the creeping, terrible feeling of a sleeping house, a sleeping street, a sleeping town and what dangers might come with she alone awake, wide-eyed. To fight this fearsome battle, she had created a creaky passageway in her head and at the end of the passageway, which took some time to reach, like putting a mesmer on herself, there was a special place of gossamer-winged fairies with ruby eyes, palaces etched from sparkling rock, velvet vales with streams threading through and she herself alighting from a white horse with a mane of flowing silver strands. Oh, each time she went to bed, the place grew grander and she fell in deeper and deeper, sinking herself until she could feel the horsehair against her legs, could feel her hands dug deep into that mane, the mane curling between her fingers, pulling her still closer.

Lying in the dark, she remembered that place, could even see it, dip her fingers into the mossy riverbanks and gaze, wonder-eyed, into the curling clouds of endless sky, remembered how easy it was to make everything else disappear.

Those trunks would have to be opened.

They would have to be opened.

My, there was so much she knew, who might've guessed, she thought. *Who might've guessed my mind could think such thoughts, know such things?*

Hospitals, she knew—oh, and there was first meeting Dr. Seeley at the hospital, remember, not dashing, but so dignified, so refined, and the way he tended to patients with tender words and gentle hands and had been so many places, had lived all over and had a snap cigarette lighter from San Francisco and cuff links that looked like little gold monkey fists and he was so patient with her, and listened to her with such care, she a flossy-headed junior nurse volunteer, nigh on eighteen years old but felt even younger—how was it she had forgotten all that?—but hospitals, yes, she knew that they would look at teeth, just like the baggage man said. That's how they find them out. They look at the teeth. It was hard to think of Ginny having dental records, but she might well.

And then there were fingerprints. She knew all about that from the time the San Diego County Hospital called her to retrieve her husband, rolled on the docks and unconscious, and no wallet but fingerprints on file with the Los Angeles Police Department from the vagrancy arrest, or the practicing-medicine-without-a-license violation.

She unfolded the train schedule.

If she did things now, she could be on the seven o'clock train. Back at work Tuesday and nearly unmissed.

If she did things now.

THE LATEST PILL, she let it roll around on her tongue, she let it scatter its dust around the tomb of her mouth, and her head tingly from the last one and from her trip to her childhood vale, she knew she had worked herself into a way of doing, a way of getting things done.

Next thing, she had walked to the five-and-dime and purchased a claw hammer, a box of matches, six towels, thumbtacks, cleaning gloves and a small jug each of borax and carbolic acid.

It was going to be the opening that would destroy her. She knew that what she would see would never be unseen, what she would see would tattoo itself in dark ridges into her brain forever. Her dark spot on the brain.

Yet she did not pause.

There was no time to pause.

Oh, Joe Lanigan, he would not believe she could ever ... Oh, Joe Lanigan, did he not always take her too lightly?

She knelt down and slid open the latches on the larger trunk, chest galloping, heart ballooning up her throat.

She felt it give, felt her fingers tuck underneath and lift.

The air seemed alive with the smell, the air itself seemed muddy, a fog, and Marion's eyes unfocused and her stomach curled on itself.

That was when she saw the blond hair, like a wig in a shop window, loosely curled and filled with shades of honeycomb, sweet butter, daffodil and, as Marion's eyes locked into focus, foamed through with black spray.

Then, dipping a gloved hand in, she had to—she had to, don't you see—she twisted her arm deep, past the shiny black shell, like a mussel plucked from the sea, that had been Ginny's face. Pushing heel of hand in, she groped deeper, sunk herself into it, fought off the smell and the horror. Her fingers touching everything, her stomach rising in her chest, she felt for teeth, she felt for hard enamel, and in finding, oh, it was an awkward move, and oh, she had to grab a hair hank to make it work, raised the hammer, and punched down hard.

She would not hear the sound. She would not hear the sound of the teeth going.

Then, digging hands in farther, hands sinking into sticky patches of horror, she pulled up both wrists, soft like tuggy blue sponges, and wrapped the carbolic-soaked towel around the bloated fingers, barely fingers, barely solid, but like some loose glove lying limp on top of a dresser. She pressed and pressed. The loops, ridges, slopes and furrows—gone.

Both hands done, she closed the trunk, walked over to the corner of the room, gloves dripping on the towels she'd stretched from trunk to door, and wept. Long, loping tears.

Then she walked over to the other trunk, which looked so small, so dainty, and braced herself for Louise, whose heart she felt beating in her own chest, and whom she now knew loved her with depths as to drown out a thousand Gent Joe Lanigans with his snide beaver coats and shallow heart.

Oh, Louise.

LOUISE'S LUSH THICKET of dark red hair.

And an eye open, turned up, glittering.

The other eye covered by a sleeve.

Something so strange, the elbow resting on her chin. How could it be, her elbow up there like that, a puzzle with the pieces pushed together wrong.

She thought of that old song played on the banjo on summer porches in houses less God-fearing than hers.

> *My darling, my darling, my sweetheart divine*
> *No feat too daring for my daredevil mine*
> *She dances 'long clifftops and tightropes for show*
> *Wraps legs 'hind her head, can kiss her elbow*

It was the thing she must've known—*he has operated on Louise, he has fixed it so we can take them away*—but now seeing it.

Slowly, with such shaping dread even through her medicine fog, she reached for the elbow, the arm and felt the arm rise light, rise, rise, rise, with her own hand. She could lift it as far as the heavens.

So terrible, so terrible, there could be no words.

Oh, Louise, love me yet.

Part Five

. . . I'm an exile sad, too sad to weep.
My fatherland is dear, but I too left it;
Far am I from the spot where I was born;
Cheerless is life, fierce storms of joy bereft it;
Made me an exile lifelong and forlorn.

—From "La Golondrina," (The Swallow)
by Narciso Serradel Sevilla,
Trans. Rev. Thos. W. Westrup, 1883

The Golden State Limited pulled into the station just after seven. A scant thirty-six hours had passed, the same bleary-eyed hobo she had noticed the day before still curled in the corner of the platform, leaning against a jutting wall, shielded from wind and the eyes of conductors.

Thirty-six hours, Marion thought, *and I have changed forever.*

She had done the things and she would not speak of them again. She latched the trunks. She soaked the towels in the borax solution. When she was sure the corridor was empty she tacked the towels to the bottom of the door, closed it and left the St. Curtis Hotel, not bothering to check out.

She left with only her purse.

No one said a word.

It was easy.

How easy it was, it shamed her more.

On the trip home, lulled by the pills and the churn of the train, she slept dreamlessly.

IT WAS NOT SO EARLY, but the streets were echoey and lonesome. The heat had already lowered fierce, settling like an iron pressing to her face and neck.

The streetcar rattled her slowly across town. She put a hand to her jaw, felt the dampness of her dirty hair. Her clothes gave off musky odors and her body too, which was radiating an unclean heat. Her eyes felt to be popping from rusty sockets.

"Lynbrook Street," the conductor bellowed, and suddenly her heart rose up in her chest.

There it was, his cool, careless fortress, indifferent and immaculate, one stray silver roller skate dangling from its leather strap on the steep slope of the front lawn.

She flitted up the lawn as fast as her shaking legs would take her.

Without stopping, nearly pressing her body against the heavy door, she raised her good hand and clapped the knocker as hard as she could, her whole body swinging into it.

He would answer her. He could speak to his actions.

"Yes?" The door opened and the prim nurse in the white collar and starched apron squinted out at Marion, eyes straining from the sunlight, that house so dark, like a funeral home or a cinema.

"I need to see Mr. Lanigan immediately," Marion said, trying to stand as upright as possible, as upright as this nurse who looked and smelled as clean as freshly boiled sheets.

"He's not here, ma'am. Shall I relay a message?" The face, unmarked, empty and serene. Serene as only a young girl's could be.

What was she, twenty? Twenty-one? Marion, *ma'am*, was once twenty, twenty-one, a million years ago.

"I will see him. I will see him now," Marion said, voice jangling wildly, a trilling hurdy-gurdy. How dare he hide himself away behind the nurse's skirts like a little boy. "Please tell him I'm here and he's to show me his Shanty Irish face."

"He's not here, ma'am. But I shall give him any message you would like to—"

Marion felt herself lunging forward. The words tumbled forth, uncontrollably. "Do you mean to tell me he's not here at this early hour? Why, he is a married man, is he not? A family man with children? And he is not at home at just past dawn? Is that what you mean to say?"

In her head, worse still, voices scurrying, saying, *This, a man so degenerate, so dissolute and perverse that he stalks the streets for girls all night like a vampire, like Jack the Ripper.*

She could not control herself.

She could not even stop her mouth from gaping and cawing and shrilling like a handsaw. The nurse, standing there so calm, so cool-browed, as if to mock her, to mock her as a hysteric, a madwoman.

"Ma'am, I do not know what you mean," the nurse said, firm and unflustered, a Sing Sing prison warden in handkerchief cap and bib. "Mr. Lanigan is in the mountains on a hunting party with friends. He returns later in the week."

Marion could hear a thudding in her head like a wood plank thwacking against a hollow wall.

"Is that what is claimed?" she said, her voice now a wheeze. "Am I to believe that?"

"I have to attend to my duties, ma'am," the nurse said, trying to close the door. Oh, wasn't life ever so easy for her? Wasn't this just another nuisance in a day of nuisances, of filling syringes, pushing pillows about, standing straight in sickrooms, counting clock ticks. What did she know of sorrow, of life?

"You tell your esteemed employer," Marion said, nearly biting her own tongue, "you tell him that Mrs. Seeley has returned home and he's to see me and if he declines, he will not like what happens. He will not like it one bit. There's things I can do. You tell him that. You tell him that."

MRS. GOWER was not home and the rooming house was hushed as Marion bolted up the stairs to her room, and her head was still doing the thudding and she felt things crawling under her nails, under her skin, and she was not going to take any more pills, and she was going to cover herself in water and never let dirt or ugliness touch her again.

Joe Lanigan, you have broken, burned and beaten me and still I am here. I wear on even as you seek to obliterate and undo me. Even as you have ruined me twice, three times over. Ravishing me, ravaging me and razing me. I stand here still.

The door whinnied open and the familiar smell of old wood and butcher polish, of mothballs and Breath O' Pine felt like a warm coat and she let it fold over her.

But as she stepped in, eyes adjusting to the light from her window, she saw something moving on the bed, and for one fleeting, appalling moment she was sure it was Louise and Ginny, spread out nude and bloodied like some nightmare come to life. A penny dreadful with bodies under groaning floorboards calling out to guilty souls.

It was only the start of a scream before she shoved her fist to her mouth and slammed the door shut behind her and the thing shifted and her eyes drew together.

"Is that you, Marion?"

And the body—the man—turned and set his feet to floor, and there was Dr. Everett Seeley. There was her husband, or was it? He looked so different. She had not seen that ruddy color on his cheeks in so long, since they married, perhaps, and those knotty cheekbones were draped softly now, his dark hair no longer baby wisping but richly toned, molasses dipped.

He rose and began to walk to her, and then she knew it was him, knew by the familiar slope-shouldered, defeated gait. His eyes, they were soft suddenly, as if with tears.

Before she could take a breath, his hands were gently on her shoulders. He tried to embrace her, but she was still clasping her purse to her chest with both arms, like some rogue-threatened waif.

"Marion, I am a few days early. When I received your last letter about your cough returning, and that you needed money, well, I was concerned. You know how it felt to me to leave you here. I shall never forgive myself for it, even as I saw no other choice. One of the mine captain's sons was heading up this way and offered me a ride, so I took it."

He was talking, but Marion could not follow, her eyes growing wider, her fingers digging helplessly.

"But, you see, Marion, I arrived last night and found you gone. Were you staying with those girlfriends of yours? Marion, do you intend to speak?"

She couldn't speak. She couldn't believe she was seeing him. She wasn't sure he was even there: But his hands, they held her arms so firmly, they spanned her, and his face, she knew it so well, or she did once. Now it was more like a photograph, like the snapshot she kept in her Holy Bible, the one where he stood proudly in front of his brand-new 1927 Model A Ford.

"Marion, you must know there is nothing you cannot say to me. Not after what I have put you through. Marion, believe me, there is nothing—"

Her knees hit the floor and stars were everywhere.

THE AMMONIA SPIRITS tickled her nose and her lashes fluttered fast. On her bed, her legs turned at funny angles, she saw Dr. Seeley, still there, squinting at her, face drawn in concern.

"Marion," he said. "Marion . . ."

There could be no dissembling. She could not reckon any more dissembling. She could not teeter one more atrocity upon the towering bank.

"Dr. Seeley," she whispered.

"Yes, Marion."

"Dr. Seeley, you must forgive me."

And she told him.

"MARION," he said to her, holding her shaking hands in his, having listened for an hour or more to her litany of mortification. The illicit lunches, the parties, the seduction, the descent into sin and, finally, the bloody night and everything thereafter. She told him as best she could.

His mouth remained open, but he could not speak, and his face—everything that had been moving in it stopped moving. It seemed to sink in on itself. It had turned old once more in that hour.

By the time she disclosed the dark day she left town with those trunks and, far worse, the things she had done to the bodies within them, his eyes dimmed and something happened. When his eyes fastened on her once more, it was as though he were looking at a stranger, an alien thing. The beast or witch that had taken possession of his dear blond wife.

Turning from her, he rose and walked to the window. She watched him, watched his stillness. She watched him for what seemed ages and more.

"Murder," he finally whispered, his hand curling over his mouth, as if to muffle his own voice. "It wasn't murder. It wasn't that."

"No, no," she said, and her voice sounded funny, a scratchy hiss. Crazily, it reminded her of Ginny's. "But it feels the same. What have I done, what have I done." She brought her hands to her face and her body began rocking. It was like a scene from a melodrama. The sinning wife's mad scene.

But he would not turn to face her. He would not look.

"Marion," he said, "it is clear to me now, and it should have been when I received your last letters, each more desperate, that you had fallen into such despair that you . . . you lost all reason. Lost all reason at all."

"I did," she rasped. "I did."

"Things happen, Marion," he said, finally turning toward her, eyes ringed red and feathered through, "when we fall off the path we're meant to follow. Because of my weakness, I took you off the path and placed you at peril, and dangers that never should have touched the farmost edges of your life have hit you square in the heart."

"I didn't wish to harm her—," Marion started, feeling her face wrenching as if she might sob. But she didn't. "I don't know what has become of me. I don't know myself." Her own words frightened her.

But looking, she could see his face softening, his eyes. She thought he must be the kindest man who ever lived.

He sat down beside her. She thought he might touch her, but it seemed he couldn't. Not yet.

"Marion," he said, "I understand the . . . the indignities you've suffered on my account. And for my behalf. I never meant for you to have this kind of life. You were not meant to have this kind of life." He looked across the room and she knew he was looking at their wedding portrait, which sat on the small dresser. "You are a pure and good girl. It has always been as it first was, as the first moment I saw you. Do you recall, Marion? At the hospital, you on the stairwell above, carrying a stack of bedding—brilliant white—and you'd stopped to look out the window on the landing. The sun was coming off the lake and you were struck by it. That's what I decided. You were struck by the light and you stopped even with arms heavy and you were looking at the light, it broke across your face and it was like some biblical illumination, it was like something you'd see in a very old book with gilded pages. That's how it was."

And then this, to bring you to this low state. He didn't say that, wouldn't say that. But should have. That's what she thought. Here she was, a ruined girl, a girl who'd let liquor cover her face, who'd let a man's hands between her knees, her thighs, who'd set herself before a man, knees on carpet, begging him to drag her down to awful places.

A girl who'd held a gun in tensile fingers and shot the life out of some slip of a thing. Shot the life out of her.

Somehow that last thing mattered less. Somehow that mattered less than that she was the girl who let a man bring his hand, dusted with that tingling white powder, between her legs, and he . . . and he . . . how could that have . . . how could she . . .

He put a hand to her lips and said, thusly, "Marion, what I see now shakes me to the core. But that is because it is me. Do you see? The shame is mine. The shame is mine. I took you from your father's parsonage. I took you from the leafy, God-loving groves of Grand Rapids, Michigan, and I sunk you in the pits of hell."

Eyes shining with sudden brightness, he added, "It is my stake to redeem you."

TAKING HER ARM in one hand and his medical bag in the other, he walked her down the hallway to the bathroom. There, he tended to her wound and redressed it. She did not wince. He watched her a moment, then said, "Marion, did he give you any medicine? Did this man give you any pills or powders?"

She dug in her pocket and held out her sticky palm, showing him the last of the pills Joe Lanigan had given her.

Dr. Seeley put his nose and tongue to one and asked her how she felt after she took them, taking her chin in his hand and lifting it and peering into her eyes. Then he dropped them down the sink drain while Marion watched from the doorway.

"Marion," he said when he returned, sitting her back down on the bed, "promise me you don't have any more of those. They will knock your nervous system to a fare-thee-well. You want to get hold of yourself. It's important, if we're to get through this, that you get hold of yourself."

"Yes, Dr. Seeley, yes," she said. But then she remembered his letters and how he always told her to settle herself, to take things as easy as she could, to come home at five o'clock and rest and eat and sleep in a decent manner. He told her, as lonely and bereft as she might feel, she must use self-control and not indulge in sorrow and malaise. The scolding, like the other one, the other one who said, while feeding her pills, *You must pull yourself together here. . . . You can't fall to pieces on me.* Both of them scolding her, reprimanding her, as if they had no part. As if they had no share in the chaos.

"Dr. Seeley, though, Everett, what do you know of it? What do you know of keeping hold of oneself?" Her voice sounded low and nasty, but she couldn't stop herself.

"Not a soul knows more than me, Marion," he said gravely. "Not a soul."

And she supposed it was true. "You've managed, then," she whispered.

"I've been simon-pure for four months, Marion. I haven't touched the stuff. I haven't dipped once."

It was the longest since she knew him, since the Indiana State Hospital when he nearly died.

"What will I do? I wonder what I will do," she said, her voice low, her face down.

"I will figure things out, Marion. I will."

And she believed he would. He was not a man who took his responsibilities lightly. He was not a man of fancy, a man of caprice. He was a sober man, a man of purpose. A man on whom whole communities could rely, a family man, a family doctor, a trusted citizen, a pillar.

Were it not for that dark spot on his brain. The spot, it was there, and you couldn't cut it out or wipe it away. It was there and changed everything.

"The dark spot," Marion murmured as she sat beside him. "Now it is mine."

At first, Dr. Seeley suggested they leave that night, take a train to Eagle Pass, Texas, and then move on to Coahuila.

Not without seeing that Mr. Lanigan, Marion persisted. *Not without that. She had to see him for herself. She had to see him and see that it was true, that he had abandoned her to this, and he would have to say it to her face.* The look in her eyes startled Dr. Seeley.

"Marion, that would be a mistake."

Marion raised her fingertips to her temples and tried to stop the shaking in her chest. "But, Everett," she said, and her voice sounded tinny, like a machine. "I think it best that I go to work tomorrow. Explain that the girls ran off with these men. I don't think we should raise suspicions."

"I suppose," Dr. Seeley said. "Yes. But in the meantime, I will be making inquiries. I will be making inquiries about this Joseph Lanigan."

"I have told you all I know," blurted Marion.

"I know you have, dear," he said, "but you may not know everything."

WHEN HE SAW HER lying bolt-straight trying to sleep, he took pity and gave her the smallest amount of chloral hydrate. She woke many times in the night and twice saw him sitting by the window, looking out. She wanted to call to him, but she could not make the words come.

She had to speak with Joe Lanigan. She had to.

DR. MILROY summoned her to his office. He told her she looked quite pale and hoped she was well. "I am sorry to have missed work yesterday," she said.

"Mrs. Curtwin tells me you have news of Nurse Mercer," he said sternly. "You mean to say she has simply gone and left her post?"

"Yes, sir," and she explained, as she knew to, that Louise and her friend Ginny had decided to strike it out in California.

"I am quite sorry, Doctor. It was all very sudden."

"I should say it is. I have not heard a word from her. Am I to assume she has vacated her position?"

"I'm afraid she has, Dr. Milroy."

"It all seems very rash," he said, shaking his head, hands

across his chest in contemplation. "She has always been a spirited woman. And her friend. The both of them. How they are. I don't understand it myself." He shook his head.

Marion began to speak but stopped herself.

"But I'm not one to cotton to rumor, not I," he went on. "And with this new development, well, I suppose it's just exuberance. Perhaps a bit too much exuberance."

"Perhaps, sir."

"She has a suitor? Does she intend to marry?"

"I can't say, Doctor. You see, it was all very headlong."

"Well, there's to be no gossip, Mrs. Seeley. I won't tolerate that. I don't want the community to think we employ the kind of women who . . . who are intemperate. Reckless."

"No, Dr. Milroy. I won't say a word."

"Fine. Please take care to empty her locker, Marion. You can forward her things along to her."

"Yes, Doctor."

"Mrs. Curtwin tells me you wounded your hand. Let me take a look. What happened?"

"Oh no, Doctor. That's not necessary. The file drawer caught it," she said, marveling at her growing talent for deceit. "It's fine."

"I'll take a look," he said, then smiled. "And I won't bill you."

"Oh no, Doctor. My husband, you know, he's a physician. He wouldn't like that. I'm sure you understand."

Dr. Milroy harrumphed, slapping his leg. "Damned if I don't, Mrs. Seeley. God bless you both for taking me as a roué."

> Tho' she stands erect in honor
> When the heart of mankind bleeds,
> Still she hides her own deserving
> In the beauty of her deeds.

The poem torn from a book and affixed inside of Louise's locker. Marion poked her head inside to read the rest. The last stanza intoned,

> But alike her ideal flower,
> With its honey-laden breath,
> Still her heart blooms forth its beauty
> In the valley shades of death.

At the bottom there was a watercolor image of a lily of the valley and Florence Nightingale.

I will not dwell, Marion said, to herself, *I will not dwell . . . I will not let it be real, not real. It is not real.*

Marion briskly shoved Louise's things—a spare uniform, a nail file, a set of hairpins—into a laundry bag. In the back was one of Louise's starched nurse's caps and as Marion scuttled it into the bag she saw a silky red tendril still clipped under the bobby pin affixed.

It was Joe that did that. It was Joe. I'll take the weight on my wretched soul for Ginny, but I had to do it to live. But I won't take Louise. Never Louise. Not Louise.

Still her heart blooms forth its beauty.

She leaned her head against the locker and took long breaths, long, scraping breaths. Her lungs, they were hurting. They were hurting like it'd come back, like the consumption had come back, coating and enrobing her lungs, seeking to tear them to bloody pieces again.

She could look no longer and swept her arm through the locker and shoved everything into the large sewing bag Mrs. Curtwin had loaned her.

Her face flared hot and cold at once and she banished thoughts of Louise, Louise struck down, but not by her. Not by her.

❦

IT WAS THREE O'CLOCK when the telephone call came.

"Marion, what do you mean coming to my home? And when did you return? I can't fathom you, Marion."

"Did you catch any bucks?" her voice slid out, cool and polite. Oh, it was a strength in her that she could steel herself so tightly, so enwalled. Three, four days prior, could she have managed such control?

"Marion, I was only gone one night. It was critical, Marion, don't you see? Everything needs to proceed as it normally would."

"That nurse of yours said—"

"Don't worry about that. What did you do? The trunks, Marion?"

"You abandoned me, Mr. Lanigan. You left me—"

"Marion, you don't know what you're saying. You need to calm down."

I am calm. You should see what's inside of me. You see the tempest in there and you would marvel at my calm. "I guess you better see me if you want to know about the trunks," she said, keeping her voice as steady as she could.

"I will come to the rooming house. I will be there at six o'clock."

"No. Not there," she said calmly.

She told him he had best arrive at the clinic, the third-floor storage room, in thirty minutes or he would not like what she would do.

❦

He was already waiting when she arrived, and he held his sennit-straw hat in his hands and she could scarce believe it had been only three days since she'd seen him last. Looking at him now, she wondered, Who was this man?

And he so tidy in his natty suit the color of creamy pistachio nougats, his Scotch-grain brogues, that great lemony sweep of hair across his forehead, an opal tiepin flashing as he turned. But he did turn and he turned toward her, and he reached out and the flesh on her arm quilled.

What had she imagined, that it would all disappear, that the feel of his hands would suddenly fall to her thoughtless as a ticket taker, a train conductor?

"Oh, Joe, I just . . ." But she stopped herself from curling into his arms like a lost kitten. She stopped herself.

"Marion," he said, and his eyes, she saw them, they were strangely blank. Blank like a man in an advertisement. Blank like a curtain had closed.

"Joe, I think you need to explain yourself. You left me to fend for myself. You have done what you said you'd never do. I had to take care of things as best I could."

"Where are the trunks, Marion?" he said, setting his hat down on one of the supply carts. "You must tell me."

"They're in Los Angeles," she said. "They remain there."

"You're to tell me everything. I need to know."

"I will tell you no more than I have. I don't know what you mean to do, Joe. But I know what you have done already."

"What have I done, Marion? Now, truly."

"The trunks are there. I left them there. I am telling all the lies. I have told all your lies, told them for you."

"Marion," he said, and there was just the faintest dampness on him. She could see it now. "Marion, I . . ." He crossed and uncrossed his arms. She could smell his heavy cologne and sense his nerves rubbing against each other. "Marion, I think you should leave town immediately. To Mexico. To your husband. It's not wise for you to stay. The risks are too great."

"But you intend to stay?"

"I have no choice. My family is here," he said carefully, "and my business. And my stake in . . . in what happened is not the same either."

"What can you mean by that?"

"Marion, you know what you did. For my share, I was protecting you."

"How can you say such things? I was protecting myself." It all seemed like an old dream now, Ginny's twisty weight on her, the look in her mad eyes, the squirming danger of her. And the blast. "You know Ginny came at me with that gun. You know the gun exploded in our hands."

"I only know what you told me. And things can get twisted, Marion. Your distinctions may not matter and, well . . . You must see now that I will make sure my name is not brought into this. I will not let it happen and it won't happen because of what I am in this town. There are levers and switches and keys and I know which way they all go. The point is, Marion, I have more money for you and it should be sufficient to carry you to Mexico and—"

"Oh yes," Marion said, her jaw rattling, her face filled with heat and rage. She had put her soul in jeopardy for this man. This man.

"Do give me those funds." And she held her hands out, palms up.

He looked at them, at her outstretched hands, and smiled a little. "Marion, I . . ." Then he reached inside his suit jacket and pulled out an envelope, as before, idling at the train station. He rested it on her palms. "My, Marion, where is my little flower, my little prairie girl?"

Marion felt her chest leap. "You have wretched nerve to say such . . . ," and her voice betrayed her, and she only let out a shallow gasp. She refused to cry for this man.

He looked at her. "I wonder if I was acquainted with you at all, or if you were some kind of cunning witch. They were, you know. Louise and Ginny. Casting spells and laying curses like backward things. Those polluted girls. But you too, I think. You find ways to get what you want."

She felt her arms give out, the envelope dropping to the floor, and she began shoving him, violently. "How dare you . . . How dare you . . ."

But he was strong and clasped her forearms together and told her to hush before she was heard.

"I'm sorry, Marion. I am. You must see." And his voice softened ever so slightly. "I did love you. I did as much as I'm able."

She looked at him. She looked at him and his eyes, not blank, but dead.

There were remembered things tearing through her, things she'd felt sure she would not summon again, most of all the way he could curl his hand under her hair and hold her face in his palm and make things happen inside her that made her buckle, made blood surge through her, brought tears to her blinking eyes.

She would not remember that again, this was the last time, and it was a battering loss.

He was leaving, he was halfway to the door. But he was not done yet. She lifted her chin high, ready for it.

"I look at you, Marion," he said, "and all I see is death. I see dead girls and sorrow. It is not fair, but there it is. I can't look at you without thinking of that night. Your beauty is blinding but behind it I see death."

There it was. There it was. And all the breath left her body, and her heart stopped, hammer struck.

But no. He could not have that too.

She bent down and picked the envelope off the floor. Opening it, she saw what looked like one hundred dollars, more than she had ever seen in her life. And all she was worth.

As she walked to the door, she tucked it cooly under her blouse. *I like to keep my money close to my heart, Louise always said, every time.*

MARION SAT AT HER DESK, her face still, her spine erect.

To her left, she saw, on top of her typewriter, the satchel with things from Louise's locker, just where she'd rested it. For one crazy moment, she thought, *I guess I had better send these along . . .*

Taking a breath, she reached over and opened it.

She could almost feel Louise just over her shoulder, coarse curls brushing up against the back of her neck, breath on her ear.

It was little more than a modest pile of papers and sundry items. Tucked between nursing association pamphlets, *Welcome to Werden! A Manual for New Staff*, old schedules, an announcement for a meeting of something called the SEIU, there was a snapshot of Louise and Ginny, their faces bursting with glee, arms nestled around each other, standing in front of a building somewhere, sometime when Ginny, wee teeth showing, was healthier, had such vim and flesh on her elfin bones and her blond curls jangling and Louise must've been laughing something fierce because her head was thrown back and her long throat so white and lovely and the two of them like sisters, like dear sisters with arms locked together forever. Forever.

And behind that, another snapshot of Ginny, this time with another girl, a blond and delicate girl. Here Ginny was sicker, head leaning, cheeks pulled across bones, eyes darkened, but with that sly grin of hers. She was seated on the sofa, as always since Marion knew her, knees bent and legs tucked to chest tightly, and the other girl, her arms were stretched happily around Ginny's legs, sweetly adoring Ginny. Ginny and her wily-angel, serene devil ways. It was adoration, to be sure, because the blond girl, cheek resting on Ginny's white dimpled knees, was Marion herself. So she knew.

Now, looking, hand wrapped round her mouth, Marion did not let out the cry but swallowed it whole. Oh, Ginny, why did you do it? Why did you come fast upon me with that gun? Slugged dope? Delirium? But it seemed a dreadful rage. Something like, *Will you two leave me now? Will you abandon me to a Bugville camp and kick up your heels across the Great Golden West without me? Why, you will . . . but not if I can stop it. Not if I can stop you.*

Marion dropped the snapshots into the satchel, but as she did she noticed, beneath them, a tidy stack of prescriptions tied with string. She pulled the knot loose and saw they were all nearly identical. Most listed Dr. Tipton as the physician, and several Dr. Jellieck, both of whom worked at the clinic. In the back of her head she remembered Louise shaking her head and saying, *These docs, Marion, they do the nastiest things when your eyes shut, or you turn corners, or, God help you, set foot on a stepladder. I got an eyeful of Dr. Tipton just last week. . . .* Dr. Jellieck, Marion remembered seeing at the party at the El Royale Hotel. The one whose large gray shoulder nearly concealed the face of the woman whom she had been certain was Louise. Friends of Joe, both, no doubt. What man in this town, what man in possession of any small measure of sway or license was not a friend of Joe Lanigan?

It was then she noticed all the prescriptions were for Veronal and chloral, scopolamine, paraldehyde and more.

Six months of them, dating from January to March 1930.

All for a Mrs. Joseph Lanigan.

It seemed enough medication for two patients or more. Enough to keep a forgotten wife watching shadows on walls in blissful nothingness, a tingling oblivion.

Marion remembered Louise saying she'd worked for Mrs. Lanigan as a private nurse for a short time.

She has the Bright's, Marion had said. And Louise: *Is that what they're calling it now?*

"MRS. CURTWIN, when Nurse Mercer started here, where was she coming from? Where was her last employ?"

Mrs. Curtwin perched her glasses higher on her nose and sighed. "Oh, she was a private nurse for a fine lady."

"And she left that position for this one?"

"Yes, she did."

"For a higher salary?"

"Mrs. Seeley, that's none of my affair."

"I just wondered," Marion said. She could feel Mrs. Curtwin's haught. She knew she must use it. "I mean, I thought I knew her well and now, the way she just picked up and left. I wonder if I knew her at all."

Mrs. Curtwin's face broke like a bubble, so easy it was. "Oh my, it's good you found out before it's too late. I can't begin . . . I shouldn't say. But you can believe when she came here, she made such ridiculous insinuations to Dr. Milroy and some of the others. Claimed the man she worked for—a very prominent businessman whom we all know well and respect and admire—was not managing his wife's health properly. Her charges were baseless, of course. She relented at last. Slander, that's what it was. She'd kept it up, she'd've been run out of town on a rail. That's what they would have done where I come from. I'm from Cincinnati, you see. We don't abide such flagrancy."

MRS. LANIGAN up high in her tower, stuffed full of a druggist's trunk, puffed like some huffing hothouse flower. And Louise seeing and knowing and no one to listen. So she makes her choice.

You choose your fights, Marion, she once said. *Some of us have fewer choices, alas.*

Louise, breath sweet filmy rum on her ear, whispering words she never said but words so true, *You must understand, Marion, I am a person of goodwill. I can count my bad deeds on one white hand. And I see your delicacy, Marion, your goodness. But it's a goodness easily worn. You haven't earned it. You haven't had to rescue it. You haven't had to scrub with horsehair brush the soft flesh on the inside of your thighs, rubbing away things left behind by three gentlemen in pale suits who caught you practicing dance steps behind the church on a summer night. Or have you? Because that, my darling, would be some stroke of chance.*

ON THE STREETCAR, she sat, hands folded, her face dry and powdery. The numbness, it was a relief, really. She felt as a shell, as a shell, and Joe Lanigan had gouged everything out and it was all gone and she was this walking, rattling shell.

With nothing left in her center, with that surging fever that had fallen on her these many months, with that fever gone, she could no longer fight off thoughts of the girls. The girls.

Suddenly, they loomed before her, gorgeous, slinking phantoms with crooking fingers.

She could see them there on the streetcar, Ginny sprawled

across three seats, blue-white skin pulsing, eyes glittering and teeth too, like some glossy vampire. Louise standing regal, red hair flaming, and one long arm reached out, dangling fingers toward Marion, smile sly and knowing, saying things, saying things, but what . . .

Oh, Louise, you had so much more to tell me. So much more and I . . .

DR. SEELEY WAS GONE for many hours and Marion had expected him there when she came home from the clinic and he was not and now supper had come and gone and Eddie Cantor sang "Ida, Sweet as Apple Cider" on the radio and Marion cleaned out her wound and looked in the mirror at the dark roots spreading through her platinum hair.

Earlier in the evening, she had planned to show him the prescriptions she had found among Louise's things. As the hours passed, though, she changed her mind. The thought of sharing yet another revelation of her lover's many sins was more than she could stand. Instead, she tucked the stack in between her underthings in her dresser drawer.

Dr. Seeley did not return home until after one o'clock, and when he did he told Marion he was so very tired and felt like the world was such a wicked, irredeemable place that only the thought of her waiting for him in their humble room made him go on. He clasped her hands in his and they were cold.

She asked him what he had found.

He told her he had begun the day by visiting a doctor at the state hospital. He asked him, colleague to colleague, about the pharmaceutical suppliers in the city.

"Oh, Marion," he said, as he ran water from the basin through his hair. "Marion, how could I have left you in a place, exposed to such dishonest men?"

"It is my fault," Marion said. "I surrendered to him. Even knowing he was a man who dallies and deceives."

"Marion, it is beyond all that," he said, shaking his head. "I paid a visit to Valiant Drugs today."

Marion's head jerked. "You didn't see him? He's never in his stores. He—"

"No, Marion, but I wanted to see . . . I wanted to see what kind of man he is, I suppose. I had some suspicions, based on what I learned at the hospital, so I went to one of his stores."

He reached into his inside pocket and pulled out a small bottle, much like the countless ones Marion had seen, had served from, had even drank from, on Hussel Street.

He set it on the bed between them. Then he reached into another pocket and set before her a vial and a packet of pills, much like the ones Louise always had.

"Understand, I did not tell the young man at the counter that I was a physician. This corn liquor, or what have you, this vial of— Marion, this one here is a barbiturate, do you understand? He's a wet druggist. I asked the right questions, I asked the right way—and you know I know the right ways. And this is what they gave me."

She nodded.

"I talked to a man buying a pint of such-named cough syrup," Dr. Seeley went on, excited. Marion could not remember him so excited. His eyes glittered. "Marion, I could see it on him. The bad stuff. He was . . . as I was. And he said before he struck gold at a card game he'd bought the rough magic down on Gideon Square, that area. He said it was the same stuff, different quality. I need to see if it goes that far for our man. He said everything is for sale there. I will see what 'everything' means."

The darkest parts of Marion's heart shimmered forth darkly. For what of this did she not know, really? And to be reminded was shameful.

She could not bear to tell him that there were no surprises here. That she had known, even as she had not really worked it through. That she had known but hadn't considered it enough to judge it wrong. That she knew and hadn't cared at all.

Do you remember, Everett, when we first met? You took me to dinner at the Rotary Club, which was the finest place I'd ever been. I took you to a meeting at the church and you had never been to anything like that before. I had to sing a song that night, do you remember? It was my turn. I had to sing a song; it was "O Africa, dark Africa, God's love has set us free" and you thought that was so funny because you had never seen anything like it before. Because you were a man of the world.

LYING IN BED, his breath fast, his fingers twitching against the mattress, his body squirming.

"Oh, Marion, when I think of this man and what he has done."

It is I, she wanted to say, but somehow didn't. The weight on her, she couldn't keep saying it, she was too tired to say it. He would never believe her anyway.

"I know," he said, and he touched her arm light as a feather, "there's probably more even than you could say."

She turned slightly and watched his profile, moonlight shot, a drooping silhouette of an aging statesman, sunken to ashy folds.

"Things he . . . Bedroom affairs for which you lack even the words. Words you don't have in your head, much less on your tongue. Such words."

She didn't say anything.

"Oh, Marion," he said, and he laid a tentative hand on her. She felt his breath catch.

That was when she understood. Understood what he was asking of her without asking.

She would give him something. Under coverlet here, she would. She knew how to now and she would do those private things for him that she had not known of just six months before. Things Joe had shown her. In the dark, under softly worn coverlet, she would.

But she knew he would hate himself for it. Not her, never her. She would give him this and this kind and good man, this noble man would only hate himself for it.

AND IN THE MORNING, trying to meet her eyes, yet not meeting them, Dr. Seeley walked her to the streetcar and then rode with her to the clinic and helped her off and kissed her soft on the forehead.

"Marion, I want you to tell them today."

"Tell them?"

"Marion, I must insist we leave . . ."

"I see." She knew he was right, but it was hard to make that matter.

"Today I will see what more I can learn about him," he said, and it struck Marion that he could not seem to say Joe Lanigan's name aloud to her. "But we would be foolhardy to remain any longer. Those bodies are bound to be found and identified, no matter how many steps you took to . . . You can tell the clinic that your husband has come to retrieve you and bring you to Mexico with him. They will understand."

"If I leave, might that raise suspicions?" As much as she knew its urgency and even after the things Joe Lanigan had said to her the day before, the thought of leaving panicked her.

And it was hard for her to look at her husband. She tried to forget the things done in that creaking bed the night before. He would not forget. Where did one go from there? Everything between them had changed twice over.

"Better to raise their suspicions, Marion, than to bear them out entire."

"You know best," she said, and she was sure he did.

What choice had she? Joe Lanigan, her corrupter, was no longer hers, would permit her to fall to the guillotine before he sullied his overcoat. It had to be.

She tried not to think of the stretch of years before her. Of the mine doctor's wife in remote Mexico, days spent without child, they could never seem to manage that either, never could seem to bring her to term. So what would it be? What would her days be? She tried not to imagine that.

Instead, she walked into the clinic as if it were any other day, as if all were not in ruins around her.

As FIVE O'CLOCK APPROACHED, Marion typed a resignation letter. She could not bear to speak to Dr. Milroy. She could not. She slipped the letter under his door and left quickly. The whole ride home she feared she might see him, even as she knew he never took the streetcar. Drove the same gleamy Packard Joe Lanigan toured around town in. The very same one.

Mrs. Gower gave her a sharp look when she walked in the door of the rooming house.

"You have visitors," she whispered. "Earlier, another man was here. From the newspaper. He said he had to speak with you and he left his telephone number. I don't like this kind of business, Mrs. Seeley. This is not the kind of house I run."

There in the frayed, lavender-cloyed living room she found

them, like gentleman callers come to tea. There were two, Officer Tolliver, whose head kept hitting the chipped chandelier, and Officer Morley, who had a mustache like John Gilbert and was very kindly to Marion and told her he had never seen such pretty eyes. They said they just had a few questions about her friends Louise Mercer and Virginia Hoyt. They asked if they might speak to her in the drawing room.

"Is there something wrong?" Marion asked, trying so hard to think. Almost convincing herself, with Officer Morley's genial face, his relaxing way, that everything would be just fine. "Have the girls gotten into trouble?"

"We're just checking into some things, Mrs. Seeley, and we were told you saw the girls before they left town."

"Yes."

"And did they tell you where they were going?"

Marion nodded. Smiled lightly. Tried not to twist the handkerchief in her hands. Tried not to tug at the bandage on her hand. Tried to make herself believe her own story. It was a good story, wasn't it?

Joe Lanigan's instructions stretched out so cleanly, like pressed sheets. It was easier each time. She told them that the girls said they had met two men and these men were very handsome and invited them to join them in their automobile on the way to Los Angeles, where there were many jobs and fine times to be had. They were the kind of girls who liked to pick up and move, you know. Anyone will tell you. Denver. Illinois. Nevada. They had been to many places. Marion, will you send our trunks along, they had asked her. And she had called a delivery service and they had come and picked up the trunks and that was the last she had heard.

"What was the address they gave you?"

Marion felt her head whirling uncontrollably. What was she

to do here? If she said Southern Pacific Station, they would call the station and the man would surely remember her, wouldn't he? He would remember her and say that the trunks belonged to a young woman and then and then . . . there seemed no way out. If they called the delivery service, what would those men say?

"They filled out the slips. I don't know. Some general delivery address, maybe?"

"They didn't intend for you to have any way to reach them?"

"They said they would write when they had an address," Marion said. "I'm sure I will hear from them soon."

"Mrs. Seeley," Officer Morley said, and he looked deeply into her eyes. His face was so kind, and he was so gentlemanly, and Marion felt safely curled in the warmth of his voice. "I don't want to alarm you, but you should know. Their landlord was concerned about the girls. It seems they owed quite a bit of back rent."

"Oh," Marion said. "The girls have slender means. We all have a rough time of it these days, don't we?"

"That we do, Mrs. Seeley. You can imagine the landlord was eager to at least gain possession of items in the home. He understood there to be a radio, silverware and some other more valuable items. I assume they shipped many of those things?"

"I assume so, yes," Marion said. She wondered where the girls stowed their pawn tickets.

"Mrs. Seeley," Officer Tolliver broke in, "you should know. There was blood found in the house. Do you know why that might be?"

"Oh," Marion managed before all the warmth slid from her face, from her head and chest. There couldn't be any blood left. She'd cleaned it from floor to ceiling. "Oh no."

"A small amount. On a pair of curtains."

A vision floated before Marion of her fingers twaining the

front curtains, looking for headlights. Whose blood might that be, she could not guess. But it was there.

"Oh my goodness."

"Did you actually see the girls leave with these men?"

"No, I never saw them leave. I never met the men."

"It may be nothing, you understand, Mrs. Seeley," Officer Morley said, one hand to her forearm, gentle. "It may be nothing at all."

"I wish I could . . . I just don't know." Everything was going to pieces and who knew what they might . . . Who knew what Joe Lanigan . . . Who knew?

"All right, Mrs. Seeley. But please, keep yourself available to us, will you?"

"Of course," she said, and her thoughts, so rambling, so jangled, stopped suddenly on an idea. "And say hello to Sheriff Healy, will you? He visited the girls often. What a wonderful man."

Officer Tolliver looked at her, eyebrows lifted. "The sheriff, eh?" And he shared a glance with Officer Morley. "Well, Mrs. Seeley, we thank you for being so helpful. You let us know when you hear from those girls, now, won't you?"

"You will be my first step," she said.

EVERETT WAS AGAIN not home and it was late, very late. Hours Marion spent going over the policemen's questions in her head. They shuttled around and she couldn't stop them. There was no way to shut them off.

As the hours passed, she tried to pack. She tried to organize herself. She cleaned her gashing wound. She replaced buttons on her husband's sagging shirts. Her face was damp. She felt a fever coming. She felt she was falling into some dire state and there was no stopping it. Her knees rubbery, she felt a faint coming on and cursed herself.

Lying on the bed was worse, though. It was a buffering quiet like cotton in her throat. It made her head go funny. Somehow, somehow, lying there, she came upon the feeling of Louise and Ginny in the room with her. She could feel them there. She could smell Ginny's avid perfume in her hair, feel Louise's fingertips on her hand. And then it was like they were beneath her somehow, under the bed, writhing, trying to crawl free. She felt if she looked to the floor, she would see their glowy white arms, splayed hands, reaching, tugging at the carpet, trying to pull themselves out.

She would have done anything for one of Joe's magic pills now.

But her husband had sent them down the drain.

Down the dark belly.

There would be decades with him. Decades.

He was a good man, a kind man.

Oh, he was.

IN THE PITCH OF THE NIGHT, the doctor returned and told her he had so much more to share about Joe Lanigan and she wanted to say what did it matter, what did it, and she told him about the police, but he did not seem concerned. He seemed to expect it.

"Marion, do not worry. Tomorrow first thing, we will buy our train tickets, and by midday we will be gone."

In early morning, as they walked down Mrs. Gower's stairwell, the newspaper on the front landing caught Marion's eye, and Dr. Seeley's too.

BLOOD FOUND IN MISSING GIRLS' HOUSE
FRIENDS SPEAK OF GAY REVELS AND WILD LIFESTYLE

With trembling fingers, Marion read about the blood found on the premises and how the police were pursuing the possibility of violence. Most of the article, however, swelled with the breathless first-person account of one Florence Loomis.

"Do you know her?" Dr. Seeley asked.

"Yes. She was a friend. She was at the house a lot, at least." The sight of plump and smeary Mrs. Loomis, tight as a drum on New Year's Eve, flashed through Marion's head. Once, she remembered her tearing her blouse open and asking Sheriff Healy to arrest her for gross indecency.

Marion looked back down at the article. There was a photograph of Louise in her nurse's uniform and one of the house, which looked grim, menacing.

"'According to Werden Clinic staff,'" Dr. Seeley read, "'the girls left town last weekend with two unidentified men on their way to California. Their belongings were shipped by a friend, Mrs. Everett Seeley, who also works at the clinic. She could not be reached by deadline.'"

Marion thought of the reporter who had come to the house, knew he would be back.

Dr. Seeley read on: "'Neighbors said the house was often the site of "gay parties" that lasted until the early morning hours, the most recent marked by frequent trips to the local drugstore for ginger ale. The women's loud voices intermingled with those of many men and kept neighbors awake for most of the night.

"'"They are a peacocky pair," said Mrs. Loomis, who befriended the young women last year. "They came to town with nary a nickel between them. They were dreadful poor and I helped them." Mrs. Loomis, who said that the girls had recently borrowed thirty-eight dollars and an electric hair-waving iron from her, added, "Good times, that's what they wanted. They had many friends to help them out. I tried to talk sense into them, but they would have none of it. I'm not surprised by any of this. They entertained many men. Men in this town." While Mrs. Loomis would not mention any names, she added that she would help the police in any way she could.

" 'One neighbor confirmed that one of the most frequent guests was Mr. Joseph Lanigan, owner of Valiant Drugs and vice president of the Chamber of Commerce. Mr. Lanigan could not be reached for comment.

" 'The sheriff's office refused to reveal any details about the investigation but police were a constant presence in the Hussel Street residence today.'"

Dr. Seeley set the newspaper down and looked at Marion. "They will be speaking to him soon."

"I know," Marion said.

"Do you know what he intends to say?"

Marion looked at him. *Your beauty is blinding but behind it I see death.* That's what he had the nerve to say to her. The stuff of tear-lashed confession magazines. That was what he had said.

"Marion, have you seen him since you've returned? Have you . . . been with him?"

"No. No. I saw him only once," she said, "at the clinic. He made me see that . . . I am alone."

"You're not alone, Marion," Dr. Seeley said. "You're not."

She looked at him and it felt a glimmer of long ago, he the elegant doctor spiriting her away, rescuing her from something, even.

"He gave me one hundred dollars," Marion blurted, ashamed she had not mentioned it before. But to have mentioned it would have meant revealing she had seen him. Seen this man whose name her husband could not bear to utter. She opened her purse and showed it to him.

"We will need it," Dr. Seeley said.

THEY WALKED STRAIGHT OUT the front door and to the street-car. Dr. Seeley said they should leave their things at the rooming house. There should be no appearance that they had gone. But they would not return.

They rode downtown to a small hotel with a fraying fringe overhang—the Kenwick Arms, the electric sign had said before its globes had burned out.

They registered as Mr. and Mrs. Leroy and it was not until Dr. Seeley had shut the creaking door behind them and the dust motes rose and settled that Marion asked him what in fact his plan was.

"Leaving town now has become hazardous. Police will be watching the train station. This way, we have perhaps purchased a day, maybe two. I have thoughts. I have thoughts. We may shore ourselves up by culling as much on this man as possible."

"How will that stop the law?"

"He has powerful friends. That is clear. After the news story he will be rounding up his horses. Marion, he does not intend to go to the gallows. We will not let him place you there in his stead."

"That is his plan, back to the wall," Marion said, surprised by the coolness in her voice. The hardness wedged tight between teeth. What had happened to her? Where was the shuddering young girl, gone forever? In some strange way, she was glad. That girl was her doom.

"That newspaper article," she went on. "What will the afternoon edition hold?"

Two hours, and Dr. Seeley went to the newsstand and returned, ashen-faced.

Marion looked at the front page. It was a muted blow; she, beaten now to smoothness, expected no less.

LOVE TRIANGLE AT CENTER
OF GIRLS' DISAPPEARANCE?

POLICE TRACE PATH OF MYSTERIOUS TRUNKS

FRIENDS SPECULATE THRILL PARTIES
FUELED JEALOUSY AMONG WOMEN

Police continue their investigation of the disappearance of local nurse Louise Mercer and her roommate, Virginia Hoyt. At the investigation's center are two trunks delivered to the Southern Pacific Station from the girls' home on Saturday. Police confirm that a friend, Mrs. Everett Seeley, was present when deliverers picked up the trunks, but they are still confirming where the trunks were shipped. Miss Mercer and Mrs. Seeley met as employees of Werden Clinic.

"Mrs. Seeley is cooperating with us," Sheriff Pete Healy confirmed. "We will be speaking with her today." The Courier was unable to locate her at press time.

Mrs. Seeley appears to have been a frequent guest at the missing girls' home since moving to the area last fall. According to several witnesses, the three were immediately attracted to each other and Mrs. Seeley regularly spent the night at the house. But it appears the friendship became troubled in recent weeks.

"There were many men at the house and there were arguments over who was the favorite among different men," said one source. "The parties were wild and unruly."

Mrs. Florence Loomis, a friend to all three girls, pointed to Mr. Joe Lanigan, prominent local businessman, as the source of much of the jealousy. "All the girls loved him. He was very kind to them. But Mrs. Seeley was particularly fond of him. She did not like the other girls spending time with him."

Other friends of the girls' intimated trouble in

recent weeks, including jealous fights and heavy alcohol consumption among the women.

"Something like this was bound to happen," said Mr. Abner Worth, owner of Worth Brothers Meat Market, who knew the girls. "Mrs. Seeley had a fiery temper and the girls were all prone to drinking and wild ways."

According to sources at Werden, Mrs. Seeley's husband, Dr. Everett Seeley, holds a position with Ogden-Nequam Mining Company in Mexico and Mrs. Seeley intends to join him. It is not known whether the girls' disappearance is connected to Mrs. Seeley's planned relocation.

Three o'clock, Dr. Seeley looked itchy, scratching his neck, and sweaty-collared, said if she felt safe, he would return to his investigation.

"Where will you go?"

"I need to see how wide the ring expands, Marion," he said, straightening his tie, twisted so thin from wear.

Marion wanted to remind him he was not a policeman, not a private detective from the Saturday matinee. She wanted to tell him none of it would matter. She thought of Joe Lanigan at his lodges, his friars' clubs, his Chamber of Commerce gatherings, his men's clubs, the smokers from which he was always returning, gin-soaked and tomcatted. What did girls like Louise and Ginny matter in the face of that, and what did she, some vagabond wife picked up for dallying and set down in a corner when done?

"Last night when I came home, it was too late," he said to her. "I was too disordered. I didn't want to worry you. Now there is no choice. Let me share all I saw, all I've learned about this man. Then you will have no doubt we will ensnare him. We must. He is a dangerous . . . He is . . ."

She put her hand on his arm. "You can tell me," she said. Even knowing there would likely be no surprises. The only surprise would be having to look full-face again at what she had blotted out, lo these months. What worse?

He told of a day and a night spent in joints, judas holes, low-down nighteries and barrelhouses, trailing the wastrels on Thaler Avenue and in Gideon Square. The sad tramps and drifting souls who seemed, somehow, to wear his own face. He saw their sorrow and their weakness and it trembled through him and he could almost not bear it. But he did. And he struck up conversations and no one questioned this shabby man with all the right words and most of all the right look in his eyes, the look of lostness. At last, a man named Farriss took him to a house on Clawson Street where he met a woman named Clara who explained how every four days, the Worth Brothers Meat Truck came to the Dempsey Hotel and you went to the third floor, room 308, and Mr. Worth, only he called himself Mr. Tanner, but everyone knew, would sell you your kit. Whatever was wanted. And sure, she knew Ginny too. Ginny used to work the Dempsey for Joe till the TB got too bad. Louise, sure, everyone knew Louise, Louise was the one before the new one. The new who? The new nurse. Everyone knew Joe Lanigan's private nurses were also his whores. His private whores, mind you. The new one, word was the new one wasn't even a real nurse, this one, she was a schoolgirl plucked from St. Monessa's.

A coldness swept across Marion's chest.

The nurse. Of course. The nurse. It was like everything else about Joe Lanigan. Seamy, rotten. Ruined.

Looking at Dr. Seeley, she pushed it all away. She looked at him.

"And you mean to go there. You mean to go to where these narcotics are . . ."

"I do, my dear," he said, and he kept her gaze. "Marion, if he can so effectively marshal the powers that be in this town to protect himself, we must put the fear in him to offer up those steel walls to you as well. He must find another goat, Marion, from among his drossy minions. It won't be you."

"But for you to move back in these worlds . . ."

"Marion, the more we know about his affairs, the more chips we have at our disposal. We need to put the fear in him. I must go."

Marion felt a tightening in the air between them. "Everett, I . . ."

"I will be fine, Marion. You know I will. I am strong for us both now. As you always have been. It is my chance. This is my chance."

Marion looked at him and he looked at her, his eyes open and waiting, asking her something that he could not say. She looked at him and she could not help but feel the largeness of the moment and it frightened her. It felt like they were spinning on an axis after a life of stillness. Or stillness after four marital years of spinning. She did not know what it meant.

"Of course, Everett. Of course." She had to say it. And she so wanted to believe it, all of it.

And maybe he was right. Maybe there was more still to uncover about Joe Lanigan, more even than she knew, enough to matter more than his rich-man, gold-cut cruelty, and maybe it could matter. Who was she to guess, given the quaking surprises of the last week, most of all the ones she'd sprung on herself. *It is you, Marion, who started the bloodbath. It is you who took hammer to teeth, acid to flesh—would you ever have guessed the limits of your own darkness?*

She handed him the hundred dollars. "You will need this, to get information."

He looked at the money. "I will take fifty dollars. But hopefully I will not need it."

"Yes," she said, and his face looked so kind and she felt a

warmth rush through her, and through her hands to his. "Thank you, Everett. Thank you."

TEN MINUTES after he left, she was on the streetcar to Lynbrook Street.

She could hear Louise's voice prickling in her ear: *It is he, it is he, you cannot let him wend so freely, smashing our girl-bones to pieces, stomping on our black-and-blue hearts while he lines his pockets and fills his mouth with sugar, sugar, sugar.*

She would need to find him out. He had set things in motion and who knew what would come next?

IT WAS NEARING four o'clock and Joe's Packard was nowhere to be seen.

Through the back windows she could see two blond-plaited girls chewing on long strings of taffy, listening to the radio. She could hear the radio faintly. Hear the girls' soft, taunting sister voices, scolding and reckoning with each other. They wore matching Easter dresses, mint green and soft-shell pink, and their backs faced the windows. The taffy was lemon yellow and they were tugging at it and laughing at the program.

Marion wished she might join them, such fun they were having, poking and prodding and nestling against each other.

It was lovely.

She turned away, the rush of feeling too great, and that was when she saw the flicker of white from the corner of her eye.

"Mrs. Lanigan, get back in this house!"

Marion backed up fast against the wall and saw the apparition, for that's what she appeared, in white, skin pallid, eyes like dark, purple-edged hollows.

Behind the ghostly figure scurried the nurse, pinch faced and grasping. Hooking one arm around the ghost, she grabbed her fast.

"Mrs. Lanigan, you know better," she said, and the ghost, the ghost who was Mrs. Lanigan, wailed mournfully.

"I don't know where. I lost my way. You're trying to make me lose my way," she moaned, her eyelids and cheeks looking so strange, puffy, like a balloon toy.

"I am doing no such thing," the nurse scolded, and it was at that moment she spotted Marion.

But said nothing.

"Oh, Jessie, put me down. Put me down. I can't bear it," Mrs. Lanigan cried. And Marion saw all her wrecked beauty, drawn tight across old bones.

Without saying a word to Marion, the nurse, this Jessie, seized the flailing woman and shepherded her, roughly, back into the house.

Marion waited.

She knew.

Five minutes later, the nurse returned.

"He's not here," she said, hand on her hip, facing Marion in front of a hedgerow. With a beckoning nod, she drew Marion farther into the corner of the lawn, away from the house.

"I know."

"What do you mean coming here? What good will it do you?"

Any guess Marion had about this nurse and the master of the house was confirmed by this, by this intimate tone. By the way her face showed possession, territorial claim.

"I am at the end," Marion said. "You replaced Nurse Mercer?"

"Yes," she said. "I did."

"And you tend to Mrs. Lanigan."

"As you can see," she said, "she's very sick."

"You keep her still. You take care of her."

"You know she is very ill. And frightened of the world too. Do you know what I mean?"

"And he has you, he has you to take care of with the medicines . . ." Marion felt her head thrumming. "And to warm his bed."

The nurse's face reddened. But she was smiling too. She pulled a cigarette from her apron pocket and slid it into her mouth.

"Oh, Mrs. Seeley," the nurse said, "you should see the things I can do. He found me, I was ready to take my vows."

"You're the wife's nurse. You're her nurse."

"I take good care, don't think I don't," she said, voice pitching. "She's so happy she doesn't know the ceiling from the floor. There's nothing wrong with it. A man has to have something. Especially a man like that."

She could hear it now: *Marion, you must understand, I cannot help myself. You are all I have that is not dead. Dying or dead. Dying and dead.*

"You don't even know what sorrow awaits you," Marion said, shaking her head. "You don't even know."

The nurse shook her head, shook her head and punched out a vicious, certain smile. "We are to be married, you know. Did you know that? He is all done with you. Yes, I know all about you. But you have your doctor husband. Why don't you take care to warm your husband's bed?"

Marion felt something rise up in her and before she knew it she had her hands on the girl, was shaking her. The cigarette fell and the girl turned white, tried to wrest herself free.

"You were his dally, but the dally is past," she said, pulling at Marion's hands, tugging from them.

"What can you know?" Marion's voice rose calamitously. "What can you know? He tosses us all aside. He tossed Nurse Mercer. He tossed her and then—"

"And then you murdered her," the nurse replied, chin jutting out defiantly. "Murdered her and the other. Those perverse girls. He has told me all about those girls." She twisted her face into a sneer, but her voice edged hysteria. "Do you mean to murder me too?"

Marion felt no jolt. There were no jolts left to be had.

Louise. Louise. Could it be that he knew exactly what he was doing as she teetered, wounded, toward them that night? With Louise gone, his easy life made even easier. No more fear she might talk of drugs and his wife and who knew what else. Who gained more than he?

Marion's voice came barreling out. "Listen, you stupid, stupid girl. Listen to me. You tell him this. You tell him: I know all about him. I know all about keeping his wife torpid and senseless up there. I know about it all and I have the proof. Louise knew too. Louise knew, and who is to say he wasn't glad for the chance to shut her up?"

The girl shook her head violently and laughed, a short bark. "He's told me you're mad. Everyone knows you've gone mad," she said, in a jerking, terrified taunt.

Marion smacked her hard across the face.

"I have phoned the police, you know," the girl said. "I have phoned them."

"You will go mad too, you wanton child. He will raze you to ruins too," Marion said, her heart battering in her chest as she turned and began to run across the lawn, to run anywhere.

"Oh, do run, Mrs. Seeley. Don't you know he's all done with you?"

Ginny's syruped tongue saying, *Meems, I never would have*

hurt you and you're such a silly fool to have shot me dead like a possum in a tree, just 'cause I cracked in two for but a minute. Don't you know, the fever on me, pen yan in the lungs, loaded up on milkman candy, watching you and Louise clinging and climbing each other, I went mad, just for a second. Just for a second and you murdered me, Marion. I wonder if you went a little mad too. I wonder if you still are. All I know is you put a big hole where my face should be. Oh, Meems, my face . . .

The weight of her sin finally fell upon her. There was nothing left with which to distract herself, no place left to hide. She had let this shallow man undo her, but she had also undone herself. *There is nothing left but to face it,* she told herself. *There is nothing left but to start paying.*

HE DID NOT COME. He did not come. And Marion felt sure it would be the police who would arrive first. She was certain of it.

By morning light, with not a shudder of sleep upon her, she felt she could wait no more, could sit in that mildewed room filled with the dread of a hundred hotel guests before her, the hectic patter of mice behind walls, the feel of dark hours careening toward final despair from a hundred, a thousand past down-at-heels nightly guests, weekly residents, no more.

She put on her hat, hair pushed beneath, and walked, down faced, to the streetcar. It was too early and the cars were not running, so she proceeded on foot. She walked along Thaler Avenue, which snaked its way fourteen blocks to Gideon Square, and everything was still and a forlorn feel was in the air.

There was a low creaking coming from somewhere in the square, and also a high singing, almost a mewl. A man crooning brokenly about a girl whose cousin was a drunkard in Cincy and died with a peach of a bun, and her uncle's a preacher in Quincy, a nutty old son of a gun. Peering, she could see the man, who was lying at the foot of the center fountain, a stone-struck phoenix rising to the heavens, and he was singing to a girl, she looked like a girl, with her arms wrapped tight around herself, a pitch of blood on her shirtfront and it was the lungs. Was anyone left in this whole lonely world with lungs not patched together as if from tattered muslin and cobwebs? They all came to the desert, like she had, they blew in from all corners, they came to the desert to build themselves anew. Isn't that what she had done, wasn't she anew?

She skittered around the square and no one bothered her, and she fancied, with her pitted stockings, her day-worn dress, the dirty tendrils of dark-rooted platinum slipping from her hat, she looked the part. She looked the part, and one poor woman, face a smear of booze-washed sorrow, offered her a glug of grain and Marion almost took it, but did not.

No Dr. Seeley. No Dr. Seeley, but she would not stop.

She called out, "Everett!" She called out, "Everett!" and got more than one answer, but never from her husband.

She wended from a lean-to on one side of the square to a tangle of boys playing three-card molly to the central newsstand opening for the day. And there was an old garage, the owner long gone, the shell of the place all intact, a few stray automobile parts hanging, and a spent cooking fire in the center. She could see four, five men and a woman folded in small corners, sleeping. One man was whittling smooth strokes of rosewood and he only nodded at Marion, who nodded back.

"Everett," she said, barely a whisper now. "Everett, are you there?"

That was when she saw a hand wrapped around a brown glass quart of Chlorodyne with the Valiant label curling off the side.

And she saw the pale face of Dr. Seeley, skin like wet paper, head resting against a stripped tire, mouth slightly open.

"Everett," she whispered, moving toward him. "Everett . . ."

She put her hand to him, the bluing lips, and his eyelids seemed to slide open, but the eyes were dead, black specks floating serene.

Then the eyes shut again.

His skin, the coldest marble she ever felt.

"Haint ever seen one take so much," came a voice in her ear. It was the man whittling the wood. "Haint ever seen such. He start with the syrup and then one came with the cubes and kit and hence he tore in with the needle too. A starving man, he."

Marion turned to face him. "And you just watch? Look at him. You just watch?"

The man looked at her. "What do you do?" he asked her. "What do you do, miss? When it's that way, there is only to watch."

She turned back to her husband, placed her fingers on his wrist and the pulse sludging, and it was like the time she found him in the bathtub at the Prescott rooming house. He spent three days in the private hospital with the doctor who promised he could wash his brain to clean the habit, but then the money ran out.

Holding his hand, she felt a panic all through.

Five seconds.

Five seconds she gave to thought. She could run for help and then, while they tended, flee. She could walk away knowing that Everett had tended himself many times after too much, much too much, had taken care of himself a dozen, perhaps a hundred times or more and always stood again. He knew what to do, he did. She knew he would want her to run. He would want her to save herself. She ran through this thought, but for five seconds only.

There were things she had done that she had never guessed she could do.

Things that had now seeped into her bones and changed her

forever. Seeped into her bones and now she was sick from inside out. Diseased and lost.

But this, abandoning him, this thing was the thing she could never do. She was glad to know it about herself. There was something left.

"WHERE IS THE NEAREST HOSPITAL?" she asked the man at the newsstand, and he told her it was two blocks and she said, breathless, "Can you summon a policeman?" and he looked at her long and hard, and said he would.

It was while turning to run back to her husband that she saw her own photograph, in clinic garb, spread across three different early editions, hanging six sheets abroad the top of the stand. All the headlines shrieked in her ears:

BLOODY TRUNKS FOUND
IN LOS ANGELES HOTEL
Two Bodies Found Inside, Believed to Be Missing Girls

BLONDE SOUGHT:
SHE SHIPPED DEATH TRUNKS, POLICE SAY
Hotel Employee IDs Doctor's Wife

She did not stop long enough to read further. She did not stop at all.

Tearing back to the garage, to Dr. Seeley, she gazed up at the phoenix wings towering over the center of the square and thought they might block out the sky entire.

Something in her lifted, something in her lifted and the weight, all the weight, it was gone. In her head, she heard strands of wavery ukulele and could see Ginny dancing, white arms curled about her like those arching wings, dancing and dancing and head tilted, smile hooking, and dancing and dancing . . .

THEY TOLD HER that her husband would be fine. They told her that he had consumed large quantities of morphine and she nodded, as if not knowing, and wondered what they must think of her that she might not know what caused the thousand thatch marks on the doctor's legs and those arms with ribbons of scars cross-threaded like a corset.

Oh, Doctor . . .

The nerve in his cheek twitched, his eyes fluttered open, and he saw her there. She could see the recognition flood across his face and it was awful. She felt awful for him.

"Oh no, Marion . . . ," he said. "No. I was trying to find out . . . I thought I was saving . . . Marion, I did try so . . . I did try . . . I . . . ." His face looked a hundred years old and his eyes filled.

Looking down at him, she rested her fingers on his chest. "Doctor, I am to blame. It is me. It is mine."

Then, quietly, he said to her, "Leave now, Marion. I will repair it all. Flee now. Go to the train tracks."

She shook her head.

"You must hurry," he whispered. Then, looking down at his whittled arm, he said, "This is my sin to bear, but I love it so"— and then the faintest of pauses—"more than you, Marion. That is too terrible to say, but it does what love can't. The world is so dark. But what the needle gives . . . I wonder if you could understand, Marion."

And he looked at her with red-ringed eyes. "It adds to truth a dream."

She saw the way he was, she saw it flickering there before her in an instant, but she shook it away, she had to shake it away. She told herself she did not understand and would not believe him.

She reached out to him, but he turned away and faced the wall. She could not get him to look her way again. She said his name a dozen times or more, but he was still.

Behind her, a doctor said that two policemen were waiting to see her. The patrolman who had brought them to the hospital had alerted them and would she see them now. He was sorry to rush her, but the detectives were quite insistent.

Standing beside Dr. Seeley's bed, she touched her fingers to his warming flesh and said something quietly to him, and the words, the voice itself came from a place she did not know and she couldn't even be sure what she'd said, other than it sounded like *you, you, you,* the last word in a song stuttering on the phonograph: *you, you, you, you . . .*

And the detectives did not wait for her, for when she turned around there they were.

THREE HOURS LATER, three hours of questions and Marion hardly managing a word, just repeating the same stories Joe Lanigan had rat-a-tat-tatted into her head and, with each repetition, the stories getting more jumbled, disjointed, a motion picture with the reels out of order.

Somewhere in her head, she wondered how they identified the bodies. She thought she heard them say something about a Los Angeles police detective matching Louise's body to missing-person photostats and a nasty voice from somewhere in the dark shanks of her head sneered, *You should've burned her face. You should've burned her face with acid or fire. My God, my God.*

She gave them nothing, could not fix her head around anything.

They asked and asked and asked.

But her head was a dust bowl.

Somewhere in her, she was building armies to prepare herself, to fortify herself because she knew it was time. She was nearly ready, nearly ready to tell everything because she felt her guilt and shame more purely than ever and knew what must be done.

But her thoughts were scattered and she worried about Dr. Seeley and her words jumbled in her mouth and she could not hold on to them. She began to doubt the soundness of her own mind.

Joe Lanigan, did you even exist? Did you live to ravish me and then disappear into thin air but to stand behind doors, voice rattling through telephones, creeping under floors, whispering commands, puppet string twisted around your heavy hands as you lift your fingers and everyone dances, dances for you?

They spoke sternly, the edges in their voices sharpening. Even that nice Officer Morley, *Detective* Morley, grew impatient—he told her she knew more, and he was asking about packing slips and train tickets, and wasn't it funny that a woman perfectly matching her description had taken that train herself to Los Angeles? Had left the Southern Pacific Station in Los Angeles with those trunks? Could she explain who this woman was if not she?

For a moment, the picture of Sheriff Healy, in full uniform and tin star, twirling Ginny around in the girls' living room, stuttered into her head.

"Sheriff Healy, is he—"

"Don't even bother," said the long-necked one, Tolliver. "Don't even bother. The sheriff knows all about you. Knows the kinds of things you girls had going on there. It went bad between you three, did it?" He zippered his fingers in the air, a perfect triangle.

Marion looked up at them and said nothing.

You must see that now that I will make sure my name is not brought into this, Joe Lanigan had said to her. *I will not let it happen and it won't happen because of what I am in this town. There are levers and switches and keys and I know which way they all go.*

And they kept talking and talking, about witnesses at both train stations, at the soda fountain on Hussel Street, everywhere. She had been seen everywhere. Everyone saw her and identified her and there was no hiding. Even people who could not have seen her said they saw her. Lever, switch, key.

"It was you, Mrs. Seeley, wasn't it?" said Morley. "It was you on that train and it was you who came to claim those trunks? And if you didn't know what was in them, why did you tell the station agent that the trunks contained game meat? It was you, Mrs. Seeley, and you knew those trunks held the remains, the butchered remains, of your friends, did you not?"

. . . and finally

Did you murder those two girls, Mrs. Seeley?

And she stuttered and started and finally gathered herself, gathered herself and summoned Louise's stalwart hauteur. She thought of Louise and she brought Louise to herself and rose tall in her chair and said, keenly, "Do I look to you, do I look to you gentlemen like the kind of person who could murder two women and do the things you've said, that you keep saying, who could cut her girlfriends to pieces and pack them in boxes and perform untold horrors upon their bodies?"

They peered down at her, these two tall men looming and hanging over her.

"And I don't think I will talk anymore. I don't think I will. I can't talk anymore now and I believe I will have a lawyer."

She was placed in the holding cell.

Joe Lanigan. Joe Lanigan. Would you really nail me to the cross?

I believe, Joe Lanigan, you would.

She sitting here behind a crossbar and what of Joe Lanigan, sprawling bedwise with his nurse-whore?

Prescription slips, tales of dirty deeds, broken-faced dope peddlers pointing shaking fingers—what did any of that matter? Who would believe her now? Who would believe this dirty thing, wasted and unclean, with drug-addicted husband, this dirty thing a monster in waiting? Who would believe her?

She would mount those gallows steps. She would.

BY THE TIME the detectives reclaimed her, not two hours later, she had toiled herself into some state.

"Where is my lawyer? Where is he?" she asked. She could not keep still. She could not stop her hands wringing. Her head was so full. Her head was so full she could scarce hold it up.

"You're not under arrest, Mrs. Seeley," Tolliver said, looming, it seemed, two feet higher than two hours before. "What would you need a lawyer for?"

"You'll have your lawyer," Morley said. "But right now, we'll have some more answers first."

She looked at Morley, and then at Tolliver. They had some bounce in them, some light in their eyes. They seemed more confident, sprightly. She felt they were circling in, circling in.

"I'd like to know where Mr. Joseph Lanigan is," she blurted before any sense or thought could stop her. But why should it stop her? Wasn't this the end of the line? Wasn't it? Grab any rope, grab and hold on. "Have you brought him in for all these questions?"

"Why would we do that, Mrs. Seeley?" Morley said, looking over at Tolliver and back at her.

"He was friends with the girls, now, wasn't he? He was friends and spent as many evenings with them as I. He's there behind everyone you mention. He's behind them all, lurking. He's behind Mr. Worth who goes to the papers and says I had a fiery temper and the girls were prone to drinking and wild antics, and all these so-called witnesses and all this. He's behind them all."

She felt her face grow stiff. Had she gone too far for nothing? Had she only ensnared herself? She stopped. She put her hand to her mouth and bit it. She bit it like an animal and her skin broke fast and blood swelled across her lips, the salt tingling. She didn't know what she was doing. She started to laugh and the sound of it was terrifying.

"Mrs. Seeley," Morley said, face turning white. "Mrs. Seeley . . ."

They bent down toward her. The way they were looking at her, like they realized suddenly they had captured a tigress, a madwoman, right there before their eyes.

SHE SAT in the holding cell. It might have been many hours, she couldn't be sure. She knew it was all over. She did.

There was a guard with a harelip and a rolling gait who kept coming in and talking to her. He told her there were reporters all the way from Los Angeles, even New York City, outside. He told her that they were trying to take pictures through the bar windows, had she seen them? He had made them stop, wasn't she glad? He waved one of the daily papers in front of her and told her that the first four pages were all about her, and wasn't that something. He said he wasn't supposed to show her, but did she want a peek? The headlines flashed before her: "SUSPECTED MURDERESS' DEATH TRUNKS HORRIFIED HOTEL STAFF" and "THE WEIRD 'SISTERS': Did Fatal Kiss Spark Blonde's Jealous Rage?"

It is all over, Marion thought, and I am somehow glad. It is my time to speak. It is my time to lay my sins bare.

"I am ready," she said. But before she knew it, her head wobbled and her chest turned to fire and she felt herself falling again.

THE POLICE DOCTOR was peering over her with his aluminum headlamp glaring like a magnificent third eye.

"I fainted," Marion whispered. She who'd not fainted in her life now twice in three days.

"Correct," the doctor said. His breath smelled of cloves. Marion thought of Christmas back in Michigan, of clove-spiked oranges dusted in cinnamon hanging on snow-pattered windows at school. Had Christmas passed this year? Why couldn't she remember the mistletoe and the holly pricking her fingers?

He kept peering.

"I'm all right," she said.

"Glad about that," he said, "but why don't you tell me now about the hole in your hand."

Marion looked down at her bullet-torn palm, then back up at the doctor, who tilted his head, watching her closely.

"I'm not talking. I'm through talking," she said, feeling peaceful, half dead. This was to be it. This was to be it and suddenly it felt so perfect. "The only talking I will do now is to confess. To confess all. I will bear the sins no longer. I will walk those gallows steps head held high."

"Mighty strong words, miss," he said, taking her hand in his and turning it over. "But I don't guess you heard."

"Heard?"

He took an alcohol-daubed swab to her hand and she cried out.

"About your husband," he said. "I guess it's to me to tell you."

She felt all the sound go out of the world and then she screamed.

TWELVE HOURS PRIOR, bleary and still broken, Dr. Seeley had dressed and found a doctor's coat, contriving to secure ten grains of morphine, and so taking, wandered out the hospital doors and hitched rides all the way to the big reservoir on the far northern edge of the city. The jump from the top of the concrete dam was more than two hundred feet and he was found by maintenance workers. The note he left on his hospital bed proclaimed:

> *To all who would listen:*
> *Ten days ago, while in the farthest depths of Mazatlán, I began to have dark notions. Mad with narcotics abuse, I became consumed by a false belief that my wife had been untrue. I determined to leave my post, traveling all the way from Mexico with the idea of entrapping her. By the time I arrived, I was fevered and unsound. Not finding my wife at home, I proceeded shamelessly to Nurse Mercer's home, knowing my wife spent many evenings there. Nurse Mercer and her friend, rightly sensing I was disordered, tried to calm me and assure me that my wife was not present. I now see they were protecting her. They saw my state and were shielding her. I became enraged. I do not know what possessed me, but for what has been done to my head from years of self-abuse. I was raving. The women were frightened and bid I leave. When I refused and attempted to force my way in, Nurse Mercer ran for a small pistol and begged me to retreat. I pushed through and I seized that gun and I shot them both dead. I shot them both dead. First, Miss Hoyt as*

she tried to stop me from harming her friend, and then
Nurse Mercer too. I couldn't stop myself. I am a fiend.

  My wife is everything to me. I forced her to assist me.
I operated on the bodies and packed them in those trunks
and forced her to take them away. She is so sweet and
lovely I knew she could move without suspicion. I
compelled her and, out of fright, obedience and love, she
helped me conceal my ghoulish deeds. I am ruined, torn
through with shame, and I can go on no more.

  It is the morphine. It is the morphine in the veins.
That first time, that first time, back in '26, I will never
forget. Everything was as never before. Strange and
beautiful. I felt, for one thrilling hour, I could do anything.
It was the most wondrous hour of my life. I wish it had
been my last.

The letter was all. When Marion read it, and she would only read it once, she wondered how long it would take her to understand the nature of her husband's sacrifice.

Part of her wanted to confess everything and clear his name—this was the biggest part. But doing so would deny his ultimate gesture.

Part of her wanted to follow him.

Part of her could feel herself falling, feel the water filling her mouth, her chest. The peace in that.

But part of her, in the winnowing corners of her fevered head, felt very, very differently. Part of her could not stop herself from thinking, hot-teared: *Dr. Seeley, you have taken something from me. I was ready. It was time. This was to be* my *redemption and now it is* yours.

"MRS. SEELEY, we know you were trying to protect your husband. We know your motives were pure and selfless. And that will not be forgotten."

That's what they told her. Mr. Quint, her lawyer, took the reins fast and handled everything.

What could be more noble, what could be a greater act of love than Dr. Seeley's keen sacrifice? On lower currents, she knew the answer: for him to have let her choose how to reckon with it, to have left it to her to choose. That would have been greater still. For she had been ready to face her crimes and, most of all, her sins. And now her chance, it was gone.

Privately, Mr. Quint did not believe his client to be of sound mind after her husband's demise. He did not believe her ramblings about Mr. Joseph Lanigan—hell, he knew Joe Lanigan, had dinner with him at the lodge once a month and went hunting with him every November. *What stories lovestruck ladies will tell. Alas* . . .

Part Six

BLONDE WIFE OF BLOOD BUTCHER FREE TODAY
January 2, 1932

Mrs. Everett Seeley, the platinum-tressed widow of the bloody trunk murderer who took his own life seven months ago following his frenzy of terror, will be released today, after serving a six-month sentence for helping conceal her husband's crimes. Mrs. Seeley confessed to "aiding and assisting" in the transport to Los Angeles of the bodies that the demon doctor hacked to pieces in his bloody rage.

Dr. Seeley claimed to have shot Louise Mercer, a nurse at the Werden Clinic, and her roommate, Virginia Hoyt, in a fit of jealous rage, believing that his wife had been seeking the attentions of a local man. The man has never been formally identified, although speculation is rampant that the man in question is Mr. Joseph Lanigan, owner of Valiant Drugs and vice president of the Chamber of Commerce.

"I knew the girls," Mr. Lanigan told the *Courier*. "I sought to help them. Miss Hoyt was sick and they were struggling to make ends meet. I tried to be a friend to them, and to Mrs. Seeley, who was lonely without her husband or family. I tried to bring cheer when I could and it appears Mrs. Seeley wrote to her husband and he misunderstood. It is a tragic consequence."

Mr. Lanigan, who just added a new store in the Country Club Park District to his growing Valiant Drugs business, has been widely praised for his generosity in paying for both girls' remains to be delivered to their families and a small shrine to be erected at the Werden Clinic.

"I'm a big Mick and I can take it," Joe Lanigan laughed, laughed all the rumors away, to all the out-of-town reporters who didn't know that, facts aside, Gentleman Joe Lanigan could never be a part of something as sordid as this, would never dip his manicured finger (oh, didn't he love his weekly manicures the cute marcelled girls at the Biltmore gave him) into such low revels, this a Lodge man, an Elk, a Mason, for goodness' sake. Didn't these Los Ang-e-lees scribes, with their pomade and shiny shoes, grabbing for ink, making the most of their small entr'acte in the crime of the decade, didn't they know our Joe?

Sure, his name tripped from tongues in ways that might, in other towns, bigger and smaller, have torn down reputation, his good name: this man, he can never now lead our school board, cannot sit on the council, run for office, run for mayor. But outsiders never would understand, would they? He is one of our own and we know things they never could in their blaring scandal-sheet Babylons. In fact, he carries a new sheen, the love object, the knightly swain, valiant is as valiant does, his acts of kindness spurring crushes, the crushes spurring jealous husbands and jealousy turned tragic, tragic. But tragedy so dogs our Gent Joe, what with that poor sick wife and he to raise two daughters virtually alone. Oh, our Gent Joe. Our Gent Joe. Who wouldn't stand beside him? He stands for us all.

I gave for you and gave for you. I would have laid down my pasteboard life for you, Joe Lanigan. But I'm through now. I'm all through. And the nails you struck across my mouth have all been pried loose and my mouth is one hundred miles wide and here I broadcast, my voice tinny, lost but no less your reckoning-day judge, what you have done to me, to those lovely girls, to my dearest Doctor, to us all. I will speak now, Joe

Lanigan, with mighty breaths, and will keep speaking until the caul you hide behind is lifted evermore.

"You'd best get on the nearest train, Mrs. Seeley. Fresh start. Heard your father wired your train fare back east. Be on that train, will you?"

"Yes, warden. Yes, I believe I will."

They gave her a new dress of robin's egg blue and her old shoes and purse and hat. Her hair was stripped of all peroxide and looked her own again but, squinting in her old compact mirror, she barely recognized herself.

Instead, she saw Ginny's plummy smirk and Louise's soft, piping cheeks and Dr. Seeley's eyes, his eyes and all the sad tenderness they could hold, that the world could hold. He had held it all, for them both.

In the tiny mirror, she saw them and felt strong.

She felt as if her shoulders held wings and she would rise, alight, feet twittering, body rising so high . . .

AT MRS. GOWER'S, the house throbbing with memories, Marion sat on the parlor sofa, waiting. Mrs. Gower had left word at the prison that she should come and retrieve her belongings. Marion wondered what could be left. But the old woman appeared with a small banded suitcase, the one Marion's father had given her on her wedding day.

Marion felt its lightness, touched its corners, its burnished latches.

"The policemen came. I gave them everything of that man's," Mrs. Gower said, her upper lip twitching. "Your . . . personal items, undergarments and such, I held them in my own quarters. It's not right for gentlemen to go through ladies' private things."

Marion nearly smiled. She was remembering something. Could they still be there, tucked between her dainties?

"I knew how he was," Mrs. Gower was saying, but Marion wasn't listening. "The doctor. Your doctor. I could see what he was."

SHE HELD THE LETTER in her hand. It had come five days before her release.

> *Dear Mrs. Seeley,*
> *I ask you kindly if you might see me. I will be at my store.*
> *Please come.*
>   —*Mr. Abner Worth*

She would see Mr. Worth. She would see Mr. Worth first. She would see him first and then she would see the other. She would see the other because she must.

She had ideas. She did not trust herself. In there, inside, she was not sound, curled tight in a cell, hundreds of letters of sympathy and calumny each day, the witchy stares of fellow prisoners, the crowded feel in her head, all the time, even when sleeping, although she did not truly sleep. She was not sound, but now she held the suitcase tight and wondered what her path would be.

THE WORTH BROTHERS MEAT MARKET was not open yet when she arrived, but she peered in the window and there was Mr. Worth, face pale at her sight.

He unlocked the door and let her into his back office. No, she did not want coffee, not even with a pinch in it, no, she did not want to pause at all. She could scarcely make herself sit in the chair opposite his desk.

The door ajar, she could smell the meat and see red edges of hanging carcasses. She could almost see them rocking, shaking even though hooked fast.

In her head she saw visions of him at one of the parties, shirt-sleeves rolled up, cranking his hand organ as she warbled, when they all asked her to sing for them and Mr. Worth, *"Twas down where the bluegrass grows, your lips were sweeter than julep, when you wore that tulip, and I wore a big red rose."*

Sitting before her now, the gin was radiating from him, seemed to be leaking from his skin.

His blood-thatched eyes settled on her and he rubbed his chin.

"Mrs. Seeley, I know I've wronged you. I know it."

Marion looked at him, feeling the wave of surprise only faintly. She could not hold on to anything long enough to truly feel it.

"It is not you," she said. "You have nothing to account for."

"When I saw what Joe was doing, I might've stopped it. I figured from the start you were a cat's paw in this thing."

"No, no," Marion said. "I know my share in this. I have faced it." Before jail, she could look at her guilt only in passing, a rustle in the back of her head. Now it was finally hers. She clung to it.

"At first he told me you murdered them both, but I knew you couldn't. It wasn't possible."

"I don't wish to talk about it anymore, Mr. Worth," she said. "I don't. It doesn't matter to me anymore." As she said it, she knew it was true. Joe Lanigan's sins stacked so high. She would not let him forget them. This was what she meant to tell him. This was what she would say when she said her last piece to him and then let him live with them, if he could. But she knew he could. That was the worst of it.

"He's got a new nurse," Mr. Worth said. "You know about the nurses."

"I do."

"The last one, the St. Monessa girl, he got tired of her. Too noisy, he said."

"I see," Marion said, looking around at Mr. Worth's desk, the cloudy bottle, the curling matches spent and piled thick along cigarette butts spread in a fan. She was beginning to feel dizzy.

"Elsie," he said. "This one's Elsie."

The name brought a hot flicker of shame to Marion's eyes. No surprises to be had, were there? She felt something sorrowful rustle in her chest. Elsie Nettle. She pictured the girl's fawn face on that long-ago night, the way her leg trembled against her in Joe's car, after everything.

"I wonder if you know this, Mrs. Seeley," Worth said, voice softening. "When he drinks, he says things. He says he's a lost man." He looked her in the eye. "Says he loves you still."

"I didn't ask for that," Marion said, hard and rough. "Don't tell me that."

"Says you brought him ruin and hellfire and yet he loves you still."

Marion, sprung back to vivid life, looked up fast and wanted to laugh. "Brought him to ruin. Oh, isn't that a fairy tale, a dreamy little love book to end all."

Mr. Worth looked at her warily, unsure. "But I wanted to say I'm sorry, and . . . your husband. I'm sorry."

He opened his desk drawer and pulled out a gun.

And she saw it was the pistol, the Colt. The very one.

"What do you have there?" she asked, thinking she might be ill. The heat, the smell of the meat, the gin swirling.

"Joe gave me this to hold," he said. "He trusted me with everything, you see, because he knows things about me. Things I'd rather not share."

He set the pistol lightly on the desk between them. "I don't want him having this over you. I don't know what he might use it for, or what you might." He looked at her. "But, on the balance, I'd have it be with you."

She was shaking. Her shoes were clacking on the floor. What did he mean by this?

"I am also afraid to have it with me," he said. "Lately I have developed weaknesses. There have been moments of despair and . . ."

Marion looked at the pistol, that same dire pistol, and felt her blood rush from her head. Blurry with heat, she took off her hat and held on to the desk edge.

"I took those girls to pieces, Marion," he said, voice so low as to be scarcely a breath. "Nights, early mornings, I think I cannot live with what I did to those girls." He looked up at Marion. "Their blood," he whispered.

"Yes, Mr. Worth," she said.

Looking at him and the heavy sags under his eyes, she wondered what he thought he was doing by giving her this. She had a head filled with bad thoughts of her own to lead her to dark places. She had no room for his. But then she realized he didn't know what to do. He didn't know what to do and he wasn't strong enough to keep hold of it anymore. He was shutting a door. By giving her the gun in this way, he was trying to shut a door.

He should know, she thought, that door never shuts. She curled her finger around the handle of her suitcase.

Reaching for his glass, he took a long swallow. "Mrs. Seeley, I do feel I must tell you," he said. "One night, end of a daylong drunk, we boys were up over at the Grand Lodge. Well, he said it to me. He said it to me."

"What?" Marion said, steeling herself, teeth gnashing to stay upright. "What did he say?"

"He said, 'I tell you, Ab, I know things now, about myself. I know what I am capable of. It is a shadow self under this one and I've seen it. You see it was a chance—Louise Mercer, she was to bleed me dry. She would not be stopped.'"

Mr. Worth looked at her. "Mrs. Seeley, he told me he shook up the delicate balance. You three girls. That delicate balance. Gave Ginny a big dose, knowing it'd get her all jazzed up. Then told her Louise was itching to get rid of her. Mrs. Seeley, you know Ginny was a jealous girl and a sick one. Joe said he thought to get her riled about you and Louise. He warned her she'd best steal away with Louise while she could. He figured they'd skip town and he'd have thrown off their snaky coils for good."

Something flashed before Marion's eyes, the moments before the murder, Ginny laying her charges before them. Louise knowing something was behind it, saying, *I wonder who's been filling your ear with tongue oil.*

Why, it was Joe, it was Joe. Of course it was Joe. "She's Pandora," Ginny had raged, "come to town with her dirty little box to bring us all to ruin." Was it not Joe Lanigan who had long ago told her, *You are Pandora. You came to town with that beautiful little box I had to, had to open.* Even now, she could picture Joe's lips to Ginny's pearly ear, warning her of the same.

Mr. Worth looked at Marion. "And he's a cold one, Mrs. Seeley. He is. He says to me, he says, 'But, Ab, I played the wrong card and Ginny went cockeyed. And I had to fix things. I did. Why, Marion already had the blood on her hands and we were nearly through. It had to end. Had to. And the end was at hand. I was to be through with them all. But then there was Louise, on her feet again.'"

And Marion saw it again, in her head, in images stuttering together:

. . . the way his arm extended, like he was batting off a fly . . . and Louise slumping to her knees like at a church pew.

"And he said, 'Ab, this here is the truth, when I look at it with sharpest eyes, which I do not often do, I cannot fairly say what was in my head. I cannot be certain of it. Does that make a monster of me, Ab? Then that is what I am. Darling, dark Louise. Maybe it was this: that I saw my chance and I blew a hot hole right in her chest.'"

THERE WERE PLACES too murky ever to see through. The bloody fury of the night and everything storming up to it, none of it was ever going to lie flat and let her run knowing fingers across it and see all the patterns and shapes and meanings for what they were. There was no essence to them. It was all mayhem and blood and now preening sorrow.

But now, sitting there with Mr. Worth, sitting quietly together, something had turned. Something had turned and she reckoned a path. It was like a fever—a yearlong fever—had broken at last. She knew, with a blooming rightness in her chest, what she would do. Mr. Worth, he was the duelist's dark second, looming up her side, rapier outstretched, retreating to his meat locker before he could even count her paces. This was all hers. All hers.

She lifted her small suitcase from the floor and set it on the desk. Mr. Worth's eyes fluttered gently as she opened its metal latches and raised the cardboard lid.

Oh, Mrs. Gower, my unlikely sister in arms, she thought. They were there, as they should be, beneath her tin of talc, her garter bands, her small cache of cotton step-ins, petal-soft—things too delicate for policemen's fingers. They were just where she'd hidden them.

Mr. Worth began clearing his throat.

Taking a deep breath, Marion pressed down on the cotton pile slightly, feeling the crinkle of paper beneath, onionskin, tied with a string. The prescription slips. She plucked beneath for the end of the string and tugged fast, her white undergarments floating to the floor.

"Here it is for you, Mr. Worth," she said. "Here is your path."

She slid the stack of prescription slips across the desk toward him, then closed the suitcase and met his puzzled gaze.

"Do you know what you are to do with these?" she asked.

He looked at them as if afraid to touch, as if they were her bloomers themselves. But finally he did, pulling the knot loose and holding the first prescription slip in front of his gin-blurred eyes.

"Veronal," he read, "sulphonal, chloral, paraldehyde, more veronal." He let his fingers run through each one.

"This is how he keeps her," Marion said, fighting off a quiver in her voice. "How Mr. Joe Lanigan keeps his wife out of his affairs. She is a prisoner to all this. His fairy dust." She pointed, waving her finger at the prescriptions. "Do you see how it is?"

"Why, the thing of it," he murmured, mouth open, a slanted *o* of slow marvel.

"And those doctors. See the names. Those are clinic doctors," Marion said. "They collude with him. And why wouldn't they? You all dance so closely, don't you? You all have fingers knotted in each other's pockets."

Mr. Worth set the slips down and reached for his glass, his hand rattling against it.

"Mr. Worth," she said. "Do you now see what you must do?"

"I see the power these documents might have," he said, gin to mouth. "I see that." But he did not look certain. She would have to make him see. To her, it was so clear.

"Who can guess, Mr. Worth, what else a hungry newspaperman might find? With a taste of fresh blood on his tongue, he might bother to raise the roof on Valiant Drugs too. There are so many hidden trails he might follow."

"Take them to the *Courier*, then," Mr. Worth said, eagerly. "You should take them."

She shook her head fiercely. "Don't you see? They won't listen to the madman's wife. The jailbird, the tainted woman. The public sinner. They will never listen to me. But you, you are one of them. You *are* them. It is your stake."

He looked down again but said nothing.

It was then that Everett's face came to her. His vain detective work, perhaps no longer vain. *Every four days,* his very words returned to her, as if her husband were whispering from his own damp grave, *the Worth Brothers Meat Truck came to the Dempsey Hotel and you went to the third floor, room 308, and Mr. Worth, only he called himself Mr. Tanner, but everyone knew, would sell you your kit.* It was his last gift to her, and she must use it.

"You know *your* share in so many of these sins of our Mr. Lanigan," she said, eyes fixed on him. "And I know them too, Mr. Worth—or is it Mr. Tanner?"

He looked at her. She made him feel it, feel her knowing. My, but she was changed. She felt Louise calling out from her own booming throat. There was a kind of glory in it.

"Mrs. Seeley," he warned, "these things are known. They are known and abided by. Encouraged. We are a small town, in many ways."

"Was it not you in the *Courier,* Mr. Worth?" she said, voice rising. "You have friends. You certainly shouted lies to the rafters when last they came calling. Was that not you, speaking of my terrible temper, of the girls' wild ways? Those girls you took to pieces?"

His face collapsed before her. She felt an ache in her chest watching it, but she went on.

"You must make your reporter believe you. You must make them all believe it," she said, voice firm, focused. "Make them see Mr. Lanigan's day is past. Make them see the profit in it, if you must. Use whatever secrets you hold to make them see."

There was a long pause, a hundred years or more, but then his chin began to shake up and down. Something was happening. His eyes sharpened.

"Can I, Mrs. Seeley?" he asked, voice speeding up. "I see. I do see. For that night, he may have us both to the wall. But not on this. And I can move things, Marion. I *know* it. I know this town just as he does, after all. I have seen all manner of things. Oh, if you knew—I have done all kinds of favors. I have worn the blinders time and again." He peered at her. "Marion, do you fathom it: I have secrets even darker than this."

She looked at him and knew it to be true.

"Can you shine the light on him, Mr. Worth? Can you take these scraps and spin silk for us?" and she felt her voice begin to break. It was all so much. "Can you do it, Mr. Worth?"

His eyes were strangely brightening. Something was lifting. His visage seemed to take new shape, those fallen features resolving themselves once more.

"I can," he said, voice rumbling, near-oratorical. "Believe me, Mrs. Seeley. Do. It will redeem me."

"It will," she said, and she knew she had given him a great gift and she felt larger. She suddenly felt like Louise's noble emissary from beyond the grave. And wasn't she?

She knew exactly what she was to do. She had set things in motion and now, now—she had given him his weapon and he hers. Abandoning the suitcase, even the purse, at the meat market, she carried only the pistol in the smocked pocket of her dress.

SIX BLOCKS AWAY, at the soda fountain, she made a quick telephone call. It was just as she guessed. He was not at home. But that was fine. It was as it should be.

Walking up Lynbrook Street, watching the three-story manse heave into sight, she felt composed, focused. But when she arrived on the doorstep and rang the bell, her breath began to catch, her chest hammering so loudly she almost did not hear the voice on the other side of the door.

"Who is it?" the whisper came, and it was Elsie Nettle's sibilant shush.

The voice so delicate, a sparrow wing rustling, Marion felt her back straighten, her head rise. She felt her blood come back, surging through her. She would do this.

"Open the door, Elsie," she said, her voice like smooth iron.

"I told you on the telephone . . . Mrs. Seeley," the voice came back. "I told you he is not here."

"I've come for you, Elsie Nettle," Marion said. "And you'd best open this door."

And she did.

It took fifteen minutes, no more. They sat quietly in the front parlor, the air heavy with motes and the tang of sulphur and tar oil. She saw the trembling in Elsie's doe eyes and knew it would not take long. In quiet tones, but with a firmness she had mastered as if overnight, Marion told Elsie that everything would change tomorrow, that the magnificent house of cards Mr. Joseph Lanigan had erected with his sweet scented hands was about to fall, *one flick from her dainty fingers, plus one butcher's thumb, and gone, gone, gone.* "You know what goes on. You tend to her. You fill her full of all those potions. If you stay, you will be lost," she warned. "You're not lost yet, or I would not have your ears now. If you stay, you will fall with him."

At first, Elsie said nothing, could scarcely raise her delicate doll head. Finally, she murmured, in the quietest of voices, "But, Marion, it was you. You delivered me to him."

"I know it," Marion said. "I put you here. I set you out for him. I did everything but lift your schoolgirl skirt for him. And now I'm taking you away. I would not leave you here, Elsie. For all the world."

And Elsie, still that mountain girl from Fool Hollow, not so broken yet, relented, even reaching out for Marion's cold hand.

They climbed the stairs to the third floor, past the gust of slow decay radiating from the sickroom in the center of the house. And Marion watched as Elsie packed her small bag with her two uniforms, two day dresses, her undergarments, everything so shabby, save a new lilac hat for Sunday Mass.

Elsie, at Marion's direction, telephoned the clinic to request a doctor to visit Mrs. Lanigan that evening, as she had quit her post and would be leaving town immediately.

Then, they walked out of the house together and Marion escorted Elsie, hand in hand, to the corner. When the bell clanged and the streetcar to the train station shuttered to a halt, she put Elsie on it, and watched her leave, the ribbon on her Easter hat fluttering behind her.

THERE WAS ONLY one step left to take. Now he would hear her, the man himself. With the pistol in hand, she would have him listen, and then she would be done. My, who would've reckoned her power, she asked herself. Not she, but there it was and she held it close.

She began walking again, in her head a million speeches unfurling, each larger and more damning than the last.

She walked to the lodge, which was dark, and to the Dunlop and the Dempsey and to the big new restaurant on Monroe and finally to the El Royale Hotel, which sparkled dustily in the foreground, reminding her of a long-ago night when a girl like her walked to that same hotel.

. . . *walking alone into the cavernous Thunderbird Dining Room, a sea of dark suits and mustaches, and "Joe Irish is looking for you, bunny rabbit," and she was fast in the arms of Gent Joe himself, tuxedo black as India ink, and she looked up at his eyes, his eyes smiling, his face doing smiling things as if there were never any such thing as shame in this world . . .*

Walking, hearing her own feet clitter lightly on pavement in the dark of the city weeknight past ten, and everything was beginning to tilt, and inside the thought of seeing Joe Lanigan, it was doing things to her, doing rough bewitchments, and she could not sort it all out and she began to wonder if she would be able to say her piece. *The words will come when I see him,* she told herself. *I will not be able to stop them.*

"I'M LOOKING FOR MR. LANIGAN," she told the bellhop sneaking a cigarette by the bank of rear doors.

The boy grinned and jerked his head toward the banquet hall, its gold-curtained entrance sprawling across the rear of the lobby.

"Thank you," she said, and she walked through those curtains, feeling their velvet tendrils. And she kept walking, through the raucous spasms of the cavernous hall, the dark flocks of red-faced men huzzahing the floor show, through the glittered, confettied folly of it all, kept walking until she found him in the farthest corner, snug behind the massive, gold-painted bandstand. As if on cue, a chorus girl in his lap.

Joe Irish, Gent Joe, Mr. Joseph Lanigan did not notice her from his dim perch and the music was loud and bumptious, and seeing his face after all this time almost broke her, almost split her into so many pieces, seeing that sheaf of yellow hair, the smile, curling and confident and filled with forget.

He was able to put things away, stow them in far places, on high shelves and in deep dresser drawers, and forget them, and forget things about himself, and he could even, when he wanted, pull them down and show them to people and calmly put them away again as if they were not his.

But she could not, she could not and how dare he put her in a creaking drawer in some hidden room he seldom went, how dare he put her there and put what he had done there too when she could not, when it flooded through her every minute of every day and when he did too and Joe still did too, still flooded and overtook her.

And he is here, and those bright girls and that sad, kind doctor are not and . . . and . . .

"It had to end," a voice muttered, her own. She began to wonder what she really meant to do. *The words will come when I see him,* she had told herself, but there was a quivery fear in her now because she no longer knew herself. The new self, the old self or that quaking self in between.

He turned and, in turning, spotted her. Oh, there it was, she caught it, she did, the gaudy fear crashing across his face. It was beautiful and made her feel she could do anything.

But he recovered in an instant and then it came again, that sly, cunning mask he could drop across his face at will. A reckless choice, but he made it anyway.

"My honey-locked jailbird, there she is," he clucked amid the din, and she thought for a moment that he might slap his other knee, the one free of the showgirl's lovesome bottom, and bid her to sit and join his bawdy party.

But he was not quite so foolish. He saw her face, saw the things in it, and quickly, cleanly removed the feathered showgirl from her roost and pushed her on her way, giving Marion his eyes, his face, newly painted sincere. She knew that dodge too. She knew all his dodges.

"You locked me away," her mouth spilt forth, "threw the key in the sand, but here I am and guess what I have done. Guess what awaits you, Joe Lanigan."

But her words, they were buffered, near soundless. There was nothing but cymbals and lurching slide trumpets and the hoo-rahs of hundreds of jostling tuxedoed men, their pleated shirt-fronts popping loose as they pressed and churned around her, one shouting, reaching out with clambering hands, "Where are the girls? I'll take this new-minted one, if you please." She pushed herself closer toward him, the two of them now shadowed beside the quaking bandstand.

Trying again, she felt a rushing in her mouth, like she might choke.

He looked at her, he waited, that bolt of lustrous hair, the violet nosegay on his suit. She fought off a fearsome wave of soft, broken memories of him and he, sensing it, raised his hand slightly, as if to reach for her own.

The sight of it filled her with fresh horror.

"I've been waiting for you, Marion," he said. "In my way, I have."

Something vaulted up inside her and she felt her body jerk forward, her hand plunging into her pocket and reaching for that pistol, which, in a dark blur before her eyes, was suddenly at the far end of her arm outstretched.

The thing jumped in her hand, the tiny Colt did, and it was only then that she knew she had fired it. A pierce in her ear and her hand had lifted so high, to the top of a thick column, a bullet wedging in the carved oak.

She spun around, gun in her hand, but the music screeched on and only a handful of men crushed right behind them could be bothered to lift their nuzzling heads from their girls, from their creamy follies. The sound of the gunshot, so thunderous in the Hussel Street living room, barely a whisper here.

Those who did see stood stock-still, one pink-faced man hissing excitedly, *It is she!*

She thought they would descend upon her, but they saw the thing in her hand, they had heard it. They could scarcely believe their eyes.

"Marion," she heard him say, and she looked at him, his face slipped to white. "Marion, no. Marion, no, don't you see?" He looked anxiously at the clutch of men motionless, fear struck, not ten feet from them. "Marion, your husband's sins, don't make them your own."

This was what he said to her. The feckless words whistling in her ear, and before she could think, her arm lifted again and she pointed this time at him, trying to rise, shirtfront showgirl-spangled. She felt the charge through her entire body as the bullet lacerated his knee, the crackling loud and victorious, the blood a glory shot.

He cried out and she had never heard such sounds from him, a dreadful bleat, and the men staggered back from them both.

It was all so stunning. She felt her body lifting, radiating. Looking around, she thought, *Have I bullets enough? I may shoot them all.*

His eyes were so wide and his face lowered, sinking into the spray of violets on his lapel.

From somewhere in the din, a recognition of the sound, a drunken voice crying out, "They've got fireworks!" and another pulling a pistol of his own, waving it gleefully as if in some Wild West saloon.

She didn't care, didn't care at all. She held that gun and felt its heat in her hand. In ways old and churchlike she knew it was not right. But part of her felt shooting him in that dark, hollowed heart of his would be the rightest thing she'd ever done. Righter somehow than anything that could be done.

"Marion," he said, voice slipping into her ear. "I know what I am. Believe it."

It was his return blow and it landed. She felt it all. He was saying, *You knew me. You knew what I was. You ran toward it. Don't forget how you ran toward it.*

She thought of Everett, at the end, staring into the dank center of things, she thought how that descent must have felt, the softest curl of oblivion, the place he'd been trying to reach since he first took hold of the needle's giddy bloom. Was that for her? To end and end and end?

It adds to truth a dream.

"No," she said, shaking her head. "That wasn't it. That wasn't it at all." The weight of the gun in her hand, his sorrowful face, she felt herself sinking.

Something rattled in her, the blood memory of Ginny, face crumpled like shiny paper. She had done such things. She had seared and hammered and destroyed. She had turned herself into such a dark thing, for him. To tear his sneer away with a hot bullet, would that redeem her now, redeem her lost friends, her direful, doomed husband?

Or would it only bury his sins, bury them with him?

And after, she would be lost to the abyss that would follow, which would swallow her. That black whorl of nothingness she now knew so well.

Fighting it, she thought of Mr. Worth, she imagined his furtive connivances, the gin-drenched whisper to the right reporters. He would not fail. It will be, she knew it. Tomorrow, the next day and for weeks to come, the newspapers will do their dance—*and they will, God help that butcher of mine,* she thought—and, with each screaming headline, all these men, these fickle, sad little gents with their hunger and their loneliness, will throw Joe Lanigan to the wolves to save their own skins. Beat back the blood, Marion, she told herself. Let these silk-coated confederates eat his black heart. It is their world. Let them to it.

She looked down at him, clinging to his shattered knee, the white of bone shining through the pants leg. He looked so small.

"Now it is your turn to watch me," she said, looking once more into those lost, careless eyes of his. "There are levers, switches, keys and I know which way they all go."

So FAST IT WAS, so slight was she, the music still caroming and the frenzy of the party, the orgiastic throng . . . a man with red whiskers—Mr. Gergen, with a mustache now?—called out, *Stop her! Stop her!*

But Marion was already pushing through the kitchen doors behind her and the dark alley beckoned forth.

SHE WOULD GET HER MIND BACK, her head on straight, her thoughts ordered, her heart thumping for something other than ardor and grief again. And when she did, this would all come storming back and she would feel the ponderous weight of everything, so fiercely it would knock the breath out of her.

But that time was not yet. And now all she felt was righteous and unbound.

Ten minutes later, by the tracks, a few yards from a pair of tramps, itching to lash on, she saw the freight train hurtling toward her. *There has to be something*, she thought, looking far off into the distance. *There is something.*

The air was simmery hot, the engine whistle wailing inconsolably. She could hear the wheels sparking, coming on so hard. The tramps, they were kicking tin cans into the ravine and getting ready to run.

She would get on that train and they would not find her. They would not want to. And if they did, it mattered not. She was gone.

Author's Note

THIS NOVEL is inspired by the true story of Winnie Ruth Judd, the "Trunk Murderess," also known as the "Tiger Woman" and the "Blond Butcher."

In October 1931, the bodies of two Phoenix women, nurse Agnes "Anne" LeRoi and her roommate, Hedvig "Sammy" Samuelson, were found in a pair of trunks abandoned at Los Angeles's Southern Pacific Station. After a four-day manhunt, twenty-six-year-old Winnie Ruth Judd turned herself over to the police, claiming she had shot her two friends in self-defense after a violent quarrel in their home.

The following day, a rambling letter written by Mrs. Judd to her husband, Dr. William Judd, was found in the drainpipe of a Los Angeles department store where Mrs. Judd had been hiding in the days following the murders. "I'm wild with cold, hunger, pain, and fear now, Doctor darling," the letter's closing lines read, "if I hadn't got the gun from Sammy she would have shot me again. Forgive me. . . . forget me. Live to take care of me, [illegible] as I am sick, Doctor, but I'm true to you. I love you. The thots [sic] of being away from you set me crazy. Shall I give up? No, I don't think so. The police will hang me. It was as much a battle as Germany and the U.S. I killed in defense. Love me yet, Doctor."

The shocking nature of the crimes set against Winnie Ruth Judd's blond angelic looks made the case irresistible to the public and popular press. Headlines screeched, " 'Hungry for Love' Her Notes to Mate Show," "Gay Revels Revealed, Narcotics Hinted in Killing," "Mind Inflamed by Drugs Blamed in Trunk Murder" and " 'Had to Fight,' Slayer Cries."

A sensational three-week trial ensued. The prosecution claimed Mrs. Judd had murdered her two friends in cold blood as they slept in their beds, and dismembered one of the bodies in order to fit them both into a pair of packing trunks for transport to Los Angeles. Their account appeared to contradict much crime scene evidence as well as Ruth's own injuries, including a bullet wound in her hand. Still, Mrs. Judd's defense attorneys, believing the fix was in among Phoenix authorities, were already planning for an insanity plea. In February 1932, Winnie Ruth Judd was found guilty and sentenced to hang.

The intervention of Sheriff John R. McFadden, however, brought a dramatic turn of events. Winnie Ruth Judd, who had not been called to testify at her own trial, divulged to the sheriff further details of the events surrounding the murders, including the involvement of a popular and influential Phoenix businessman.

A hearing was convened by grand jury request, finally permitting Mrs. Judd to tell her story. She recounted a harrowing argument with her two friends that became so out of control that Sammy Samuelson threatened her with a gun: "[Sammy] had the gun pointed right at my heart. And Sammy used to take spells . . . and she would look—oh, she didn't look like herself at all . . . and she had the gun pointed right at my heart, and I grabbed the hand with the gun." A struggle ensued and the gun went off, wounding Mrs. Judd and killing both Miss Samuelson and Mrs. LeRoi. Mrs. Judd went on to claim that the crimes had been concealed and the dismemberment arranged by one J. J. "Happy Jack" Halloran, one of the town's civic leaders and Mrs. Judd's rumored lover. She said that Halloran persuaded her that she must not go to the police. "Why, he scared the life out of me," she told the court. "He told me not to call my husband or the police. I must not

mention this to anyone, that he would take care of this himself."
She added, after her arrest, he promised her if she kept quiet about
his role, she would be protected.

THE GRAND JURY ultimately requested that the Arizona Board
of Pardons and Paroles commute Mrs. Judd's death sentence to
life imprisonment, claiming it was manslaughter, not premedi-
tated murder. At the same time, the jury indicted Jack Halloran as
an accessory to murder.

In a bizarre twist, however, Halloran's attorney made the case
that the state, by putting Mrs. Judd on the stand as a witness,
proved a prima facie case of self-defense. Halloran's lawyer suc-
cessfully argued that no murder meant Halloran could not be an
accomplice either. The judge agreed and Halloran was set free.

Then, despite the grand jury's findings, the Board of Pardons
and Paroles denied any commutation of Mrs. Judd's sentence.

A mere three days before her scheduled execution, Mrs. Judd
was granted a sanity hearing. Declared insane, she escaped the
hangman's noose and was transferred to the Arizona State Hospital for the Insane in Phoenix, which would be her home for the
next thirty years. Her husband remained steadfast in his support
of his wife until his death in 1945.

Over the years, Mrs. Judd escaped seven times from the hospital, the last escape in 1963 lasting more than six years, during
which time she took on a new identity, as Marian Lane, working
as a beloved servant for a wealthy San Francisco family.

In 1971, Winnie Ruth Judd was judged sane by medical
examiners and released on parole. She died at the age of ninety-
three in 1998.

OVER THE YEARS, I've returned to the Winnie Ruth Judd case many times. Again and again, I wondered what might have happened to her if those trunks had not been found so quickly, if she had returned to confront her betraying lover, if circumstances had been such that she could have put her survival skills (so in evidence in her multiple escapes) to the test rather than surrender to questionable authorities. After reading *Winnie Ruth Judd: The Trunk Murders* (1973) by J. Dwight Dobkins and Robert J. Hendricks and Jana Bommersbach's *The Trunk Murderess: Winnie Ruth Judd* (1992) and press coverage of the murders in the *Los Angeles Times* archives and elsewhere, I began to reimagine Winnie Ruth Judd's story, with a different final act.

In doing so, I had to make some choices in terms of how much I should deviate from history or, in this case, history, lore and legend and the many blurry spaces in between. After all, the "true story" of what happened between Winnie Ruth Judd, Anne LeRoi, Sammy Samuelson and Jack Halloran on that long-ago October night remains a mystery. There are those who believe Mrs. Judd was responsible for both deaths, pointing to her history of emotional problems. Many believe her self-defense story. Others claim that Halloran murdered both girls, convincing his lover to take the rap for him and promising, with his connections, she would never go to prison. By the time she realized she was being set up, it was too late.

With no definitive answers, I invented my own. I began with the basic foundation of fact and rumor, and navigated an imaginary path forged by the elements of the story that so captivated me, most especially the powder keg at the center of the case: the various attachments, triangles and jealousies between the three women and the one man, all of whom depended, in ways small and large, emotional and economic, on one another.

The characters that emerged bear many surface similarities to their real-life counterparts but are ultimately fictions. Like Marion

Seeley, Winnie Ruth Judd was left in Phoenix by her doctor husband, William Judd, whose drug addiction led him to work for a mining company in Mexico. Dr. Seeley's fate, however, diverges wildly from that of the real-life Dr. Judd's, although it is inspired by his paternal loyalty to her. Like Louise Mercer, Anne LeRoi was a nurse at the same clinic where Winnie Ruth Judd worked and various details of her employment are the same. Jack Halloran was, like Joe Lanigan, married with children and was a successful businessman and pillar of the community, but the rest is pure fiction. Ginny Hoyt, other than the tuberculosis she shares with Sammy Samuelson, is an invention. Press reports delineating the contents of Miss Samuelson's diary, however, include excerpts from the poem "The Teak Forest," which appears at the beginning of Part Four, as well as various song lyrics and verses throughout the novel.

Because we have only Mrs. Judd's accounts of the murders themselves and because her recollection of Anne LeRoi's death has always been dim, this novel's version of those events is heavily imagined. Many of the details leading up to the murders, however, draw extensively from Winnie Ruth Judd's accounts, from interviews, testimony and her late-in-life conversations with author Jana Bommersbach. For instance, one of the precipitating factors in the women's fight that Friday night was Anne LeRoi's and Sammy Samuelson's anger that Mrs. Judd had invited a new nurse at the clinic out for an evening with Jack Halloran, at Halloran's suggestion. The accusations the women made (e.g., that the nurse had syphilis) are drawn from Mrs. Judd's accounts, as is Ginny's sudden rage.

Finally, the question of how the women's bodies ended up in those famous trunks that so captivated public attention draws on Mrs. Judd's account that Mr. Halloran told her Sammy Samuelson's body had been "operated on." According to at least one source, the doctor rumored to have carried out the dismemberment appeared at the prison in which Mrs. Judd was being held after her trial, "drunk as a skunk, waving his hat around and yelling he was the only man alive who knew the truth about the Winnie Ruth Judd case." A few months later, in June 1932, the doctor died of a heart attack.

The story of Winnie Ruth Judd, Anne LeRoi and Sammy Samuelson is actually a hundred stories or more. Researching it, I came upon so many "side" tales, moments large and small, that lingered with me. Moments like this small, haunting story that appears in *The Trunk Murderess*:

Virginia Fetterer, the daughter of an Arizona legislator, recalled to the author a long-ago New Year's Eve in the late 1930s when she came upon Happy Jack Halloran, Mrs. Judd's betraying lover, at the Adams Hotel in downtown Phoenix.

It was a night of jubilation, with street bands, and "everyone wandered around drinking and dancing and visiting with friends in a town where everybody knew everybody." Ms. Fetterer and her friends approached the Adams Grill, the hotel bar, and Halloran and his friends were coming out:

> Somebody asked [Halloran] a question, like if he
> could take care of a problem. And he was bragging
> that, sure, he could fix it. Then he said—I can't recall
> his exact words, but it was to the effect that if you
> knew the right people, you could fix anything in this
> town. He laughed and said that Winnie Ruth was out
> in the state hospital paying for what he'd done. He
> was bragging about it. Then, she said, a drunk Jack
> Halloran staggered away.*

The Trunk Murderess: Winnie Ruth Judd by Jana Bommersbach, Scottsdale, Ariz.: Poisoned Pen Press, 2003.